Deborah Sheldon is an award-winning author from Melbourne, Australia. She writes short stories, novellas and novels across the darker spectrum. Her titles include the noir-horror novel *Contrition*, the bio-horror novella *Thylacines*, the dark fantasy and horror collection *Perfect Little Stitches and Other Stories* (Australian Shadows "Best Collected Work 2017"), the crime-noir novellas *Dark Waters* and *Ronnie and Rita*, and the creature-horror novel *Devil Dragon*. Her work has been shortlisted for numerous Aurealis Awards and Australian Shadows Awards, long-listed for a Bram Stoker, and included in "best of" anthologies. Other credits include TV scripts, feature articles, non-fiction books, and award-winning medical writing.

Visit Deb at http://deborahsheldon.wordpress.com

Deborah Sheldon's titles published by IFWG Publishing Australia

Dark Waters / Ronnie and Rita (novellas, 2016)
Perfect Little Stitches and Other Stories (collection, 2017)
Contrition (novel, 2018)
Figments and Fragments: Dark Stories (collection, 2019)

FIGMENTS AND FRAGMENTS

Dark Stories

By Deborah Sheldon

Figments and Fragments: Dark Stories

All Rights Reserved

ISBN-13: 978-1-925956-21-4

Copyright ©2019 Deborah Sheldon

V1.0

Stories first publishing history at the end of this book.

Printed in Palatino Linotype and Signo.

IFWG Publishing International
Melbourne

www.ifwgpublishing.com

For Allen and Harry

Table of Contents

Basket Trap

It took Helen about ten minutes to make a basket trap with her shirt. She knotted the sleeves and tied the shirt wide open to a couple of branches that she had rammed deep into the riverbed. In time, fish would swim into the shirt and be unable to turn around. She waded out and climbed the bank. Standing waist-deep in the water had rinsed some of the blood and semen from her jeans and singlet. For now, preserving forensic evidence was the least of her worries. She berated herself again for choosing such a remote area of Brazil for her holidays, when she could just as easily have picked Rio de Janeiro or somewhere back home in Australia.

She checked her watch: just after 11am.

By her rough calculations, she'd travelled about ten kilometres, so the men who'd snatched her from the train station had a search area of some 160 square kilometres if they wanted to find her again. To further confuse a human tracker, assuming they had one or even cared to go looking for her, she'd taken the least obvious route: northwest into the forest, rather than east along the road to the coastal township. She could rest for a while.

She lay with her hands behind her head. Her throat felt dusty, but the sunshine would take some twelve hours to sterilise the river water in the plastic bottles that she'd found in the garbage along the banks. Smoke from a fire was too risky, and since air-drying any fish she caught would take the best part of a day, the decision on whether to keep walking or to stay here and make camp was already made for her. Good. She was too tired to keep running anyway.

Helen's eyes began to close. Three or four of the men had taken turns on her all night and she hadn't slept. Somewhere beyond the trees, a finch whistled. A breeze ruffled the canopy overhead.

She fell asleep and dreamed that she was on the Wimmera plains, a flat expanse of Victorian countryside covered in wildflowers, and Dad was by her side. She was practising her tracking skills on rabbit spoor, and it didn't seem strange that she was a kid again instead of a grown woman approaching thirty. Dad started to point his walking stick, trying to tell her something, but she couldn't hear him and grew afraid.

She woke with a jolt. Nearby was the riverbank. The shadows had lengthened. The noise came again, a rustling in the underbrush. She rolled onto her stomach and looked up into the gun barrel. Only it wasn't a gun barrel; it was a red brocket some five metres away, a deer that tensed at Helen's sudden movement but didn't bolt. They stared at each other with wide eyes. Then the deer carefully lowered its sleek head, took a mouthful of grass, and retreated into the forest.

She dozed. When next she checked her watch, it was nearly 3pm.

Her ad hoc basket trap held two catfish, each about the size of a rat. She dropped the fish to the riverbank and hung her shirt in a tree to dry. A fallen branch served as a club and she set about scaling and gutting her catch. The men had taken her backpack but she still had her penknife. Why they hadn't frisked her, she didn't know. Maybe they were too used to snatching foreign women who had nothing but hotel keys, a few notes, loose change, and tour maps in their pockets.

She ate one of the fish raw; the other she needed to preserve. It had been years since Dad had taught her to make fish jerky and the task took her some time. The strips of fish were draped on sticks in the full sun. To keep off the flies, she tented her shirt over the top. Then, light-headed, she sat down hard.

She was still hungry. Vegetation surrounded her but she didn't know which species were edible. She thought again of her father. Of all the survival skills he had taught her, Dad always said the most important was keeping a cool head.

Daddy, can I ask you something about your tour? Mum always says

I shouldn't ever ask you anything.

I tell you what, sweetie. I'll answer if I feel like it, is that okay?

Okay. When they found you, they hurt you, didn't they?

Yeah, they sure did.

That's why you need a walking stick.

That's right.

What did they do?

Lots of things. But that was a long time ago and it doesn't matter now. So tell me, what's the most important thing to do when you're in a tight spot?

Think about the people you love.

Right, but there's also hanging tough. Never forget that. Don't start carrying on like a baby and you'll be all right.

And she had kept a cool head. She'd tamped down the terror until it was nothing but a knot in her stomach that helped her stay frosty, that showed her the moment to make a break for it.

She gave a silent prayer: *thanks again, Dad, for insisting on your access weekends.* Mum had never approved of Helen's camping trips with Dad, afraid that Helen would follow too closely in his footsteps, but Dad was a soldier, not a killer. Too bad that Mum had never seen the difference.

Helen checked her watch: nearly 6pm. She lay down, dropped once more into a dreamless sleep, and drowsed in and out of torpor, sweating, her teeth chattering.

It grew dark and then light. For all she knew, animals had taken her fish. Occasionally she saw parakeets and toucans. Once, she thought she saw a family of marmosets leaning over and peering at her, but then again, maybe not. Seeing things that weren't there was a bad sign. Maybe she wouldn't make it out of here and scavengers would scatter her bones. One day, a hiker might chance upon what was left of Helen and move on, assuming that her remains belonged to a wounded deer that had sought shelter long ago.

When she at last woke up with a clear head, the sun was already high in the sky. She had to get moving. Her plan was to hike to the sugarcane territory in the south, and hitch a ride northeast to the coastal township where she could raise the alarm. The image of those men behind bars galvanised her, but when she got to her feet, dots sprang across her vision.

Grabbing onto tree branches, she made it to the riverbank. She drank all the water from one of the bottles but could only pick at the fish strips, her appetite gone. Perhaps this was another bad sign. Packing the rest of the bottles and the fish into her shirt, she slung it over her back and headed south at an ambling pace. Conserving what remained of her energy was now the only thing that mattered.

Hours slipped by, hours of endless repetition. The curves of the river fell behind. Unseen birds peeped and warbled. The valley was thick with palm trees, and the grass was as green and shiny as fresh limes and was dotted with orchids.

Mint grew wild in the undergrowth, and as she walked through the stems, the aroma conjured roast lamb lunches and lazy Sunday afternoons with the potbelly stove throwing off heat, and the wind and rain beating at the kitchen windows. Dad was carving the roast. Mum was sitting with her elbows on the table and her chin propped on her interlaced fingers. She was smiling with that soft look she used to have for Dad before his nightmares got out of hand and the memories claimed him, before he moved away to live in a caravan and drink beer for breakfast.

Dad offered Helen a plate that steamed with slices of mint-scented lamb. She reached out, salivating, and cactus needles stabbed into her hand. As she stumbled back, her legs gave way.

The ground hit her. As she lay amid the leaf litter, she looked about at the forest, blinking, dazed.

"Get a grip, you idiot," she said, and her voice creaked, a frightening noise. "Stop it right now."

She watched the grey, scudding clouds. Rain was coming. If only she had a poncho. Her forehead was burning but it wasn't fever, she decided; she wasn't sick, goddamn it, only famished. Low blood sugars were messing with her mind. She ate a piece of fish jerky without much interest and started walking south again.

A faint yelp echoed over the forest.

Helen's heart kicked into a gallop. It couldn't be a farming dog, since the only farms around here grew sugarcane and soybean. So it had to be a tracker dog, which meant the men were hunting her after all.

When the dog barked, Helen broke into a run.

She sprinted hard, taking high choppy steps through the underbrush, fearful of breaking an ankle, vaulting over logs and crashing through low-lying branches. Then she tripped and fell full length on her front, knocking the wind from her. For a moment she lay gasping, air burning her throat, the taste of copper on her tongue. She sat up.

To the southeast was a low hill. She abandoned the strewn water bottles and jerky, grabbed her shirt and bolted. In the ten minutes it took to reach the hill, a stitch had her doubled over and panting. She scrambled and clawed her way to the peak and glanced back across the valley.

There was nothing but the coils of river winding through the forest, and beyond, a shimmering blue sliver of ocean. She forced herself to look again and finally, there they were down at the riverbank where she'd slept, two tiny figures, a man walking behind a dog on a long leash.

A strange calm settled into her and she sat down.

She had done everything she could to throw off a human tracker: taking a circuitous route to the township rather than the beeline, wading through the river, keeping to deer tracks, doubling back from time to time. But to a dog, her scent would light up the forest like the flashing bulbs on a trimmed Christmas tree. Then there was the fever. No use denying it now. And travelling slowly would allow the tracker to catch up in no time at all.

As she dropped her head to her folded arms, Dad's voice came back: *Don't start carrying on like a baby and you'll be all right.*

She whispered, "It's no use, I can't outrun them."

So kill the dog.

"Oh yeah? How? I could never get close enough." Helen croaked out a laugh. "This is ridiculous, Dad, you're not even real. I'm just hallucinating again."

But she did think about killing the dog. Then she thought about it some more. There was an hour until nightfall: the man would soon be setting up camp. The wind carried light drizzle, and no dog could follow scent in the rain. Helen got to her feet.

By 4am, there was nothing left of the campfire but a few stirring embers. The man was tucked into a sleeping bag, an arm folded under his head for a pillow.

Helen recognised him. Three days ago, this small, middle-aged man had introduced himself as a taxi driver, offering in broken English to take her to a nearby hostel. Helen had followed him through the crowd to a van parked outside the train station. Once she was in the van, a man in the front passenger seat turned and showed her a gun. They had taken her to a shack at the edge of town where other men were waiting.

And now, beside the dying fire at the riverbank, the driver was snoring peacefully. She withdrew the penknife from her pocket, opened its blade and kicked the sleeping bag.

The man startled, and rubbed at his moustache with a slender hand, mumbling, "*O que está acontecendo?*" What is happening?

Then he gaped at her. Neither spoke for a long time. At last, the driver sat up and cut his eyes around the camp.

Helen said, "Your little beagle is dead. *Cachorro morto.* I waited in the rain, came up downwind and clubbed it with a log. I don't know any words for that. *Cachorro morto?*"

"Yes, the dog he is kill. Me also?"

"No, I just want your boots."

He frowned, shrugged, and contorted his mouth like he was going to cry. "*Sinto muito, eu não entendo.*" I'm sorry, I don't understand.

"Boots. Your shoes," Helen said, and patted one of her feet. "*Sapatos.*"

"Ah," the driver said, and nodded and smiled. He picked up the tattered pair of sneakers by the campfire and tossed them to her. Helen couldn't comprehend his flurry of words, but the beseeching tone was clear.

She lifted a placating hand, and said, "It's okay, *senhor*. Without your dog or your shoes, you can't follow me, right? No *cachorro*, no *sapatos*, you no *seguir*."

"Yes, no follow. Okay missy. It is deal, okay?"

The driver laughed and clapped a few times, then thrust out a hand for her to shake. Helen nodded and took it, smiling, and he wrenched her towards him and threw his other arm about her neck and rolled her beneath him.

The campfire embers hissed through her shirt and burned her back. The driver tightened his grip. Helen slashed over and over with the penknife. For a time, the only sounds were their harsh gasps and the clattering of the campfire stones under her writhing body. Then the driver cried out and his grip around her neck loosened. He started to gurgle. Helen shoved and his weight shifted. She crawled some distance away, fighting for breath.

After a while, the gurgling noises stopped. For the longest time, she couldn't bear to look. A finch whistled. The sky paled and the horizon showed pink through the trees. Helen looked behind her at last. The driver's eyes were dull and his blood glistened like treacle.

"Didn't you hear me, you stupid bastard? I wasn't going to hurt you."

And then she wept, but not for long.

Later, much later along a path, sugarcane bristled in shiny rows and the sun blazed butter-yellow. Helen's vision blurred and ran red. Unexpectedly, Dad stepped out onto the path, his arms wide open to her.

Her breath caught. "Oh Dad, I've done a terrible thing."

A female voice replied, "*Quem está lá?*" Who's there?

Helen squinted into the bright light. A woman and a girl shimmered like luminous deities, each figure perfect in the cast of her shoulders, the glow of her hair. Godlike, they reached out with their long beautiful hands and caused the ground beneath Helen's feet to turn into water.

Helen sank down and the darkness crowded over her.

The mother and daughter at the sugarcane farm had called for the town's doctor. After four days in the city hospital getting treatment for dehydration, exposure and a kidney infection, Helen was well enough to be discharged. She went straight to the Australian embassy.

The deputy chief-of-mission was a fat man with ears that stuck out. The room was small and papered brown. Through the window came noises of the street: motor scooters, the odd shout, canned music from a transistor radio.

The deputy's pen hovered over the documents on the desk. "And your passport?" he said.

"In my backpack."

"The backpack that was stolen on the hiking trail?"

"That's right."

"Ah, the same old same old, thievery in this area is terrible. It could've been worse, believe me, the tales would turn you grey, but what can you do?"

"Get out and never come back."

"Wise words, that's for sure." The deputy scratched his pen across the form. "Okay then, done, I can get you an interim passport and book you on the next flight." He looked up and smiled uncertainly. "Are you all right?"

She was thinking about the river, which held the driver and his dog, both weighted down with stones. Catfish would be pecking at the man's moustache and sucking the meat from his face, reducing him to bone.

She said, "I just want to go home and put everything behind me."

"Of course. Sign here."

She took the proffered pen with shaking fingers. During her last visit with Dad, he'd sat mute and gaping at his trembling hands as if they'd held invisible horrors. She was her father's daughter after all, but whether or not she could avoid the bottle and the madness, Helen had no way of knowing.

She scrawled her name and put down the pen.

Risk of Recurrence

Dr Wainscott tries to smile, then says, "I'd very much like to talk about it with you."

"Okay," Bernadette Fry says. "So tell me why you did it."

She shifts her weight on Dr Wainscott's couch and hunkers down like a child settling in for a story. Transfixed in his armchair, Dr Wainscott mentally scrabbles for an answer that could satisfy her. Unfortunately, he can't think of one.

Bernadette Fry had walked into his office for the first time about a year ago, her hair uncombed and her gaudy dress too tight. Dr Wainscott had gestured at a seat and she'd dropped into it, fat shimmying. According to her file, she had no chronic illnesses, prior surgeries or major health concerns—apart from this one. Her mammogram pictures were clipped to the light box on the wall.

Dr Wainscott removed his glasses. "If I may call you Bernadette," he said, and indicated the pictures with a roll of his wrist. "Now, Bernadette, this image is of your left breast and this one is of your right. These spongy areas suggest normal breast tissue. And this little spot here, on the left..." He tapped the arm of his glasses against a starfish shape. "Do you see?"

"Yeah."

"That spot isn't what I would consider to be normal breast tissue."

"So, I have cancer."

She said it as a statement rather than a question, which surprised him. He leaned back in his chair and said, "Yes, Bernadette. I believe the lump you found is what's known as *invasive ductal carcinoma*."

"But you're not sure?"

He put his glasses on his nose. "I've been the cancer surgeon in this town for close to thirty years. I would think, Bernadette, that after all the cases I've treated, I can recognise breast cancer from a mammogram, don't you?"

Bernadette Fry didn't respond. Her grey eyes took him in and waited.

Dr Wainscott opened his diary and checked his schedule. He picked up the handset on his desk phone, flipped the intercom and asked his secretary whether Friday morning at the hospital was clear. She put him on hold, then got back to him and said yes, theatre two would be available on Friday at eleven o'clock and should she book it for him? He said yes, hung up and made a note in his diary, wrote a few lines in the medical file, then regarded Bernadette Fry.

The arrangements had taken him some five or six minutes — more than enough time for most patients to be pulling handfuls of tissues from the dispenser on his desk — but she was humming and looking at a wall-mounted poster on skin cancer awareness.

"I can perform your operation on Friday morning," he said, and she stopped humming and turned to him. He said, "I'll do a lumpectomy. Most of your breast will remain but you'll need radiotherapy. That's a kind of x-ray that kills off any remaining cancer cells. But don't worry about that now. We can talk about further treatments after you've recovered from surgery."

Bernadette Fry stood up in a single motion, quick for her size, and the raft of disturbed air carried a scent of sweat and sunscreen lotion. Dr Wainscott took off his glasses.

"Don't you have any questions?" he said.

She stopped at the door. "Okay, what time do you want me at the hospital?"

Friday at eleven o'clock sharp, nurses delivered Bernadette Fry prone on a gurney into operating theatre number 2. The anaesthetist knocked her out. Dr Wainscott removed her tumour, along with a thick margin of healthy tissue just to be sure, and dropped the grey and red mess into a kidney dish for the nurse to take to the pathologist.

Next, he opened Bernadette Fry's armpit on the same side and scooped out two lymph nodes, stained blue from the pre-op injection, and tossed them into another kidney dish. Then he paused to reflect.

With just a few swipes of his scalpel, he had saved the life of Bernadette Fry.

After a full day in theatre, Dr Wainscott drove home in a contemplative mood. The traffic at about 5:30pm was light, as always—with a population of just 48,000, peak hour lasted no more than ten minutes.

His Edwardian-style bungalow sat on the only hill in town. He eased his Mercedes into the single garage, parked, took the interior door straight into the kitchen. At the bar, he fixed a whisky and soda. Then he changed into shorts and a singlet, sat on the balcony and worked on his drink and then another, watching, as he did every night, the lights from the street lamps and houses below coming on and pinpricking the dark.

Like any other Victorian town, this place had its Main Street, turn-of-the-century clock tower and rash of truck stops. But it had one distinguishing feature: a tourist attraction named "The Big Broccoli", which Dr Wainscott could see from his balcony. Back in the 1970s, one of the mayors had authorised its construction in honour of the town's major export. The concrete and steel fabrication was a twenty-foot tall sprig of its vegetable namesake, and housed a gift shop that stocked items such as broccoli magnets, t-shirts and stubby holders.

Behind the gift shop in a separate building was the Big Broccoli Bistro, dubbed "the Triple B" by locals. The Triple B had always been a low-rent pub for drunks and gamblers, but in the past year or so, new management had transformed it into one of the district's most popular restaurants. And new management— according to the anaesthetist who had gossiped to Dr Wainscott over the various unconscious bodies in theatre that day—was none other than Bernadette Fry.

Dr Wainscott finished his second drink and thought about making a third. On the horizon, clouds were bunching in a dark scrum, threatening havoc, but he knew that the much-needed summer rain would head east as usual and waste itself in the ocean. He went inside.

"**S**he refused chemotherapy."

"Come again?" Dr Wainscott said.

"She wants to keep her fertility. To be a mum someday, I guess."

"But she's over forty. And what man would have her?" Dr Wainscott went to the urn to make a coffee he didn't want. Behind him at the clinic's staffroom table sat his long-time associate, medical oncologist Emily Ta. Since she was close to fifty and didn't have any children herself, Dr Wainscott hurried on and said, "Doesn't she realise the cancer could return? Hasn't she seen the graph? You showed her the graph, didn't you? Granted her lymph nodes were clear, I accept that, but does she understand that cancer cells can travel through blood as well as lymph? Did you tell her?"

"Of course."

He stirred his coffee, dropped the teaspoon into the sink and said, "Well, isn't that rich? Isn't that just a show and a half?" He stuffed his hands into the pockets of his white clinician's coat. "Did she seem upset?"

Emily shrugged. Dr Wainscott abandoned his coffee on the draining board and left the room.

Apart from Emily Ta, Dr Wainscott's only other associate at the clinic was radiation oncologist Jason McDougall. Dr Wainscott had arranged to have their regular Tuesday meeting at the Triple B rather than the clinic staffroom, and Jason was late. Dr Wainscott bought a whisky and soda and tucked himself into a booth that had a line of sight to both the bar and the front door.

The remodelled Triple B was a kind of sports bar, but it didn't feature the memorabilia of famous Australian athletes; instead, it showcased players from clubs around the town and surrounding districts. Photographs, local newspaper clippings and significant items of small-time glory filled every wall. Next to Dr Wainscott's booth, hanging in a mahogany frame complete with an engraved silver plate, was the jumper worn by the sixteen-year-old captain of the town's A-side football team during their Grand Final win last season.

At first, people had come to the refurbished Triple B to bask in the public homage to their sons, daughters and friends, but they had returned for the menu. According to the anaesthetist, you needed to book a table for Saturday night at least one week in advance, regardless of who you were.

Dr Wainscott took a gulp of his drink and surveyed the bar. And there she was, like the shock of cold water, emerging from a rear office doorway: Bernadette Fry in a loud print smock, breasts jouncing against her belly, frizzy hair wrestled into a topknot. Dr Wainscott hunched down in the booth. He couldn't hear her, but he could see her well enough. She chatted to her bar staff, laughed, then shouldered through the rear office door and was gone.

"I can't believe it, sir, you're drinking."

Dr Wainscott turned. Jason McDougall, standing a metre or so from the booth, must have entered from an unseen side entrance. Dr Wainscott scowled. Jason had the pinned pupils and jittering intensity that suggested drug addiction, and a personality that made Dr Wainscott miss the previous radiation oncologist, a diabetic smoker who had retired to Queensland last year with his fourth or fifth wife.

Dr Wainscott swallowed whisky and soda. "Give me the radiation summary for Bernadette Fry."

"Yes sir," Jason said, and took a seat at the booth. "Twenty-five treatments for the whole breast and five boosters to the tumour bed, which amounts to thirty treatments altogether over six weeks with weekends off, assuming the machine doesn't break down."

"Did she have concerns? You haven't listed any in her file."

"None."

"None whatsoever? All right, fine. And I see you've written her down for Wednesday morning checkups. I'll be sitting in."

Dr Wainscott raised his glass in an unusual display of camaraderie, and Jason blushed and grinned in return.

The oncology wing of the local hospital featured the only external-beam radiotherapy machine for hundreds of kilometres. Finished in a baby blue powder-coat, and nicknamed *the Blue Whale* by its technicians, the monster filled a cavernous room, and could swivel on mighty pivots both horizontally and vertically above its fixed stretcher. The Blue Whale had cost over two million dollars and she was a beauty, according to everyone on staff.

But three weeks into her radiotherapy treatment, Bernadette Fry complained of gastritis. The next week, she added heartburn and reflux to her list of grievances. The week after, she grumbled about abdominal bloating and what she delicately described as "changes in bowel habits".

Dr Wainscott blamed these symptoms on stress and Jason agreed. At her sixth and final checkup, Bernadette Fry said, "I rang a Melbourne expert in radiation side effects and she reckons it's the radiation."

Jason looked at Dr Wainscott. Dr Wainscott ignored him and said, "What you're talking about, Bernadette, is called *mucositis*. It only happens if the alimentary tract is in the direct path of the radiation. In your case, the alimentary tract is clear."

Bernadette Fry didn't argue. She took off her shirt and bra and kept quiet during the brief medical examination. The radiation damage was mild—peeling skin, a blackened crescent of blistered flesh in the armpit and beneath the breast, charring of the nipple—and Dr Wainscott dismissed her. In her medical file, he wrote,

"Patient is delusional and in need of psychological help. Will advise breast-care nurse accordingly." Then he slid the manila folder across the desk so that Jason could sign the entry.

But according to the breast-care nurse, Bernadette Fry refused the offer of free psychological counselling. Soon after that, the hospital's patient advocate called Dr Wainscott and Jason into a meeting.

Bernadette Fry had complained that those responsible for her cancer care were negligent and lacking in compassion. In her written statement—which the Patient Advocate allowed Dr Wainscott to read—Bernadette Fry noted that the doctors had not investigated her gastrointestinal symptoms, an oversight that the Patient Advocate could write into Dr Wainscott's record despite three decades of consistent and exemplary life-saving.

Dr Wainscott placed Bernadette Fry's statement on the Patient Advocate's desk and composed himself. He could hear Jason breathing rapidly in the chair next to him.

"We examined her," Dr Wainscott said, "and her symptoms were imaginary."

The Patient Advocate shelved Bernadette Fry's complaint.

Dr Wainscott paced his balcony with a drink in one hand and cordless phone in the other. He said, "Harvey, if we do nothing, it's her blood on our hands."

"You're telling me she's suicidal?"

Dr Wainscott downed a slug of whisky. It was strong without the soda and he shuddered.

"Are you still there?" Harvey said.

"Yes, yes, I'm here. Listen, Harvey, you're the chief clinical psychiatrist; don't tell me you don't have the shove to get a favour or two."

The following week, just after the lunchtime rush on a Thursday, two police officers turned up at the Triple B and took Bernadette Fry to the psychiatric unit of the local hospital. She asked to be booked as a voluntary patient. Within an hour of her admission, a staff doctor gave her the mandatory physical examination. Two hours after that, she was brought before Dr Harvey Bennet and two of his colleagues and put through a detailed psychiatric assessment. Based on their joint findings, Harvey Bennet and his colleagues immediately released Bernadette Fry.

The police officers who had taken her from the Triple B were the same ones who drove her back there, and both of them accepted her offer of nachos and beer on the house.

About six weeks later, Dr Wainscott was at his office performing a follow-up review with a patient when his secretary buzzed the intercom; the Public Advocate was on the line. Dr Wainscott apologised to his patient for the interruption and took the call.

"Bernadette Fry didn't like her visit with Harvey," the Public Advocate said. "She's got the Health Services Commissioner on side."

"All right, thanks for letting me know," Dr Wainscott said, and felt the sweat pop to his face.

He called an emergency meeting after lunch. Jason came to the clinic staffroom with a bag of muffins and ate steadily during the wait for Emily. She arrived at last, clutching her handbag and a rolled-up magazine, but remained in the doorway.

"Did that Fry woman complain again?" she said.

"I don't know," Dr Wainscott said, "but I suppose it would be prudent if we made a plan."

"For what?" Jason said.

Dr Wainscott stood up, clattering his chair. "This is serious, this is a Victorian government thing, the Health Services Commissioner has the power to shut us down."

"Us?" Emily said, and slapped the rolled magazine against her thigh. On her way out the door, she said, "If it's that Fry woman again, it's got nothing to do with Jason or me."

Dr Wainscott returned to his office and called his union rep, who wasn't any help. At the end of his working day, Dr Wainscott drove his Mercedes towards the glowing green dome of the Triple B. In the car park, he killed the engine and sat for a while. Against the fence, a breeze idled at fallen maple leaves, stirring them into a lazy circle; it was the start of winter and still no rain.

Inside, he sipped at a double whisky for nearly twelve minutes before the door behind the bar opened to reveal Bernadette Fry, resplendent in a purple velvet dress. Her expression flat, unreadable, she crooked a finger and he followed her around the bar and through the doorway. The whiff of cleaning products brought an operating theatre to mind. The staffroom was crammed with fridge and sink, formica table, two vinyl chairs and the bulk of her voluminous body.

"Take a seat," Bernadette Fry said. "Coffee?"

He shook his head. While she boiled the kettle and fixed herself a drink, Dr Wainscott looked at the curios of meaningless sporting achievement that decorated the walls. Almost at eye level was a black-and-white photograph of a fat person, comically spherical in a wetsuit, brandishing flippers and a mask and standing on the deck of a boat. Then he realised that it was a shot of her, the hood of the wetsuit concealing the wiry hair to fool him, but before he could lean in for a better look, Bernadette Fry sat at the table.

She had to angle her chair into the middle of the room because her thighs wouldn't fit between the table legs, and he thought momentarily of how it might feel to press his feverish face against those soft, velvety knees. He waited for her to speak, but she appraised him with distant eyes and said nothing.

Finally, he said, "Bernadette, my dear, have you thought about what you want?"

She smiled with one side of her mouth. "Yeah, a scan of my whole body."

"But I was told you weren't interested in chemo."

"Not for that; to see if I have cancer anywhere else."

The tension went out of his shoulders. He actually smiled and meant it. "All right, Bernadette, it's a deal. CT or MRI?"

"Which is better?"

"It's much of a muchness, really."

"Then either one, and I don't want to pay for it."

Within a fortnight, Bernadette Fry had her CT scan at no charge.

Just over one week later, the Deputy Health Services Commissioner of Victoria called Dr Wainscott at his office to tell him he was required to attend a hearing in Melbourne and that he may bring his lawyer if he wished.

Dr Wainscott thanked the Deputy Health Services Commissioner, hung up the phone with great care and paused, his mind reeling.

So it had come to this, somehow, for a surgeon who couldn't walk down Main Street on a Sunday morning without at least one ex-patient, brimming with unshed tears, stopping him to shake hands or kiss his cheek. Shocked, Dr Wainscott felt wetness on his own lashes. This single glitch, somehow, might mean more than the miracle of one thousand lives that still ticked on earth solely because of him.

He had no choice but to call her. Bernadette Fry, her voice cool and remote, wished him good luck and hung up. Dr Wainscott returned the handset and leaned over until his forehead rested on the desktop. He closed his eyes and focused on the pulse fluttering at his throat. After a time, his secretary knocked on his office door and delivered the mail. One of the envelopes held Bernadette Fry's CT scan results and the significance of this coincidence forced Dr Wainscott to pray for the first time since childhood.

Then he opened the envelope and read the report. Bernadette Fry had her answer. The telephone was near his right hand. And at his left hand, underneath the desk, sat the paper shredder.

Dr Wainscott recalls this moment of indecision. He tries to smile, then says, "I'd very much like to talk about it with you."

"Okay," Bernadette Fry says. "So tell me why you did it."

The daylight has drained from Dr Wainscott's lounge room but he can't move from his armchair to switch on the lamp because he is trussed with duct tape. Bernadette Fry, sitting in his couch with the coffee table between them, is reduced to a silhouette.

The balcony is behind her and the town, with its points of warm yellow light streaming from the hundreds of homes below, is beyond his view.

At last, Dr Wainscott says, "We both took things too far. You nearly cost me my licence. The Health Services Commissioner went through me like a dose of salts, my dear, and the legal fees were horrendous."

She says, "You told me the scan was clear."

"Did I? Then it must have been."

Bernadette shakes her head. "This morning, I tracked down a copy of that report from the hospital. The report they posted to you. The one you called me about."

"I don't remember."

"You don't remember my liver tumour?"

Bernadette raises one of her hands, the hand that's holding the spear gun, and Dr Wainscott's chest seems to shrivel in on itself as if anticipating the terrible blow. He shouts, "It was six months ago and I don't remember, I swear. Please don't, Bernadette, please. For God's sake."

Despite the dark, Dr Wainscott can see Bernadette Fry lower the spear gun. Her hand, resting on her thigh, angles the weapon harmlessly at the floor. Dr Wainscott can breathe.

Then she says, "Listen to me very carefully. Tell me the truth right now and I won't shoot. Hurry up or the deal is off."

Dr Wainscott, sweating through his clothes, stares into the wild halo of her hair and says the first thing that comes out of his mouth.

Family Album

This is a snapshot of my father's greatest joy, his 1962 blue and white Nash convertible, taken outside the old homestead just before I was born. From left, my dad, Stephen Clarke, who farmed wheat in those days, then my mother Wilma. I'm the bump under her apron. The man with the dog, which I think was a collie, is Uncle Paul. He's dead now, but he opened the town's first hardware store. And the toddler next to him is apparently my sister, Jenny, who was killed by the dog in this picture three days after the photograph was taken.

Farm Hands

The door of the employment agency flew open and two men walked in. They each wore a backpack. The thinner man approached the counter.

"Can I help you?" the woman behind the counter said.

"Well, I'd hope so. We're looking for work, aren't we, Murray?"

Murray, round-shouldered and doughy, shambled to the counter, his face pinking with a sudden blush. "Yeah. We're not fussy, but doing something physical would be bloody good. You know, like, something on one of these farms."

Carl Jensen, standing at the far end of the counter, stopped scrolling through the list of casual job applicants on the computer screen and watched the men. They looked barely out of their teens, maybe twenty or twenty-one.

The woman said, "It's wheat and sheep farms around here. Either of you worked on a farm before?"

The thin man turned to Murray and smirked. "So we need a resume now to work up a sweat in the sun? Who knew it was so competitive? Do you think they want character references too?"

Murray snickered. Carl Jensen walked over.

The thin man said, "What's your issue, Grandad?"

"I've got to replace one and a half kilometres of fence. I pay twenty an hour, cash. I've a caravan out back for fifty a week; dinner is another fifty if you want it."

The thin man held out his hand. "Sweet. I'm Leon. This here is Murray."

Carl Jensen, with Leon and Murray crammed next to him in the ute, drove the line of bitumen through the flat landscape. Green wheat rolled in the breeze. Every now and then the ute flashed by a paddock of sheep, the startled animals motionless like features in a painting.

Leon said, "So Carl, wheat or sheep?"

"Wheat."

"Oh yeah? So what's with the fence? You scared the wheat'll get up and walk away?" Leon nudged an elbow into Murray's side and panted with silent laughter. Murray sniggered in response.

Carl said, "The elements rust the wire and rot the posts. I've got sheep on one side of me, horses on the other. Animals wreck fences all the time."

"So why not hire a fence contractor instead of busting your back and ours?"

Leon was watching him with the dark, alert eyes of a bird.

Carl said, "Wheat farming isn't just about wheat, it's about figuring costs. A fence contractor charges nine seventy-five a metre. If I get my own post-hole digger, I can do it for six."

Late morning at the homestead, Carl showed them the four-berth caravan, a hangover from decades past when Carl used to take his wife and children on holidays. His wife was long dead, his children long gone.

Leon and Murray decided to take the accommodation, which included a daily shower in the homestead's bathroom. Since they didn't have a vehicle to get into town, they also agreed to dinner; simple fare, Carl had warned. Chops or sausages, accompanied by mash and carrots, nothing fancy, with maybe an apple pie for dessert.

Carl gave the ute key to Leon, and said, "The farm equipment company is south of the township. I'm going on the back roads. Follow me closely or you'll end up getting lost."

Carl took the truck. He headed out on the ruler-straight road and the ute stayed about fifty metres behind him. An abandoned farmhouse raced past, sagged and broken, hulks of wrecked cars scattered out front. Carl heard the ute's horn and looked in his rear-view mirror.

The ute took a sudden hard left onto a dirt road that ran between paddocks. Swearing under his breath, Carl pulled over and swung a clumsy U-turn. By the time he got to the dirt road, the ute was pluming dust about a kilometre ahead.

Minutes later, the breeze whisked away the dust to reveal the ute parked at the side of the road. Carl stopped his truck, leapt from the cabin. The ute's door flung open and Leon jumped out.

Carl said, "What are you doing? Let's go, dickhead, you're on the clock."

Murray opened the passenger door of the ute and eased himself out, staring at Carl with wide eyes. Murray stood next to Leon. Carl saw that Leon, hunched with his mouth set, held a knife.

Carl put his fists on his hips. "You planning on robbing me?"

"That's right. So give me your cash and I won't hurt you."

"Listen boy, I don't have time for your bullshit, I need that fence up by the weekend. Now do you want the job or not?"

"I don't think you get it, Grandad. You're in deep shit."

"Boy, the only one in the shit is you."

Carl squared his shoulders and worked his boots into the gravel. Leon rushed him, punched the knife into Carl's arm, and sprang back.

"Oh God," Murray said.

Carl saw blood flowering over his shirtsleeve. There was no pain. "I don't understand," he said. "Why did you take the job when you had no intention of doing the work?"

"Give me the money."

Carl hesitated. The breeze picked up, caressing his sweating face. He reached into the top pocket of his shirt and threw the notes. Murray, breathing hard, scrambled over the dirt and gravel to gather up the strewn money. Then he stood up, and thumbed through the notes.

"Two-fifty, a lousy two-fifty," he said to Leon, his face blanching. "You told me farmers always use cash."

27

"And the rest of it," Leon said.

"That's it, that's all I have."

"Crap. A post-hole digger must be worth thousands."

"To buy, yeah, but I'm just hiring it for a couple of days."

The wind had died and there were no sounds. The field on one side of the dirt road was wheat, on the other side, sheep. A ewe watched from the fence, working her jaws on a mouthful of grass.

Leon said, "What about the money for the posts, the wire?"

"I've got credit with the store."

Carl's shoulder had begun to throb and his arm felt heavy. A runnel of blood tickled along the hairs on his forearm.

Murray said, "Oh shit, what're we gonna do now?"

"Search the truck, the old bastard's lying, it's got to be here somewhere."

Murray staggered to the truck. He wrenched open a door and climbed into the cabin, the truck lurching on its shockers. Carl could see him through the cabin's back window. The boy's head appeared, disappeared and appeared again. Murray struggled backwards out of the cabin and stood splay-footed, gasping and shaking his head.

"So there's nothing? Nothing?" Leon began to pace in circles, his nostrils pinched. After a while, he leaned against the truck with his back to them and bowed his head.

Carl said, "If we can just go into town like we were supposed to, we can forget this whole thing."

"Really?" Murray said. "But what about your shoulder?"

"It's nothing."

"You sure?" Murray raised his eyebrows. "Well, Mr Jensen, that'd be pretty big of you to let it go like that, I mean, to turn the other cheek and everything after, you know, after this."

"Misunderstandings happen, I realise that. Okay?"

Leon spun around, flung himself on Carl and hit him over and over while Carl flailed his arms and Murray shrieked. It was over in seconds. Carl fell and rolled onto his back. Wispy strips of cloud were chasing each other across the sky. Carl's eyes fluttered shut. He smarted and stung all over. Murray was still yowling, high-pitched, like a girl.

"Shut up, shut up," Leon shouted.

"Oh my God. Is he dead? Did you kill him?"

"Shut up, will you? Get a grip."

"What did you do that for, Leon? Didn't you hear him? He said that if we drove into town like we were supposed to—"

"Shut up, I had to do it; we would've got done no matter what."

Murray made sounds like he was crying. "Oh shit, he's not moving. Mr Jensen?"

"Come on, let's go."

"What?"

"The ute, get in."

"We're gonna leave him here?"

"I'll drive the first leg."

"What? But what about Mr Jensen?"

"Just get in the ute, Murray, I swear…"

The ute's engine started up, revved hard. Gravel sprayed over Carl. He opened his eyes. The ute, churning dust, was fishtailing along the dirt towards the main road. Carl flopped onto his stomach and gathered his arms and legs beneath him. He got up, slid along the side of the truck to its open door and leaned over the front seat. He groped at the centre console for his mobile phone. It took him some time to figure out that the battery was flat. The charger cord hung from the socket for the cigarette lighter. He patted along his pockets for the keys. They weren't there. He looked up through the windscreen and saw, in the distance, the ute's brake lights come on.

He pushed himself off the seat and kicked through the blood-spattered dirt where he had fallen. The keys weren't there either. The ute completed its U-turn. Carl pitched himself at the truck, leaned into the cabin, and grabbed the tyre lever. He backed out, slammed the door. The ute came to a stop facing the truck. Leon and Murray emerged. Carl showed them the tyre lever.

"You're a tough old prick, aren't you?" Leon said, and rushed at him.

A scalding heat flashed across Carl's throat and then he was down. Leon and Murray loomed above him. Murray, sobbing, had the tyre lever.

"I'm really sorry, Mr Jensen, it's just that I can't go to jail, you know? I'm not cut out for it, I can't do it."

Murray raised the tyre lever. Carl closed his eyes, saw his field of wheat shining green in the weak August sunshine, the heads rasping across his outstretched hand, the breeze hissing through the stalks.

There was nothing for a time.

A whooshing, roaring sound made Carl struggle to open his eyes, his eyelids sticky and caked. Flaming orange wheat had come to life, twisting and thrashing in a wind he couldn't feel, throwing off heat. Carl propped himself on an elbow. It wasn't wheat, but fire. His truck was on fire. His boots and jeans were smoking, the flesh on his arms and face popping and lifting.

Carl pushed his heels into the dirt and scooted himself backwards until the burning vehicle receded into a gentle campfire over which he could warm up the pan of beans and sausages. Glenda came out of the bush with their two boys. He saw that a strand of hair had fallen from her ponytail and he wanted to kiss her.

Carl heard voices. He opened one of his eyes. Clouds were speeding across the sky. The truck was belching smoke. The voices came nearer. He looked around for Leon and Murray. Instead, he saw Glenda.

"Honey?" Carl said. "Is that you?"

Glenda squatted by his side and said, "Jesus aitch Christ, I don't believe it. Carl? Jesus, what the hell happened? Brendan, call an ambulance. We've got Carl Jensen over here and he's still alive."

"Glenda?"

"No, it's me. Frank, Frank Whitby. I'm here with Brendan and the CFA truck. Someone driving past saw the fire and called us out. Holy Mary, mother of God, just hold on, can you hear me, Carl? Help is coming."

Carl nodded and went back to the campfire where Glenda was smiling at him, and his boys were plucking sausages straight out of the pan. After lunch, they would go swimming, then try their luck with the fishing rods, and get redfin or cod for dinner.

Blue Light Taxi

You stumble from the bar, giggling. The street is a blur of tram tracks, shop fronts and parked cars. There must be stars overhead, but the streetlights are too bright for you to see them.

"Wait," you shout, and laugh, doubling up.

Far ahead, the two detectives, striding to a Holden sedan, stop and look around. You turn to the couple behind you. What are their names again? They are talking, not making sense, every syllable floating off like a balloon. The earth tilts beneath your stilettos. One of the detectives, the chubby-cheeked one, suddenly has his arm pressed around your waist, his sweating hand on your hip. You smell whisky and cigarettes.

"Come on, you can't call it a night," he says. "We've got that party, remember?"

You say, "Just help me to the car, Hedgehog."

The chubby-cheeked detective sniggers. Hedgehog is your name for him; you came up with it during your fifth or sixth or whatever champagne. His short hair is gelled into needles, and he's pear-shaped, a waddler, a stout little hedgehog on hind legs. You giggle again.

He says, "Can you walk? Do you want me to carry you?"

"Oh, no, I hope she's not sick," a female voice says.

You glance at the couple: the greasy-faced girl with her scruffy coat shedding nylon faux-fur from its lapels; the skinny boy with his straight-leg jeans, long fringe and cardigan. They are very young. Older than you, of course, but so cloistered and middle-class that when you and the detectives used them for laughs they didn't even know it. But they bought drinks too, so what the hell.

"I think she needs coffee," the chubby-cheeked detective says.

You push away from him and dash along the footpath towards the other detective, who has his hands on his hips, his suit jacket pushed back to reveal his crumpled shirt, his paunch, his shoulder holster, the butt of a .45. Your stiletto heels clack and smack against concrete. Each footfall sends shock waves up your legs. The world is sliding. The detective catches you by your elbows, straightens you up.

"Know what you look like?" he says. "A baby horse, all legs and no balance. I was waiting for you to face-plant."

"Oh yeah? What would you have done?"

"Left you there."

Under the streetlight, he's a lot older than you thought, maybe fifty. He wears his thinning brown hair to his collar in a style too youthful for the lines around his eyes and the yellow of his long teeth.

You say, "If I'm Baby Horse and he's Hedgehog, then you're Mister Fox." You laugh but he doesn't.

He looks over your head and says, "What about them?" and lets go of you.

You turn. The couple is right there, staring at you. The girl especially seems fascinated, like she's never seen anything like you before. It's a look you already know from high school, you with your sneer and your piercings, those scars along your arms. Cliques of girls look at you that same way every lunchtime and recess when they walk on by.

"Hurry up, let's go," says the chubby-cheeked detective, standing at the Holden sedan. Then he snatches a parking ticket from under the windscreen wiper and flips it to the gutter without even looking at it, without even commenting. A warm thrill diffuses through you.

A V8 packed with teenagers and thumping rap music ploughs past. A bottle smashes against the footpath.

"Arrest them," you shout, and lean against the Holden, closing your eyes.

You're bundled into the back of the car. You crawl along the seat and slump against the window on the far side. The boy gets in next to you, the girl takes the other window seat, and the detectives are in front with the older one behind the wheel. The sedan pulls away from the kerb.

"Oh my God," you say, peering around the driver's seat to point at the two-way radio and handset recessed into the dashboard. "Is this an unmarked cop car?"

"Aw, don't tell me this is your first ride in a blue light taxi," says the chubby-cheeked detective. "A fine, upstanding girl like you."

"Wow," you say, "have you got lights and sirens?"

"It's a frigging cop car, isn't it?" he says, and snorts through his nose. "How many have you had tonight, honey? Bottles, not glasses. You're way past counting glasses."

Yes, I am, you think. *I'm way past counting anything anymore.* For a few seconds, thoughts of home come to you, but staccato, each one quickly lost, beads on an open-ended string. It doesn't matter. You don't want to think about your family.

"What's the fastest you can drive?" you say.

"Depends on the traffic," the older detective says.

"Well, I can't see much traffic right now."

The older detective turns his head to catch your eye. He smirks. The chubby-cheeked detective gapes at you joyfully and slaps his thigh.

The older detective says, "She's a bit of a firecracker, isn't she? We're gonna have to watch her, mate, what do you reckon?"

"Oh yeah," the chubby-cheeked detective says. "Oh, shit yeah."

"Come on," you say. "*Come on.*"

They glance at each other. You become aware that you're holding your breath. A small male voice says, "I don't think we should." Startled, you look around. It is the couple. You forgot about them, yet here they are, two church mice.

The acceleration slams you off balance. The siren and strobing lights almost stop your heart. Then you grab the back of the driver's seat and hang on, whooping.

The car takes a corner, tyres screaming on the bitumen. You

point at the red light up ahead and yell, "Don't stop." The car blows through the intersection. You point again, yelling, "Drive on the wrong side," and the car fishtails over the line. The posted limit is sixty, but the speedometer quivers over one-twenty-five.

The chubby-cheeked detective, his eyes bright, murmurs, "Oh, honey, you're loving this, right?"

You point at a one-way sign and yell, "Turn into that street," and the car does. You are god of this machine. The rush threatens to take off the top of your skull.

There is a sudden dazzle of headlights.

The older detective leans on the horn and the headlights slew out of the way. You blast past a hatchback, a shocked face at the window, and your laugh is wild. The detectives are laughing too. You remember Mister and Missus Church Mouse and how much you hated their white-bread sensibilities but you're expansive now, all forgiving, gracious, and you turn to them, a benevolent deity.

It's a scene from another movie. The girl appears to be crying. The boy's lips are pulled back from his teeth. The couple is shrunk into the seat, clutching at each other.

The car lurches to a halt. It is a red light. A semi-trailer is lumbering across the intersection.

The girl flings open the door. The couple tumbles from the car and sprints down the footpath, coat tails and cardigan flapping. Their animal panic makes you understand that you should be bailing right along with them, that these detectives should be watching the pitching frills of your polyester dress as you also run to safety.

"I guess they've changed their mind about the party," the older detective says, and turns off the siren.

"Aw, stuff 'em, so what." The chubby-cheeked detective gets out of the car, shuts the back door, and climbs into the front passenger seat again.

The older detective turns off the spinning blue and red lights. The car has pulled in its teeth and claws. Now it's just another vehicle on the road, a plain Holden sedan. Your heart rate drops, your eyes fill. You've had enough but the night isn't over yet.

"Ready, honey?" the chubby-cheeked detective says.
You nod.
The light turns green.

Lunch at the Trout Farm

They drove for an hour to reach the hills, and some twenty minutes along a gravel road. The steering wheel jittered beneath Tom's sweating hands. Maybe his wife Donna was right and they were lost after all, but then the sign-posted gate appeared out of the scrub.

"Well, finally," Donna said, and reached into the footwell for her handbag.

Jake, in the back next to the picnic hamper, started bucking in his seat. "Oh my God, Dad, are we here?"

"We sure are," Tom said. "Who needs a cake? We're gonna catch us a happy-birthday trout, aren't we mate?"

"Don't build it up too much," Donna whispered.

"Wow, Dad, this is the best birthday ever."

The dual-cab ute bounced and rattled down the driveway for a time with nothing around but red earth and gum trees.

"Welcome! No dogs! Take your rubbish with you!" Jake said, reading the hand-painted sign hammered into the car parking area. "What's the time? Hey, if I was at school right now, I'd be in the art room doing a dumb painting or whatever."

Donna twisted around in her seat. "All right, that's enough. Don't get used to this, Jake. It's a one-off, okay?"

"Okay, Mum."

"He's grade one, what difference does it make?" Tom whispered.

Donna gave him a brief look over the top of her sunglasses. Tom tightened his grip on the steering wheel. Despite Donna's reservations, he'd pulled Jake out of school so they could have this family day, a rare event given Tom's long hours. His painting and decorating business was nearly a year old, but just scraping by. In fact, each of his three employees made more money than he did.

Tom parked the ute and they got out.

Donna said, "Uh-oh. We're the only car here."

"That's because it's Monday morning."

"It looks closed to me."

"I rang the bloke yesterday. He knows we're coming."

"Oh no, is it closed?" Jake said.

"Of course it isn't closed, all right? Look, here's the bloke who runs the place."

Out of the weatherboard house on the edge of the car park appeared a pear-shaped man in navy overalls and gumboots. He had a limp. They waited for him.

"Tom, is it?" the owner said. "So, you made it all right?"

"I just followed the directions you gave me over the phone, and here we are," Tom said, and let out a hearty laugh.

"Well, it was much further than we were led to believe," Donna said.

"Well, that depends on how fast you drive," the owner said, and smiled. "Now, let's get you folks started."

They followed him out of the car park and through an area equipped with shade cloths, barbecues and wooden picnic tables. Jake skipped around them and kept looking up to catch glimpses of parrots flitting about the gum trees. It occurred to Tom that today was his son's first time in the countryside, and the realisation, unexpectedly, choked him up.

They approached a wooden shack. A framework crammed with fishing rods was attached to one side of the shack. The owner stopped and sorted through the rods, selecting on their behalf without asking. Beyond the shack sat two giant, rectangular ponds. They looked to Tom like flooded graves, and in a way, he supposed they were; the trout in those ponds were already as good as dead.

And in less than a minute, the owner had doled out the fishing equipment, taken the entry fee in cash, and left them to it.

"Terrific," Donna said. "Now what do we do?"

"Fish," Tom said.

"Yeah, no kidding. I thought we were supposed to get a lesson."

"I guess that was it." Tom watched the owner limp back to the weatherboard house and disappear inside. "We'll be okay. It's not that hard."

"Christ, that bait really stinks," she said.

Jake leant his rod against the shack. "You'd better catch all the fish, Dad. I'll probably just get a hook in my eye."

"Come on, mate, you'll be fine," Tom said, and gave what he hoped was a reassuring smile. "Now, which pond do you want to try?"

He picked up their rods and equipment and waited. A hand-written sign hammered into the grass between the ponds stated, "No throwing fish back". Tom could feel the sweat starting to run again.

Donna shrugged. "I don't care. I'm not fishing, anyway."

"All right then, Jake, 'plate-sized' or 'banquet-sized'?"

Jake jumped up and down, chanting, "Banquet, banquet, banquet."

"I packed two salads and a bread stick," Donna said. "Just how much trout are we expected to eat?"

So they went to the pond with the hand-painted sign, "Plate-sized 500g or less", and looked into the water. Smooth, opalescent shapes skimmed just under the surface.

"Which one's going to be yours, Jake?" Tom said.

"Oh, boy, what are we waiting for?"

Tom pulled a nub of fish bait from the block. It was cold and dense like clay. He moulded it around the hook at the end of Jake's fishing line, and handed the rod to the boy.

Jake held it like it was about to explode in his face. "What do I do?"

"Okay, first, just try to relax," Tom said. "Put one hand in front of the other on the handle."

Donna said, "Tom, when was the last time you did any fishing?"

She had on her sunglasses, so Tom couldn't read her expression. "Just get the camera ready," he told her. "Jake's about to catch a fish."

Jake giggled. Donna opened the zip on her bag and rummaged inside it.

Tom held his son's slender wrists and began to swivel the boy's arms back and forth. He said, "When you throw out the line, you've got to try and snap the rod, like this, you see? Like cracking a whip."

"How's that going to help him?" Donna said. "He's seven years old, he's never cracked a whip in his life."

"But he's seen it done," Tom said. "Haven't you mate?"

"Not really."

"Don't worry, you'll be fine. Donna, get the camera ready. Jake, let's cast. We're gonna aim for the middle of the pond, all right?"

"All right."

Tom thumbed the bail arm on the reel and released the line. Gripping Jake's wrists, he pulled back and swung the rod as quick as he could despite the dead weight of his son's arms. The grey nub of bait wobbled out on a scrap of line, and plunked into the water less than a foot away from them.

"Well, that sucked big time," Jake said, his cheeks reddening.

"It doesn't matter," Tom said. "That was just a practice run."

"I can't do it, Dad."

Tom wound in the line and jammed the rod back into his son's limp hands. *Please let this work.* Then they cast again and, sweet relief, the bait arced away and landed in the middle of the pond with hardly a splash.

"Oh, yes!" Jake shrieked. "Boy, Dad, was that a great cast or what!"

"Brilliant. Okay now, start turning the handle, slowly now, keep it going…"

The sudden pull on the line staggered the boy. Tom could have screamed his joy to the heavens but, instead, grabbed the net and yelled, "Reel it in, Jake! Lift the rod!"

"Oh my God!" Jake squealed, laughing. The thrashing fish broke the surface, submerged and flailed again, while Jake wrestled the rod and struggled to keep his footing. "Dad, help me!"

Tom took hold of the fishing rod with one hand and, with the other, dipped the net into the water and scooped out the fish. It flapped, gasping, a runnel of blood trailing from its mouth.

"Look, Mum, look! It's a monster!"

"Well done, Jake," she said. "What a team you two make."

Tom smiled back at her. He took the pliers from the bucket and, with a flourish, removed the hook from the fish's mouth. Then he grabbed the stumpy wooden truncheon from the bucket and hit the flopping trout hard on the head. *Thock*. The sound of it was surprisingly hollow. The trout quivered, then stopped altogether.

Donna showed the digital photos. Not only was each shot perfect, but the series of shots was perfect, too—the cast, the fish on the hook churning the brown water, the fish in the net—and every snap lit by Jake's flushed and beaming face. Tom was in each photo, of course, thickening through the middle and thinning on top, but he looked happy as well.

"Excellent work," Tom said, and kissed Donna on the lips.

Jake caught another trout, and then Tom had a go. Donna and Jake went to the ute for the picnic hamper while Tom knocked on the door of the weatherboard house and asked the owner to clean their catch.

He followed the owner to the wooden shack. Inside was a set of scales, a cash register, and a stainless-steel table with a high lip on all sides. The owner weighed the fish and Tom paid in cash.

The owner bent down and turned a hidden tap, which started a continuous flush of water along the tabletop. He used a thin blade to decapitate the fish and take its fins. Then he ran the blade along the belly. A tumble of blue and red guts fell out. The running water swept the parts along the table and into a sunken trap. Tom was glad that Jake wasn't here to see this.

Donna had set the picnic table in the meantime. Tom returned with the cleaned fish. He watched Jake, who was at the other end of the clearing playing on a swing and slide set, and said, "Do you reckon he's having a good time?"

"Only the time of his life, by the look of it."

"Are you having a good time too?"

Donna turned away. "Don't get started on that again. Not on his birthday."

Tom took the bottle of oil and barbecue tools from the hamper, and carried the fish to the nearest barbecue. The grill plates were crusted in grease, dead bugs and bird droppings. The neighbouring barbecue was just as filthy. A minivan pulled into the car park and about a dozen Asians got out. The owner limped from the weatherboard house and led them towards the ponds.

Tom went back to the picnic table. "The barbies are dirty, but it doesn't matter. I'll cook on aluminium foil."

"Oh, yeah? Then I hope you packed some, because I sure didn't."

Tom hesitated, stumped.

Donna stood up, her mouth in a tight line. "I never cook on the barbecue. That's your job. How am I supposed to know about foil?"

"Don't worry, it'll be okay. I'll peel the skin off once it's cooked."

Donna threw up her hands and sat at the table with her back to him.

Tom headed to the bank of barbecues. Across the clearing, Jake hopped off the swing and started climbing the ladder to the slide. Tom took some time choosing the least grotty barbecue. He pushed the ignition switch and nothing happened. Cursing, he selected another barbecue. That wouldn't light, either. Maybe there was a trick to it, or he was supposed to use matches, which he didn't have anyway. He glanced at the pond area. The owner was still occupied with the tourists. Tom would have to walk all the way over there and ask for help, or he could pack the fish and drive his family home, but either option meant first explaining his failure to Donna.

He pressed another ignition. *Click, click, click.* This wasn't going to work. He looked over at his wife sitting with her arms crossed, and then he looked over at his son whooping as he hammered down the slide, and Tom had no idea what to do next.

Road Rage

Darren's car stank of cigarette smoke. Chrissy didn't say anything. With her suitcase on the back seat, she accepted her brother's kiss on the unmarked side of her face and told him he looked good, which wasn't exactly true; he'd gained a lot of weight since she'd last seen him on Christmas Day.

Twenty minutes into the drive from her inner-city flat to his suburban house, Darren lit another cigarette. Chrissy lowered the passenger window. The late autumn air bit at her wounds and tightened her stitches. She closed the window and took smaller breaths.

Darren turned the car from the main road into a street lined with tired brick houses and yellowed lawns. When Chrissy saw Darren's place up ahead with its deep veranda built under the roofline, she wanted to sob but didn't know why. Her old self, the twenty-six-year-old accountant who had moved fearlessly in the world, was only three days in the past but felt much further away than that.

Unexpectedly, Darren stopped the car. He lurched into reverse. They drew level to the front yard of a house where a middle-aged man in a dirty t-shirt and jeans, smoking a cigarette, paced in apparently fruitless circles. Darren braked. The man faced them, squinting. He had lank hair hanging to his shoulders and a droopy moustache.

Chrissy said, "Oh, for God's sake..."

"Open your window," Darren said, and she did. He leaned over her and shouted, "Hey, mate. That your red Commodore on the road there?"

"What of it?"

"You've left your lights on."

"Aw, thanks mate. Cheers."

Darren coasted the car a few metres and turned it into his own driveway.

"Who the hell was that?" Chrissy said.

"A neighbour I've nicknamed *Maniac*." Darren sniggered. "His car's a piece of crap and he goes nuts when it doesn't start. You know he lives there with his parents? They chase him out of the house sometimes. One day his mum went after him with her walking stick, can you believe it? Yeah, they fight with that dirtbag all the time."

"What about?"

Darren shrugged and cut the engine.

Chrissy trailed him into the shade of the veranda. "That man, Maniac," she whispered. "He's watching us."

"Don't worry," Darren said, unlocking the front door. "It's bright out there and dark under here. He can't see us. No one can."

She followed her brother into the house. Like the car, it reeked of cigarettes. Chrissy decided before she'd even closed the door that she would spend most of her convalescence on the veranda. She walked into the living room. The lounge suite and redwood entertainment centre with its stereo, amp, DVD player and plasma television were gone. In their place, centred in the expanse of carpet, were a canvas chair and a portable TV.

Chrissy said. "Things have changed a fair bit since Christmas lunch."

Darren put down her suitcase, propped his hands on his hips and surveyed the near-empty room with surprise, as if he hadn't noticed anything wrong until now. "Yeah, it's not much, is it? Brenda took everything that wasn't nailed down. I haven't had time yet to replace the stuff."

"In five months?"

He laughed. Chrissy smiled too, but gently, so as not to strain the stitches.

They ate dinner early: five-thirty. Darren had to leave at six o'clock for his night shift at the printing factory. They sat at a card table, set up where the dining table used to be, and ate Darren's preparation of chops, peas and mashed potatoes. She noticed that he had red, blue, yellow, black ink spattered over his uniform, ground into the calluses of his hands, staining the quicks of his fingernails.

"Stop staring at me," he said.

"I'm sorry."

"You'll be fine. I'll be back tomorrow morning around seven. We're not allowed mobile phones in the factory, but I'll give you the number for the mounting department. Just be patient and let it ring." He put down his knife and fork and picked up a chop to gnaw at it. "You're studying me again."

She touched his arm and said, "Thanks for letting me stay here. It won't be for long, I promise, I just didn't know where else to go."

He took his plate to the sink. "You could always ring Mum and Dad, if you feel like talking."

She nodded, watching the spots of fat congeal on her plate. After a time, she heard the front door open and close and his car start up. The engine drone moved out of earshot.

Chrissy slept in the single bed in the spare room.

Darren got home just after seven o'clock in the morning. She made him bacon and eggs, which he chased with a couple of beers and a smoke. He showered and went to bed for the day.

Chrissy put the canvas chair from the living room onto the veranda, and piled books and magazines along the balustrade, but found she couldn't concentrate on reading. The wind kept blowing scraps of a woman's disembodied voice bellowing *five, six, seven, eight*, over and over, as if counting the beat for a roomful of dancers or marking time for a band, but Chrissy couldn't see any cars parked on the street or in nearby driveways. Then an elderly man puttered along the footpath on a motorised scooter. He had a scruffy Pomeranian on his lap, its leash trailing. The dog, smiling broadly with a long, hanging tongue, seemed to be enjoying the ride. These things were hard to understand.

When Chrissy returned to the veranda after lunch, two police vans were parked in the street. She ducked back into the shadows. Maniac was sprawled on his front lawn with his hands cuffed behind his back. Of the four uniformed police ranged around him in a loose circle, one, a woman, was holding the garden hose and watering his face.

Chrissy approached the balustrade and clutched the railing. She couldn't hear a thing. The five in the tableau were relaxed and calm. No one was shouting. She figured that the first divisional van with two coppers hadn't been enough to contain Maniac, and that backup had come. A dose of pepper spray must have knocked the fight out of him. Maniac struggled to a sitting position, his jeans and flannelette shirt sopping. Two of the officers grabbed him by his elbows and hauled him up. They steered him into the back of a van. The female officer ambled to the tap and turned off the hose. Then the police got into both vans and drove away.

Chrissy watched Maniac's house for a while, waiting for something else to happen. She considered waking up Darren to tell him. Instead, she rang her parents. They weren't interested in the neighbour's arrest. Mum said that Darren lived in a bogan area anyway, so what can you expect, and no wonder Brenda left, and have the police caught *That Psychopath* yet? Then Dad got on the phone and said that he had a right mind to climb out of his sickbed and jump on a plane and speak man-to-man to the detectives handling her case and demand to know why they weren't doing anything.

Chrissy said, *Dad, it's only been four days*, and Dad said, *Yes, but how many Mercedes-driving psychopaths could be rampaging around Melbourne?* So Chrissy told them she would come out to see them once the bruising and swelling had gone down. *Kiss kiss*. She hung up, trembling.

Over dinner, she said to Darren, "Why do you think they arrested Maniac?"

"Who cares? He'll be back soon enough. He always is."

The next morning, while she cooked bacon and eggs for Darren, they got into an argument. Chrissy had meant to talk about going furniture shopping but had somehow said, "Why did she leave?"

"Brenda? Jesus, how should I know?"

"Didn't you ask her?"

He flicked his cigarette into the sink, and crossed his arms. "She reckoned she didn't want to be with me anymore."

"But why not? Was there someone else? Did you have a fight?" Chrissy turned from the stove to see that he was smiling and frowning at the same time. She continued, "Weren't you getting along?"

"We were getting along fine."

"That doesn't make any sense."

"Who said it had to?"

"But everything happens for a reason."

Darren started a long, jeering laugh. Chrissy fell quiet.

"Really?" he said. "Everything? What about the stranger that pulled you out of your car and beat the living crap out of you? What's the reason for that?"

Darren stalked from the kitchen and down the hall. She heard the shower and later the click of his bedroom door closing. Nonetheless, he kissed her on the top of her head before he left for work that evening.

That night, the sudden blare of a car horn jolted Chrissy awake. She fumbled with the lamp and checked her watch: 3:42am. She lay back in bed and waited. The horn didn't stop. It clamoured on and on and on. The screaming pitch yowled in and out of her ears, making her nauseated. Voices shrilled over the din. A female yelled, *Make it stop, turn it off.* A male shouted, *Get away from my fuggin car.* Feet drummed along the footpath. There were more voices, a yapping dog.

Chrissy went to the kitchen and grabbed the phone. Darren's work number was taped to the cupboard. She could barely hear the ringing over the car horn. The phone rang out. She pressed redial. While listening to the tone, she went onto the veranda. The blatting came from a red Commodore parked across the road and two doors down: Maniac's house. The car had a lazy handful of flames working its way around the bonnet. People were watching from porches and lawns. No one was trying to put out the fire. Chrissy pressed redial.

Then the car horn stopped. Its sudden cessation unbalanced her for a moment. The fire must have burnt out some wires. Now she could hear the neighbours on the street, talking and swearing. Chrissy hung up the phone and thumbed the redial button. The bland tone rang out again.

The fire licked inside the Commodore's cabin, lapped at the seats, and took a firm hold. Two frail and small figures stood on Maniac's lawn. Chrissy realised in a panicky rush that the car was Maniac's; these figures must be his parents. But where was Maniac? She studied each dimly lit silhouette on the street but couldn't spot him. Maybe he was still in the lockup.

Intermittent lights winked across the scene. A police car, ambulance and fire truck pulled up. The officers stood around while the Commodore burned and smoked. As if galvanised by the arrival of emergency services, Maniac's elderly parents tottered to the roadside, gesturing and flouncing and weeping at the conflagration, while the police and ambulance officers, unmoved, watched their performance. The fire officers strolled to the rear of their truck and began unfurling a hose. Chrissy hung up the phone and didn't press redial.

And then, there he was, Maniac, standing bow-legged and sure on the nature strip like he'd been there all along, the lights from the emergency vehicles throwing staccato blinks of red and blue over him. His parents were slapping their tiny hands at his back, but Maniac ignored them and strode towards the Commodore. He seemed to be smiling, or maybe grimacing, it was hard to tell. Chrissy held her breath. Like a mad conductor of a hellish orchestra, Maniac raised his arms at the flames engulfing his car as if willing them higher. Chrissy couldn't help but stare at him, spellbound, because his clawed hands surely held the answer to everything.

The Caldwell Case

He was wearing a balaclava, but you didn't have to see his face to know he was dead. The body lay sprawled across the kitchen tiles like a sack of mud. The detective named Higgins used his foot to nudge the body, and then he said to the uniformed officer standing by the kitchen sink, "How'd it happen?"

"Beaten to death."

"Okay. Where's the weapon?"

"There isn't one," the uniformed officer said. "Just bare fists, so they reckon." He inclined his head towards the doorway that led from the kitchen to the lounge room. Higgins turned and looked.

The husband and wife were sitting on the couch. Police officers milled around them and two ambulance officers were unrolling blood pressure cuffs and opening bandages, but the couple stared, unseeing, into the middle distance, with the same blank eyes.

"Their kids slept right through it," the uniformed officer said. "A neighbour has taken them for now."

"Okay," Higgins said. "Is the husband a boxer? Black belt? What?"

"Neither." The uniformed officer reached behind him and picked up a plastic bag from the kitchen bench. In it was a pair of handcuffs in pieces. "And the offender had him cuffed from the get-go. The fireys snipped him out just before you blokes got here."

"That's even more impressive," Higgins said, and took the bag and put it in his suit pocket.

"No, you've got it wrong," the uniformed officer said. "The husband didn't kill the offender. Apparently, it was the wife."

Higgins frowned, laughed, and then frowned again. He turned to take another look at the small and shivering woman. "You're joking. That's what they told you?"

Moving to make way for the forensic photographer, he went into the lounge room. The husband had his arms around the wife, weeping silently into her neck, and whispering over and over that he was sorry. She sat, staring at nothing.

Higgins sucked at his lips, and wondered why a pleasant, middle-class couple from the suburbs would want to lie to the police.

The couple, Mr and Mrs Caldwell, was ferried by ambulance to the local hospital just before sunrise. By the time Higgins arrived at the hospital an hour or so later, Mr Caldwell was sitting in the casualty waiting room, and there was no sign of his wife.

Higgins bought a couple of cans of cola from the drinks machine in the corner and sat down next to him.

"John Caldwell? I'm Detective Sergeant Higgins from the Homicide Squad. I was at your house a little while ago. Remember?" Higgins offered one of the cans. John Caldwell took it. He was tall and heavy-set, with bullish shoulders. Higgins took note of the red weals around the husband's wrists and said, "Back at the house, you were apologising to your wife. What for?"

John Caldwell emptied his lungs in a drawn-out sigh. "Because I didn't protect her."

"No other reason?"

"It's my job to protect my family. And I didn't do that." He rolled the can between his big hands. "They've had Megan up in X-ray for ages. What do you think is taking them so long?"

Higgins opened his cola and took a swig. "I'm sure everything is okay, but hospitals always make doubly sure. I'd like you to tell me what happened."

"Well, I don't know much. A noise woke us up about four o'clock. I told Megan to stay in bed. I went down the hallway, and something hit me over the head. The next thing I remember seeing is Megan standing over the man's body."

"And you were wearing the handcuffs at that point?"

John Caldwell nodded.

Higgins watched the nursing staff behind the counter and sipped at his drink. After a while, he said, "How did the offender get in?"

"I don't know. He must have broken in."

"No, he didn't. All your windows and doors were intact."

John Caldwell shrugged. Then he said, "I put the bins out last night. Maybe I forgot to lock the back door."

"Okay, that makes sense. Do you lift weights, Mr Caldwell?"

"I've got some equipment in the garage."

"If I searched your house, I wouldn't find receipts for a balaclava and handcuffs, would I?"

John Caldwell stared with bewildered eyes.

Higgins watched closely, then reached into his jacket pocket and pulled out a business card. "Call me if you think of anything else," he said, giving John Caldwell the card. "Someone from my office will be coming by in a little while to talk to you some more and drop you home. Okay? Wait here."

Higgins followed the signs along the corridor to the X-ray Department. After asking around, he located Mrs Caldwell's casualty doctor, a stout woman with her hair scraped into a tight bun. Higgins and the doctor stood in a doorway to keep clear of the staff and patients walking the corridor.

"Look, I'm sorry but we're prepping Mrs Caldwell for surgery," the doctor said. "You won't be able to speak to her until later this afternoon."

"What's the surgery for?" Higgins said.

"Pins, screws, plates, possibly external fixators; we'll have to see how bad when we open her up. She's got multiple compression fractures and comminuted fractures in both arms."

"She's got what?"

"The bones in her hands, wrists and forearms are shattered and compacted." The doctor smiled. "All right, put it this way, Detective. Imagine she dived out of a double-storey building and landed smack on her fists."

Higgins said, "Is there any other way she could have hurt herself like that? Apart from jumping out of a double-storey building?"

"She told me she was defending herself against a burglar."

"Apart from that, too."

The doctor appraised him with cool grey eyes, and then gazed at the ceiling for a time. "The degree of splintering suggests that whatever hit her, hit a lot of times."

"What about a mallet?" Higgins said. "Swung by a big bloke, smashing her flush on the knuckles?"

"I suppose that could do it, yes."

Higgins thanked the doctor and gave her one of his business cards. In the squad vehicle out in the hospital car park, he called the Coroner's Court and was told the autopsy on the Caldwell offender hadn't yet begun. Then Higgins drove back to headquarters where his detective inspector was waiting for him.

They sat in Detective Inspector Naylor's office. Naylor was an older man with forty years of service and a puffy red face. He had taken to gnawing on a paperclip since quitting cigarettes.

Higgins said, "The offender is Craig Spencer. He's got priors for theft and assault. He was charged with rape a few years back but got off."

"And the torch and knife found in the kitchen?"

"Covered with the offender's fingerprints, for what it's worth," Higgins said. "The butt of the torch has Mr Caldwell's blood type on it. We're still waiting on DNA analysis to be sure."

"So, no one's found the offender's vehicle yet?" Naylor said.

Higgins shook his head. "And I don't believe he went to the Caldwell house on foot."

"Meaning?"

"I think the Caldwells knew this man. I think they invited him over. John Caldwell picked him up in his car, brought him home and killed him. We're digging into the husband's background. We'll find a connection somewhere."

Naylor worked the paperclip from one side of his mouth to the other. "Has the husband got any injuries to his hands?"

"Only from the handcuffs. He would have used a weapon."

"Then how do you explain the wife's injuries?"

Higgins wiped his hand over his face. He was tired after only four hours of sleep. "I haven't figured that out yet. But she could have done it to herself to cover for her husband. I had a bloke a while back who faked a holdup on his store. He shot himself in the leg."

Naylor took the paperclip from between his teeth. "You're getting ahead of yourself, aren't you?"

"No vehicle for the offender. No forced entry. No key for the handcuffs found on the offender or anywhere else in the kitchen or back yard, and a dodgy story from the Caldwells. It's a set-up, plain as day."

Naylor chewed on the paperclip.

Higgins stood up. "If you want me, I'll be at the Coroner's Court."

The pathologist, Eva Daniels, was slated for the Caldwell offender, and she was on her coffee break when Higgins arrived. He joined her in the tearoom and took a couple of pastries from the servery for his breakfast. They sat at one of the tables by the window.

"I've only had time to give your offender a quick once over," Daniels said.

"And what do you reckon?"

"Off the top of my head?" she said, and laughed. "All right. That he picked a fight with a bodybuilder in the throes of a steroid-induced psychosis."

Higgins nodded and took another bite of vanilla slice. "Could a woman have done it to him? With her fists?"

"I wouldn't think so, but it depends on her size and strength."

"I could tuck her under one arm."

"In that case, I'd say no. But don't quote me until I've done the autopsy. I'll call you when I know more."

Higgins got up. "Thanks. You've helped me already."

"Hang on," she said and pointed at his face. "Icing sugar."

Higgins winked, wiped his mouth with his jacket sleeve, and left the tearoom. He drove home to his sparse one-bedroom flat and slept for three hours. When he got up, he showered and dressed in a clean shirt and suit, then made some calls to other members of his squad. No one could find any connection so far between the husband and the offender. Higgins suggested they try to find a link between the offender and the wife. After a quick cup of instant coffee, he drove to the hospital.

Megan Caldwell was out of surgery and recovering in a private room. Higgins checked in at the nurses' station and had to wait while they paged Mrs Caldwell's orthopaedic surgeon. For five or so minutes, Higgins eavesdropped on the nurses discussing their weekend plans, until the surgeon strode over to the station and thrust out his hand. Higgins took it. The surgeon's palm was smooth, as if dusted with talc.

"Good afternoon, I'm Dr Falk."

"Thanks for meeting with me," Higgins said. "They tell me you just spent five hours putting Mrs Caldwell back together."

"She had extensive bone fragmentation. There'll be permanent nerve damage, unfortunately. Further surgery might help, or physiotherapy, but I doubt it."

"Can I talk to her yet?"

"Yes, she's coherent," Dr Falk said, and hesitated. "I hear she killed her attacker. Is that true?"

Higgins shrugged.

Dr Falk leaned close. "I have an interest in this kind of phenomenon."

Higgins quirked an eyebrow. "Aggravated burglary?"

"Superhuman strength. Anecdotally, the human body is capable of incredible feats, if given the right stimulus."

"The right stimulus?"

"Mortal danger," Dr Falk said. "Do you mind if I sit in on the interview?"

Mrs Caldwell's room was on another floor. Dr Falk went in the room first, introduced Higgins, and then took a seat against the wall.

Higgins stood by the bed. "Hello, Mrs Caldwell. How are you feeling?"

"I don't know," she said in a thready whisper. She looked small and grey against the white of her bed sheets. Bandages and tape covered most of her hands. The visible skin on her fingertips was a purple and black mottle. A metal frame ran the length of each forearm; pins from the frames pierced her flesh.

"I'd like to talk to you about what happened," Higgins said, and took out his notebook and pen from his jacket pocket. "Do you think you're up to it?"

"I can try," she said, and her eyes brimmed with tears.

Higgins opened his notebook and clicked his pen. "Mrs Caldwell, can you please tell me what happened last night?"

She turned her heart-shaped face to the window and began speaking in a soft monotone. "We heard something," she said. "John went to look. He told me to stay in bed, but I didn't. John got to the kitchen. I saw the man hit him over the head. John staggered and fell by the front door. I ran to him." Her eyes fluttered shut. "My legs were shaking so hard."

"Then what happened?" Higgins said.

"The man pushed me and I hit the sink. He put handcuffs on John." Her mouth twisted and she pressed her trembling lips together. "I told the man I'd do anything he wanted, if he left my family alone. He held up the knife. He said he would cut them."

She broke into sobs and turned her head against the pillow in a futile attempt to wipe her tears. Dr Falk leapt from his chair, grabbed a fistful of tissues from the box on the side table, and dabbed at her eyes.

"It's all right, Mrs Caldwell," Dr Falk said. "Detective Higgins is trying to help you."

Higgins waited until Mrs Caldwell stopped crying. Dr Falk patted her cheeks with the tissues one last time, and took his seat. Mrs Caldwell again stared towards the window.

"What happened after the man told you he would cut them?" Higgins said.

"I'm not sure. There was a great rush inside me. I felt an explosion somewhere. I can't explain it."

"Did time slow down?" Dr Falk said. Higgins looked over at him and frowned. Dr Falk sat back in his chair.

Mrs Caldwell said, "The man seemed to be moving in slow motion like he was underwater. It was so easy to hit him. He couldn't keep up with me. When he slashed at me with the knife, I had all the time in the world to move out of the way."

"That's called tachypsychia," Dr Falk said to Higgins. "The distortion of time perception is a classic sign of the survival reflex."

"Okay, fine, let's talk about that later," Higgins said, and Dr Falk nodded and looked away. "Mrs Caldwell, what happened next?"

"I kept hitting and hitting."

"You didn't feel any pain?"

"None at all. And I couldn't hear anything either, except for this weird roaring sound."

Dr Falk held up a finger and whispered, "Tunnel hearing, also known as auditory exclusion. Another classic sign."

"Dr Falk, would you please…" Higgins said. Dr Falk raised both hands in a placating gesture. Higgins said to Mrs Caldwell, "Then what happened?"

"The man fell. I knelt on his chest and kept hitting him. I had to stop him. My children were asleep in the next room. Don't you understand?"

Higgins put his notebook in his jacket pocket. "Mrs Caldwell, are you trained in any type of martial art?"

She shook her head.

"What about self-defence lessons? Anything of that nature?"

She shook her head again.

Higgins said, "I'm going outside to talk to your doctor for a minute. Okay?"

She nodded and locked her gaze on the window. Higgins and Dr Falk went out to the corridor. Higgins closed the door.

The doctor's face was flushed and animated. "The survival reflex is hormonally driven. Adrenaline mainly, but other chemicals are involved, we're not sure which. Research is so scanty into this field."

Higgins took hold of Dr Falk by the arm. "That woman doesn't weigh more than fifty kilos. Are you saying it's possible she bashed a man twice her size to death?"

"I'm saying it isn't impossible. Every physiological response she mentioned is supported in the literature. The trouble is that we don't understand the capability of the human body under extreme stress."

Higgins let go of the doctor. "I've been on the force for eleven years, and I've never seen anything like this. A woman can't punch that hard."

"And I've been a surgeon for nearly twenty. And I say that people can find it within themselves to do almost anything if enough is at stake."

A voice called out, "Detective Higgins."

Higgins turned around. John Caldwell was walking towards him. He had a dark-haired boy around three years of age propped on one hip. A girl of about six held his other hand.

"Do you need to talk to me about anything?" John Caldwell said. "I want to see my wife."

"No, it's okay, go ahead," Higgins said.

John Caldwell opened the door and went into his wife's room.

"I've got to make some rounds," Dr Falk said to Higgins. "I'm off at seven, if that helps."

The two men exchanged business cards. Higgins took the lift to the ground floor and went outside, where he made a few calls to his crew. They had found no connection so far between the offender and Mrs Caldwell. Higgins paced around the hospital entrance and tried to make sense of it. Then he called Detective Inspector Naylor.

"I need a couple of warrants," Higgins said. "One for the Caldwell house; I think we'll find the keys for those handcuffs tucked in a drawer somewhere. And the second warrant for the Caldwell bank records. If they're living beyond their means, we might find the connection."

Naylor said the evidence was weak, but he would try for the warrants anyway. Higgins hung up and swore under his breath. Then his mobile rang. It was Eva Daniels, the pathologist, saying she had completed her autopsy on the Caldwell offender.

"The head and neck have more than two dozen small puncture marks," she said. "They correspond exactly to the solitaire diamond in Mrs Caldwell's engagement ring."

Higgins sucked on his lip. "The husband could have put that ring on his pinky."

"The knuckles left a distinct bruise pattern," Daniels said. "The fist is seven centimetres across, consistent with the hand-size of your petite female victim."

Higgins stopped pacing. "Go on."

"From the bruises on the offender, I can distinguish between most of the punches. I got Mrs Caldwell's x-rays sent over from the hospital. There are changes in the bruise pattern on the offender's skin that correspond with the progressive bone fracturing in Mrs Caldwell's left and right hands."

Higgins didn't say anything for a long time.

"Are you still there?" the pathologist said.

"I'll be over in a little while." He hung up, pocketed his phone and walked into the car park. The late afternoon sun warmed his face. The sky was clear blue. He noticed the leaves on the elm trees that lined the car park were turning pumpkin-yellow. Then he called Naylor and told him to forget about the Caldwell warrants.

Higgins knocked on the door of Mrs Caldwell's hospital room and John Caldwell opened it.

"Is there anything else we can tell you?" John Caldwell said.

Higgins walked into the room. The girl was standing on a chair and leaning over her mother. The boy was sitting on the bed with a box of tissues, drawing out one tissue after another and tossing them into the air. Mrs Caldwell looked at Higgins for the first time. She had colour in her face.

"The investigation is over," Higgins said. He took out his wallet and fished around for a business card. He gave it to John Caldwell and said, "Numbers for Victims Services. They offer counselling. It might help."

"Thank you," John Caldwell said, slipping the card into the pocket of his jeans. "Do you have any more questions for us?"

"I may need to call you at some stage, but that's about it for now."

"Will I be charged with anything?" Mrs Caldwell said. "Am I going to jail?"

"No," Higgins said.

John Caldwell held out his hand and Higgins shook it. "Thank you, Detective."

Higgins backed to the door and left the room. He paused in the corridor. After a while, he walked back to the room. Mrs Caldwell's door was fitted with a rectangular window.

Through it, Higgins could see John Caldwell bent over the pillow with his cheek resting gently on the top of his wife's head. Now the children were cuddled against her, each framed by one of her bandaged and pinned arms. Mrs Caldwell pressed one long kiss on the girl's forehead. She turned to the boy and kissed him on the forehead, too.

Higgins headed for the lift and thumbed the button for the ground floor. The lift took a minute to arrive. During that time, Higgins wondered, briefly, if he would ever be given the chance to love someone, anyone at all, as much as that woman loved her family. Then the lift doors opened and he stepped inside.

Beach House

Rosemarie kept her hands in the ten-and-two position on the steering wheel and stuck to the speed limit, while cars overtook her in streams. In a while, she would have to park to check the street directory again. She hadn't visited the old beach house in thirty-eight years and just about everything along the route was unrecognisable. For one thing, the narrow road with unsealed shoulders was now buried somewhere beneath this dual carriageway. Fast food restaurants, service stations and shopping malls cluttered the roadsides, while double-storey houses with double-garages and landscaped gardens and potted hedge plants kept whizzing by her. The empty kilometres of coastal scrub were gone.

She shouldn't have agreed to go.

But her sister, Thelma, had collared her at a moment when Rosemarie was off-centre and unprepared, staring at the shiny lacquered coffin with its sprawl of lilies across the lid and their big brother, Graham, locked inside. Thelma had said, "We've got to sort out Graham's stuff. I'll meet you at the beach house Saturday, all right?"

"Wait. Can't we meet somewhere else? What about Graham's flat?"

"Don't be silly. Here's a key. Get there after lunch."

Rosemarie had nodded and taken the key. Her sister had walked away before Rosemarie could offer a retraction. Revisiting the past was something she strictly avoided. Old photographs, songs from her youth, bumping into somebody she went to school with, all these unpleasant things gave her a kind of vertigo.

And yet here she was driving to the beach house, the place Mum had willed to Graham. Which was fine, so what? Graham had been Mum's favourite anyway. But one thing nagged in particular: why had Graham given keys to Thelma? Rosemarie had hosted her brother and sister for the last twenty-six Christmas lunches in a row. Wouldn't they be a disparate bunch of strangers with nothing to say to one another if Rosemarie hadn't made such an effort, a beaming, straining effort, for all those years?

Her cheeks warmed as if slapped. She rolled down the window.

Before she could check herself, the tang of briny air swept her back to the family Holden FE sedan; she and Thelma, Graham and baby brother Pip leaning over the parcel shelf to watch the sandy roadside drop away every now and then to reveal a glimpse of the sea. On those weekend trips to the beach house, Dad had liked to wear what he called his driving hat, a battered Fedora with a magpie feather in its band. Mum used to lean her head on Dad's shoulder, chain smoke, and sing along to the radio, even the advertising jingles. Rosemarie and her siblings waved at cars, cheering when the driver and occupants waved back, booing if they didn't. And always on those long drives, the children elbowed each other and kicked bare feet, fighting for more room in the back seat. She could still remember the cowlick in Pip's strawberry blonde hair, the dimple in one cheek but not the other.

Rosemarie closed the car window.

After wrong turns and breaks to consult the street directory, Rosemarie at last aimed her battered Corolla down a series of side streets and pulled the car into the dirt beside Thelma's Ford. She cut the ignition, listening to the engine ticking and clunking, the breath whistling in and out of her nose. The gum that had been a sapling the last time she laid eyes on it was a massive old man with limbs stretching into the sky. The gravel road was sealed. The empty block over the road had units on it.

The beach house was the same.

The front door opened. There was her sister, Thelma. From this distance, Thelma looked like an old woman—weary, hunched in the shoulders—and Rosemarie got out of the car and held her head high to lengthen her neck and minimise her jowls.

"You're late," Thelma said. "You got lost, didn't you?"

"No, of course not."

Rosemarie grabbed her suitcase, but hesitated at the beach house doorway. The buckled lino with its faded flower pattern made her giddy. Carefully, she stepped inside. The kitchen was orange laminate and brown stained-wood trim, forgotten details that now seemed as familiar as Rosemarie's own face.

"I'm staying in our room," Thelma said. "I've made up a bed in the boys' room for you."

Rosemarie followed Thelma into Graham and Pip's old room. The walls held a smell of salt, mildew and rotting seaweed. Rosemarie put down her suitcase and stood at the window. The open curtains revealed the scrappy patch of back yard with its wire fence, heath-studded dunes beyond, a couple of seagulls floating in the blue, sluggish rollers lolling against the sand. The last time she was here, Dad had been pacing the beach in the moonlight, wailing and pulling at his hair, and Mum, across the hallway, had been sobbing behind a closed door.

Rosemarie said, "I haven't been here since we lost Pip."

"I was here a month ago. Graham let me stay whenever I wanted."

"Really? I had no idea."

"We never mentioned the beach house to you because of, you know, because of what happened."

Rosemarie said, "Don't you ever think about Pip?"

"No, but obviously, you do."

Rosemarie shook her head, but she could track how her every step, every decision, every lost opportunity was a direct result of that one event, which made her ponder sometimes how things may have turned out if that one event had never happened. She said, "Did Graham talk to you much? I didn't even realise he was so unhappy."

"Unhappy? No, he got his love of booze from Dad. It's a disease. Don't go thinking it was Graham's long-winded way of killing himself." Thelma winked. "Come with me. I want to show you something."

The master bedroom was filled almost to the ceiling with stacked boxes. The bed Mum and Dad used to share was gone.

Rosemarie said, "What *is* this stuff?"

"Crap, mostly. Anything we can't sell we'll donate or chuck out. It's going to be a hell of a job. Didn't you know he was a hoarder?"

Rosemarie opened the nearest box: cheap dinnerware. The next box held a dozen bottles of sherry. Another had spice jars; another bottles of red and green peppers suspended in oil, years past their use-by date. Rosemarie, pulse beating in her ears, flung open more boxes: wine glasses, ballpoint pens, tinned tomatoes... She picked up a shirt, still packaged in plastic with its arms pinned behind its back, and said, "Poor Graham. I didn't even know he was dying."

"So? We've always lived our own lives."

"But I could have helped."

"How? His liver was knackered. What could you have done? Forget it. Let's just go down to the shore."

The sisters walked to the beach. On the way, Rosemarie decided to reveal her own terrible news at the water's edge. She had planned to tell Thelma during Graham's funeral but it had seemed inappropriate at the time, like she would be stealing Graham's thunder. Maybe here, with memories of Pip, was the best place.

They took off their shoes and padded over the sand. Rosemarie, watching her feet, dodged rubbery clumps of seaweed and broken shells until the water foamed at her toes. Only then did she look up and take in the green, heaving expanse.

"Do you ever think that Pip is still out there somewhere?" she said.

But Thelma was already far away, skirting the ocean.

Rosemarie retreated up the beach, gathered the hem of her dress beneath her and sat down. Next to her ranged the footprints of some unknown bird, perhaps a shearwater. She could see a raft of them lifting and dropping in the surge far beyond the breakers, a grey and white stippling across the water.

What happened to Pip thirty-eight years ago had happened right here.

Rosemarie closed her eyes.

The afternoon is hot and blustery. The waves curl, tuck and froth at the sand. Graham gathers driftwood to build a kindling pile that Mum, back at the beach house, would never let him light, while Thelma plays chasey with the sea, dashing away and squealing whenever the water reaches for her. Rosemarie, with the sun nibbling at the back of her neck, pokes a stick into a hole in the sand, hunting for the crab beneath.

Rosemarie looks up.

Five-year-old Pip is laughing inside Dad's hug. They're enjoying the same old game. Dad's arms are brown, his legs milk-white. He drops Pip into the water. Pip lands with a splash. His laughter seesaws on the breeze as he staggers out of the surf.

"Do it again, Daddy. Do it again."

Dad swings Pip in circles, around and around, then launches him at the sea, a little further out this time, the boy's skinny limbs flailing in the air. Pip goes under the waves. *Plop.*

And doesn't come back.

Rosemarie forgets about the crab. She lets go of the stick. The breath hooks in her throat. Any moment now, Pip will bob up and dog-paddle to the sand while she gasps in relief and Dad holds out his arms, ready to keep playing the game. But when too many seconds crawl by, Dad and then Rosemarie run to the spot where Pip went under. They screech for him, claw at the waves with their hands, kick at the sandy bottom, but nothing, there is nothing.

And Rosemarie, air bellowing in and out of her, feels how big the sea truly is: how far it stretches from one side of the planet to the other, how it gapes all the way back to the sky and plummets to the bottom of the earth. She yells to Graham and Thelma but they're too far away, the wind is tearing the words from her mouth and they can't hear her. Rosemarie stamps and hollers in the spray and knows that her little brother, small enough to carry on her back while he makes choo-choo noises on each riser up the stairs to bed, is lost. (And Rosemarie is right. Pip never shows again. *Fish food* says a boy at school the following week, and Rosemarie gets suspended for breaking his front teeth against her knuckles.)

Telling Mum is the worst. Rosemarie hangs back at the door of the beach house, wishing for Mum a few more moments. The others stumble in. Minutes pass. Rosemarie hears the shrieking and later, the sobbing through the closed door.

Police come and go.

Mum and Dad forget to offer dinner. The remaining kids forget to feel hungry. Rosemarie, unable to sleep, sits at Pip's window and watches the phosphorescence gleaming along the dark waves, sees the silhouette of Dad patrolling the beach in the moonlight, stumbling, falling. Worst of all is thinking of Pip reaching heaven and having no one there to greet him.

"Look at this," Thelma said, her old-woman voice nearby without warning. "I found it on the rocks over there."

Rosemarie opened her eyes. Thelma was squatting beside her with a puffer fish lying on a piece of driftwood, her hands wrinkled and spattered with sunspots. All of a sudden, Rosemarie hated her sister wildly, furiously.

Struggling to her feet, slapping the sand from the back of her dress, Rosemarie yelled, "Throw it back in. Hurry up."

"What for? It's probably dead."

"Just throw it in, goddamn it."

"Don't you want to have a look first?"

Rosemarie grabbed the piece of driftwood from Thelma and launched the puffer fish at the water. The breeze dropped it short. Waves licked at the fish but instead of drawing it back in, only pushed it further up the beach. Next, Rosemarie tried to use the driftwood like a hockey stick. As she kept flicking the puffer fish at the sea, the waves kept nudging it out again.

Thelma got a fit of the giggles.

At last, Rosemarie flung the driftwood aside and grabbed the fish by its tail. She threw it. The fish arced high through the air, plunked into the sea, disappeared. Thelma was still giggling. Rosemarie grabbed her shoes and marched towards the beach house. She was pacing around the kitchen table for at least five minutes before Thelma came back inside. The sisters faced each other.

Thelma slung her shoes at the floor and said, "What's wrong now?"

"That wasn't funny."

"Yes, it was. You should've seen yourself."

Rosemarie said, "I've got something to tell you."

"What?"

Unexpectedly, Rosemarie found that she couldn't answer.

Thelma huffed, put one hand on her hip and set her mouth in a tight line. "Okay, so what's the big secret?"

"Actually, I've changed my mind. This isn't the right atmosphere."

"For God's sake, spit it out."

Sweat prickled at Rosemarie's lip. Many times over the past week, she had pictured telling her only living relative about the cancer diagnosis, about how the prognosis was bad, as bad as you could get, but she hadn't anticipated a scene quite like this. She craved solicitude, compassion. Finally, she said, "I don't want you to be angry when I tell you."

"Angry? Why? What have you done that would make me angry?"

"That's not what I meant. It's bad news. Maybe you should sit down."

"Just tell me what you want to say."

The floor canted beneath Rosemarie's feet, but she didn't want to be the one who needed a chair. The world felt large and cold around her. She steeled herself.

Then she told Thelma.

S tubbornly, the memory refused to fade. Something in Rose-marie's chest would always tighten whenever she looked back on that moment at the beach house. Telling Thelma about her diagnosis—her death sentence—turned out to be far worse than the surgery, the pain, the indifference of medical staff or the side effects of drugs. Thelma had taken the news so well that she hadn't needed to sit down; so well, in fact, that Rosemarie couldn't bear to even look at her. Rosemarie had grabbed her suitcase and fled. Thelma hadn't tried to stop her. The sisters never spoke again.

In her last weeks, as her mind and body unravelled, Rosemarie comforted herself in the night whenever she couldn't sleep by imagining Pip waiting for her in heaven. Pip would be happy to see her. They would stroll, hand in hand, along a coastline that framed a calm, blue sea. Pip would show her how to find hermit crabs in the sugar-white sand. She would be part of a family again.

With this soothing vision, Rosemarie found that she could fall asleep and not dream of the beach house.

Man with the Suitcase

The sun comes up and steams the dew from the railway tracks. The only person waiting for the train at this hour on a Sunday is a middle-aged man with a suitcase. He is slumped on a bench when the teenaged boys creep down the stairs.

The one with the knife, whose name is George, smirks at his twin brothers and says to the man, "You're up early."

The man looks them over and says, "I haven't gone to bed yet."

"Oh, yeah? That can't be good at your age," George says. His brothers snicker. George drops his smile and lifts the knife. "Let's have it, mate."

The fight is over quickly. The man picks up the suitcase and takes the stairs out of the station.

George stands, puts a hand against his bleeding nose and kicks at his brothers who lie sprawled and groaning. "Come on or we'll lose him," George says. "If you don't get up right now, I'm telling Mum."

They take the stairs to the street. There's no sign of the man with the suitcase. The brothers jog across the road.

Sitting in a parked car nearby are two men. They exchange glances.

"You see that?" one says, and the other nods. The two men continue to watch the brothers.

The brothers enter a café and approach an older woman hunched over a plate of cooked breakfast. She is fat and shaped like a beanbag. She throws down her cutlery and scrapes her chair from the table, slaps at George and yells, "Where's the suitcase?"

The twins back away.

George says, "Mum, you didn't tell us Rudi could fight."

"What? Rudi did this to you?"

"There wasn't nobody else with him Mum, so yeah."

Mum, stricken-faced, drops into her chair. "Georgie, if we don't have the suitcase, we don't have nothing, understand?" The waitress approaches and offers towels to the bleeding brothers. They take the towels without acknowledging her. The waitress retreats to the kitchen and Mum whispers, "Now she's gonna call the coppers because of you dickheads."

Outside, the men in the parked car are still sitting patiently, waiting. The one with glasses is reading a paperback. The skinny one watches the door of a bakery. The man with the suitcase comes out of the bakery, eating a croissant.

The skinny one says, "Sarge."

Sarge looks over his glasses and closes his book. "Well, he's a lot thinner than he used to be."

"I thought Zef the Clog wore his hair a little longer."

Sarge laughs. "Come on, Nash, a man can't get a haircut? It's Zef the Clog all right. Why else would the Frenelli boys be after him?"

"I suppose," Nash says. "Think he's carrying money or drugs?"

"Who cares? Let's take it, whatever it is."

Nash twists the key in the ignition.

Meanwhile, as he walks along the footpath, the man with the suitcase takes his mobile phone from his pocket. Its display window is broken. He shakes the phone and pieces rattle. He drops the phone into a bin and surveys the road, and here comes a yellow taxi. The man waves his arm but the taxi cruises past. He watches it go. A ringing sound turns his head. It's a young woman on a bicycle, thumbing her bell. He smiles and she smiles back. He watches her as she cycles away.

A car brakes into the kerb in front of him. Two men leap from the car. Sarge takes him by one arm and Nash takes him by the other, and they bundle him through the door of a laundromat.

George is watching from the café window. He says to Mum, "The cops have just nabbed Rudi."

Mum pales and says, "Go get Monster."

"Where is he?" George says.

"In the dunny out the back. Hurry."

In the laundromat, Sarge and Nash wrestle the man to the rear of the room. A young man with his hair gelled into a mess looks up from his washing basket and shapes his mouth into a soundless *oh*. Nash jerks his thumb at the front door. The young man dashes out of the laundromat.

Now they are alone. Nash stands by the front door. Sarge pushes the man towards one of the plastic chairs. The man sits, places his suitcase on the floor between his feet, and rests his hands on his knees.

Sarge points at the suitcase. "You delivering this to the China-man?"

"No."

Sarge looks around to Nash. They both grin. Sarge says, "So, tell me what's in it then."

"Clothes, toiletries. A present."

Sarge says. "For the Chinaman?"

"No, for my sister. It's her birthday."

Sarge folds his arms across his paunch and shakes his head.

Nash says, "I read in his file that Zef the Clog was smart. An IQ of 130, wasn't it?"

A petite man with a crazed look on his face bursts through the doorway. He wheels a one-inch galvanised water pipe in his left hand and a chain in his right. Nash, who was knocked to the floor during the petite man's entry, gets up and reaches for the police-issue Smith & Wesson revolver strapped to his bony hips.

Sarge takes a lashing of chain around the back of his skull, and staggers. The man with the suitcase ducks the swing of pipe and sprints across the laundromat to the door. Nash drops the gun and scrambles for it.

Once on the street, the man hesitates, checks both ways. A sedan lurches to a stop in front of him and the passenger door is flung open. It rocks on its hinges.

"Get in!" someone yells, and he gets in, the car taking off before he has the door closed.

The man looks at his salvation. The honey-haired woman in a pantsuit twists the wheel, stamps the brake and executes a controlled slide around the corner on the amber light. She guns the car up the road, takes another turn and another, then slows down, eyeing the rear-view mirror.

He says, "I haven't seen driving like that in a long time."

"Thanks, but I can't take the credit; it's standard training." She flicks him a quick up-and-down glance. "I expected a woman."

"Oh? Why's that?"

"Isn't it obvious?" she says, and takes another corner. "Bent male cops always blab to women, don't you find?"

"Well, I've never really thought about it. So where are we going?"

She shoots him a look. "You've got the stuff, haven't you?"

"Stuff?"

"Tapes, photographs. The dope on Sergeant Turner and Senior Constable Nash, it's in your suitcase, right?" When he pats the suitcase, she giggles and says, "Wow, you really had me worried for a second."

One more screeching turn and they're back where they started, on the same street but further down. She rams the transmission into park and rips on the handbrake.

"You've moved the car about fifty feet," the man says.

She points at a shop door marked *ABC Accounting*. "They're in there."

"Who?"

"The Feds, who else?" Her smile fades. "You know what? You never gave me the code word."

The man gets out of the car and shuts the door. He scans the street both ways.

She gets out the driver's side, yelling, "You're under arrest, whoever you are."

He says, "Wait."

Because across the road coming out of the café are the fat woman and her three sons: they're looking straight at him.

A marked police car, lights flashing, parks outside the cafe. Mum and her boys start crabbing sideways along the footpath.

Mum hisses, "I told you that waitress was gonna call the coppers, didn't I? Now look what you've done."

"Sorry, Mum," George says.

"Get in here," Mum says, and she ushers her three sons into the newsagency. She peers through the floor-to-ceiling window at the man with the suitcase backing away from a woman in a pantsuit who's waving a pair of handcuffs in his face. Mum puts on her glasses, looks again. "Now, just hang on a minute," she says, and grabs at her huge bosom where her heart might be. "Oh sweet Mary, that's the bloke? The tall one with the suitcase?"

"That's him," George says.

Mum slaps him hard enough to stagger him. "That's not Rudi, you buffoon."

Two uniformed officers get out of the police car. They adjust their utility belts, straighten their hats and saunter towards the café. A scream spins them around.

Across the road, a mother with a pram, still screaming, is running away at speed. A group comprising a man with a suitcase, a woman in a pantsuit, and a petite man holding a pipe and a length of chain, are circling each other.

Then the woman in the pantsuit pulls a Glock semi-automatic pistol from the holster hidden within her jacket, and aims it first at the petite man and then at the man with the suitcase, as if she can't make up her mind. Other pedestrians, the few out at this early hour, shrill and scatter.

The uniformed officers draw guns and duck behind their parked car. One of them shouts, "Police. Drop your weapons."

The woman in the pants suit lifts both arms. "Federal police officer."

"Holster your weapon."

And she does.

"You with the pipe and the chain," a cop shouts. "Drop 'em and get on the ground."

Mum leans from the newsagency door and shrieks, "Monster! It ain't Rudi, it ain't him!"

The uniformed officers wheel around. Mum and her boys startle and duck back into the newsagency at a run, aiming for the rear door. One of the uniformed officers gives chase. Out on the road, Monster has turned on his heel and is dashing along the footpath with surprising speed for someone with such delicate legs.

"I got him!" the woman in the pants suit yells, and bolts after him, and the remaining uniformed officer jumps up and follows her.

The man with the suitcase takes the car belonging to the woman in the pants suit. He doesn't speed. He stops at the red light. He scrolls through the radio stations until he finds a song he likes. He puts a hand on the suitcase lying next to him in the passenger seat.

The light turns green and he drives off. It's still early and there is hardly any traffic. He notices in the rear-view mirror that a car is closing the distance at a rapid rate. Then the speeding car taps its nose against his boot in a perfect PIT manoeuvre. He loses the back end, spins the car, ploughs it up the footpath and spreads the bonnet around a telegraph pole.

The airbag deploys. Then he lolls back in the seat, blood coursing from his lip, as the car behind him screeches to a stop and parks. His door opens, and Sarge and Nash pull him from the vehicle and fling him onto the footpath. The man rolls onto his back and stares up at them.

"What's so funny?" Sarge says.

"Nothing," the man says.

Sarge and Nash look at each other. Both are dishevelled, bruised and bleeding.

Nash reddens and says, "He had a pipe and a chain. He came out of nowhere."

Sarge shoves at Nash. "Shut up."

The man gets to his feet. Sarge grabs at the man and runs him against the ruined car. The man bounces off and ends up on the footpath again.

"I ought to put a bullet in your back," Sarge says.

The man sits up. Nash takes the suitcase from the passenger seat and places it on the bonnet of their unmarked squad car and opens the suitcase. Nash and Sarge lift out items one at a time and drop them to the road: shirt, jocks, t-shirt, a pair of socks, another shirt.

"What the hell is this?" Sarge says. "Some kind of joke?"

The man shrugs. Sarge holds up a little box wrapped in gold paper and tied with ribbon.

The man says, "That's the present for my sister I told you about."

Sarge drops it to the ground. "Oh, crap."

"I told you his hair was too short," Nash says.

"Shut up."

Nash goes to the back of their squad car and takes out an expanding manila file. He opens it and riffles through it, while Sarge glares down at the man sitting on the footpath. Nash finds what he's looking for. He walks the photograph over to Sarge and they both study it for a long time.

At last, Nash says, "It's definitely not him."

"Christ." Sarge doubles over as if hit by pain. He straightens and stamps around in a circle, cursing, then turns to the man. "Stupid prick. I ought to shoot you."

"Maybe you should save your strength for Zef the Clog," the man says.

Sarge lunges, but Nash manhandles him to the squad car.

"You'd better get out of here," Nash yells. "And don't tell anyone about this, all right? Don't even try it."

Their car peels away from the kerb in a bloom of tyre smoke. The man gets up, repacks his suitcase and closes it. He walks along the street to the strip shopping centre. He stops at a public phone housed inside a half-egg of plastic perched on a pole. He puts the suitcase next to him and thumbs coins into the slot and calls a number. It answers on the second ring.

He says, "Cat? Dog. Uh, sorry, can't remember what I'm meant to say next. What? No, the mobile's broken." His mouth sets into a line. "Okay, look Penelope, I know it's you, you know it's me. Yes, I'm late. Yes, I've still got it. All right, I'll see you in half an hour."

His only warning is a creak of unoiled gears and then the woman on the bicycle leans over, snatches the suitcase and pedals away. The man is too surprised to call out. He barks into the phone, "Give me an hour," and he drops the handset and sprints after the bicycle.

Shootout at Cardenbridge

Police work in the Victorian town of Cardenbridge, population 950, is undemanding—Saturday night drunks, the occasional theft of agricultural equipment, loose cattle on the highway—which is why Sergeant Maggie Drummond mistook the *pop-pop-pop* sounds and bright flashes in the farmhouse doorway for Chinese crackers. It was, after all, the eve of Australia Day. She had already cautioned a number of revellers for discharging fireworks.

Maggie Drummond, 48, stopped the police car near the veranda and cut the engine. She and her new partner, Constable Nick Theophilus, 22, got out of the car. Both windscreens exploded.

The officers scrambled behind the car. Ordinarily, a car is an effective shield against gunfire, but a noise like a ball peen hammer striking a water pipe told Maggie different. She looked up and saw bullet holes flowering across the car boot. She knew that the shooter in the farmhouse doorway had armour-piercing ammunition.

Her thoughts dashed from one realisation to the next in under a second. The radio and mobile phone were inside the car, so they had no way to contact the Cardenbridge station. Even if they could, the only backup was their third and final staff member, Senior Constable Garry Brown, 65. And if Brown put out a general call for assistance, it would take at least twenty minutes for police to arrive from neighbouring towns, while the ferociously armed and expertly trained Special Operations Group were in the city of Melbourne, some two hours' drive away.

She had no choice. Maggie unholstered her police-issue .38-calibre handgun and peered out from behind the car. Aiming at the farmhouse's open doorway, she wondered if she would have time to see the bullet that would kill her.

The day before, two armed men wearing balaclavas robbed the Central Bank in Landon, an affluent suburb in Melbourne's east. At about 11:30am, the men closed the door of the bank, shot some fifty rounds into the ceiling and walls to ensure cooperation from terrified staff and customers, and forced the bank manager to open the vault. Within sixteen minutes of entering the bank, the robbers left with approximately $80,000 in cash.

Daniel Whitney, 24, and Mario "Mark" Antonelli, 30, had met seven months previously at a gymnasium in Melbourne's north, where they became training partners. Their similar backgrounds fostered a close friendship: both came from violent and broken homes, had dropped out of school, and had prior convictions, Whitney for theft and assault, Antonelli for drug offences. They cemented their partnership over a crime spree, robbing two building societies and a chemist, with the latter involving the near-fatal shooting of a shopping mall security officer.

Whitney and Antonelli bought the two weapons involved in the Cardenbridge shootout—the HK91 copy semi-automatic rifle and the 9mm Beretta 92F pistol—from a member of an outlaw motorcycle club some two weeks before the bank robbery.

Neither Whitney nor Antonelli had experience with guns. Most of Whitney's crimes had been committed with a hunting knife, while Antonelli's crimes were considered "soft".

After robbing the Central Bank, Whitney and Antonelli headed northwest in a stolen Ford sedan. It is not clear where they stayed overnight. Police theorise that the robbers planned to steal a fresh car at their next stop, Cardenbridge, then drive north to Brisbane. Whether the robbers got lost along the 1100 kilometres of dirt roads in Greater Cardenbridge and just happened to stop at the Hogan farmhouse, or if they deliberately picked the location, is anyone's guess. But just after 8am on Sunday January 27, the stolen Ford bumped and rattled down the unsealed driveway of the Hogan property.

"**G**et up, bitch. Get up now."

Jessica Hogan opened her eyes. At the foot of her bed were two men she didn't recognise. The larger one hauled her out of bed by her hair. The men, she would later discover, were Daniel Whitney and Mario "Mark" Antonelli, among the most wanted felons in Australia.

Whitney pushed her down the hall and into the lounge room. Jessica began to cry. Last night, she had told her son, Benny, there'd be "hell to pay" if he wasn't back from the party by 10am. The wall clock showed 8:20am. The men tied her hand and foot with string they found in a kitchen drawer, then went outside.

Jessica could see them through the lounge room window. They stood at the open boot of their Ford for perhaps half an hour, and seemed to be discussing something of great urgency, although Jessica couldn't hear them.

During this time, unknown to Jessica and her assailants, 18-year-old Benny came home from the party. From the mouth of the driveway, he saw the strange men and stopped his car. Something about the look of them made Benny turn around and head to the police station in town. Sergeant Maggie Drummond agreed to check on Benny's mother. Constable Nick Theophilus offered to go along for the ride.

Whitney and Antonelli finished their heated discussion, and brought their luggage inside the farmhouse: a zippered sports bag and two suitcases. Then the two men helped themselves to breakfast and switched on the television.

Minutes later, Jessica caught the sound of tyres crunching along the driveway. She prayed that it wasn't her son coming home, prayed that whoever it was out there would leave. Whitney and Antonelli ran to the window. Relieved, Jessica saw that it wasn't Benny's station wagon, but a marked police car.

Antonelli froze and blanched. Whitney, galvanised, unzipped the sports bag, and pulled out the Beretta and the HK91. He threw the Beretta to Antonelli, who fussed with it like he'd never held a gun before. Whitney pulled back the bolt on the HK91. Jessica shut her eyes and braced herself, waiting for the bang. It didn't come.

She looked around. Whitney had opened the front door and was trying to sight through the rifle. A longtime rabbit hunter, Jessica noticed he was handling the weapon all wrong, failing to brace the stock against his shoulder, among other basic errors. Antonelli, standing slightly behind and next to Whitney, shook the Beretta at arm's length as nerves got the better of him.

The car stopped a few yards away. The engine cut out.

Whitney cursed under his breath. Antonelli was making a strange *huh, huh, huh* noise, like he was close to weeping. Jessica saw Maggie and Nick get out of the car, and tried to scream a warning. Her throat had frozen. She realised that the double murder of the Cardenbridge police officers might be the last thing she would ever see.

Whitney let loose a torrent of gunfire.

Keeping as much of her body behind the car as she could, Maggie aimed her six-shooter at the muzzle flashes in the doorway, and returned fire. She squeezed off shots at one-second intervals. A steady whine of bullets flew past. Something hot thumped into her right leg. Then she noticed there were two sources of muzzle flash, and she shifted her sights.

Jessica saw Antonelli fly backwards and slam into the hard-wood floor. Whitney didn't react, intent on reloading. Aghast, Jessica watched as Antonelli rolled over and began to crawl towards her, trailing a widening ribbon of blood. Then he passed out.

Shots continued from the HK91, concussing Jessica's eardrums. The puddle of Antonelli's blood, as dark and shiny as varnish, spread across the floorboards.

Maggie hesitated. She had counted each of her shots—only one left—so she emptied the last bullet into the doorway, dropped her arm to her side and waited for death or deliverance.

Seconds passed. Above the sound of her breathing were the screeches of airborne cockatoos, the clopping of hooves on hard-packed dirt as the property's horses galloped in alarm, but nothing else: no gunfire, no snap-and-clack of weapons being reloaded.

She turned to Nick—who was crying, his gun still in its holster—and cautioned him to stay behind the car. She took his weapon, approached the farmhouse. Once inside, her eyes adjusted quickly to the relative dimness.

Sprawled on his back near the doorway lay Daniel Whitney, his broken face masked in gore. To Whitney's left was Mark Antonelli in a spill of blood, his lifeless gaze staring at infinity. And beyond Antonelli on the couch, begging with frightened eyes, was Jessica Hogan.

Jessica wailed, "Oh my God. You've been shot."

Maggie looked down. Shards of muscle and flesh hung from a rip in her trouser leg. A scalding wetness—her blood—was beginning to pool in her shoe.

Nausea rushed over her. She collapsed onto the couch. Seconds later, Nick crept into the farmhouse. He surveyed the dead assailants and ran to the couch. Maggie remembers Nick leaning over her, pressing his hands against her wound to staunch the bleeding, and sobbing over and over, "Help is coming, Maggie, everything's okay," while Jessica's hysterical voice chattered about towels and boiling water. Maggie wondered *Who's having a baby?* Then she fainted.

As soon as he received the frantic radio message from Nick, Senior Constable Garry Brown put in emergency calls to the Cardenbridge ambulance service and every police station within one hundred kilometres. Before lunchtime, the Hogan farm had more than sixty detectives, coronial staff and forensic specialists on site, the bank's money had been recovered from the boot of the stolen Ford, and Maggie was undergoing surgery in the nearby Blake Regional Hospital.

(Later, forensic testing would show it was Antonelli's Beretta that had inflicted her gunshot wound. According to Maggie's surgeon, these tests were unnecessary: a shot to the thigh from Whitney's HK91 with its armour-piercing ammunition would have sheared off her leg.)

Every newspaper and television newscast around the country lauded Maggie as a hero. The Victorian Police Chief Commissioner awarded her the Gold Cross of Valour. The shootout put Cardenbridge on the map, and a year later, tourism is still thriving (To date, new businesses include four restaurants, a hotel, two motels, a bowling alley and a nature park, while the Hogan farmhouse is a popular stop for out-of-town ghouls).

Maggie walks with a pronounced limp, and must lean on a walking stick when tired. Doctors consider her disability to be permanent. Maggie doesn't mind, however, saying, "Just getting an even break in such a bad situation is miracle enough for me."

Parrots and Pelicans

Anna's grandson, Jayden, was hunched in her lap. He cried like this often. After a time, Jayden flung his teddy bear aside and said, "Can I go to the park now?"

"All right, but if that little savage from over the road turns up, come back."

Jayden ran his nose along his sleeve. "Nana Anna, why is Matt's dad so angry?"

"How do you know his name is Matt?" Anna demanded. "I told you not to play with that child. Have you been playing with him?"

Jayden, his face a wet smear, slid off her lap and ran from the lounge room. The front door opened and closed.

Anna got up from the couch and moved from one window of her unit to the next to check Jayden's progress along the footpath. Her bedroom overlooked the park next door. Its meagre playground was one of the reasons her daughter Gail had picked Anna's place, or so Gail had said, but perhaps the real reason was because there was nowhere else for five-year-old Jayden to go. He was to stay with Anna until his divorcing parents decided who would take him.

Anna stood at her bedroom window and watched Jayden. He ambled across the grass and stood with his hands in his pockets to survey the play equipment. Then he scaled a ladder and whooshed down the slide. Anna sat on the bed and picked up the phone. Gail answered almost immediately. The call was brief.

Gail, weeping, eventually agreed to come over at dinnertime.

Anna got her handbag and locked the front door behind her. She glanced over the road. The rental house was still and quiet, as if abandoned. No sign of the little savage. She walked to the park and found Jayden sitting on a park bench.

"Guess what?" she said. "We're off to the shops to buy bird-seed. We'll have parrots in the birdfeeder from now on, big bright red ones. How would that be?"

Jayden didn't say anything. He was a cautious, quiet child these days. Together, they walked to the end of Anna's street and crossed the road to the shops. She allowed him to post her letters in the mailbox, introduced him to each of the shopkeepers. The man at the newsagent gave Jayden a chocolate. In the supermarket, Anna bought the smallest bag of wild birdseed she could find. Jayden handed the money to the worker at the till. Anna let him keep the change.

By the time they left the supermarket, Jayden, skipping, was chattering about ways to attract pelicans to the birdfeeder, and Anna was laughing, noting proudly how so many passers-by were smiling at them, admiring them; perhaps even envying them.

And then an old woman fighting to steer a shopping trolley blocked their path. Her handbag gaped just enough for a vinyl purse to fall to the ground.

"Excuse me," Anna called. "Hello? Wait a minute."

The old woman didn't hear. Jayden darted ahead and grabbed the purse. Holding it high, he caught up to the woman, and waved it at her. She heaved the shopping trolley to a stop.

"Oh, aren't you a good boy?" she said, taking the purse. Bent over, she winked at him, brought her yellowed face close to his. "You're in for a surprise tonight."

Jayden quailed. Anna approached and clutched hold of his hand.

"He's been well raised," the old woman said, nodding at Anna.

Anna hurried Jayden past the shopping trolley. They walked fast, both of them slightly breathless. After a time, Jayden glanced behind.

"Was she a witch?" he said.

"What? No. Why would you think that?"

"She said I'd get a surprise tonight. Did she give me a wish? Is she a fairy?"

"Don't be silly," Anna said.

At home, they went into the back yard to the Japanese maple tree. Anna took down the birdfeeder. Jayden piled handfuls of seeds into it. Then she hung it back up on the tree while Jayden hopped and sprang about on tiptoe.

"Parrots," he yelled, his face angled to the sky. "Come and get your dinner."

Anna laughed. "We'd better go inside or we'll frighten the birds."

Once inside, Jayden stood at the floor-to-ceiling kitchen window and watched the birdfeeder. Anna ran a load of washing and tidied the house while she had the chance. Then she lay on her bed. She had just dozed off when Jayden entered the room.

"They're not coming," he said. "I think we got the wrong seed. There's nothing out there but dumb old pigeons."

He knuckled tears from his eyes and pulled up the hem of his t-shirt to wipe his nose. Anna was too tired to chastise him for it.

"I think I'll go to the park," he said, and dashed from the room.

Anna sagged back onto the bed. Making promises about the parrots had been a mistake. A flock of them flew over every morning after sunrise and flew back again before dusk, but the birdfeeder was hidden under a canopy of leaves. Perhaps she could hang it from the clothesline for a few days until the parrots spotted it. Or perhaps Gail would come over tonight and take Jayden home.

Anna got up and crossed to the bedroom window. Jayden and that boy from the rental property were crouched at the bottom of the slide in a huddle, either shaking hands or holding hands, she couldn't tell. If Gail didn't take Jayden, he would soon be running wild with that little savage, roaming the streets and rooftops like an animal. Anna rapped on the window. The boys ducked out of sight.

After a few minutes, she heard Jayden come in. She went to the kitchen. He was slumped at the table with his face propped on his fists, staring at the birdfeeder with its untouched heap of black seeds.

She said, "If I see you with that little savage again, I'll box your ears."

Motionless, Jayden kept staring at the birdfeeder as if he hadn't heard her.

Later, he only picked at his dinner. The light faded. The screeching flock of parrots passed overhead. Anna had forgotten to hang the birdfeeder on the clothesline. And where was Gail?

"Keep eating your tea," she said to Jayden, and went into her bedroom and closed the door. Gail's voice, when she answered the phone, was fuzzy from too many wines. She wouldn't be coming. Anna hung up, opened the door. Jayden was in the hallway. "Were you listening to my conversation just now?" Anna said.

He got up and ran to the lounge room. Anna could hear him crying as she washed the dishes. Through the window, the glistening black sunflower seeds kept drawing her eye. She should have stuck to bread crusts and pigeons, and be done with it.

"Nana Anna," Jayden called, sounding frantic. "Come here, quick."

She threw the sponge into the sink. "What is it now? Can't you see I'm in the middle of something?"

Jayden was standing frozen by the lounge room window. Anna approached. In the dying light, she saw the little savage tearing laps across the rental property's lawn, his father gaining at every turn.

"Not another thing," Anna said. "I just can't take one more blessed thing."

The father swung his arms, ready to bat the boy to the ground. The boy leapt against the fence, sprang up the rails and vaulted onto the carport roof. The father ran for the ladder at the rear of the carport.

"It looks like they're going to play tiggy up there again," Jayden said.

Anna put her hands on his shoulders and steered him into the kitchen. "Low-life creatures like that thrive on an audience," she said, directing Jayden into a chair. "If nobody watches, I bet they'll give it away. Now, how about some ice cream?"

They sat together at the table and ate.

When the shrieking started, they both jolted in their chairs and gaped at each other.

"Stay here," she ordered, and hurried to the lounge room window.

The boy stood on the nature strip with his hands locked behind his head. He ignored his red-haired mother as she flapped her arms and wailed in their front yard. The boy was looking the other way, towards his father, who was strangely suspended in mid-air between the carport roof and the ground, lolling his head, shrieking over and over. Squinting through her glasses, Anna tried to make sense of the father's apparent levitation.

"He's stuck on the gate," Jayden said, standing beside her.

"Go on," she said. "Get away from the window."

Looking again, she saw that it was true. The father must have slipped from the roof and landed on the pointy spikes of the wrought-iron gate. Anna could just make out the vertical rods as they disappeared into the father's flank and thigh.

Oh God. The fright of it pinned her vision. For a moment, the floor wavered under her feet.

She began to steer Jayden away from the window. And then the slapping of feet on asphalt made her turn. The boy was running straight across the road at her, hoping to bring his ghastly family drama right through her front door. When the knocking started, she panicked and decided not to hear. Jayden raced to the door and opened it.

"Please help, we don't have a telephone," the boy said.

Anna took jerky steps to the kitchen and, for the first time in her life, rang triple zero.

Time passed. The ambulance arrived. Anna went onto the porch. Jayden had an arm around the boy's shoulders. While officers struggled to lift the father off the gate, neighbours came out on the street to watch and fret. Meanwhile the boy, *that little savage*, appeared unmoved. Surely, Anna thought, this situation couldn't get any worse.

Then the red-haired mother exited the rental property and began to plod across the road. Anna wanted to retreat inside. However, the mother kept Anna in her doleful sights the whole way. Finally, the mother reached the porch.

"I'm sorry," the mother said. "We don't know each other. But please, could you look after Matt? The ambos want me to go to the hospital with them."

"Look after...? Well, to be honest, I'm not sure that I can."

Jayden threw his other arm around the boy and hugged him. "Come on, we're having ice cream. You want some?"

Jayden led the boy inside. The red-haired mother smiled wanly. Trapped, Anna stepped backwards through the threshold and slammed the door shut.

Jayden and the little savage were sitting at the kitchen table.

When the little savage realised that she was glaring, he put Jayden's spoon back into Jayden's bowl, and wiped ice cream from his mouth with the back of his hand. "I didn't push him," the little savage said.

Anna set her teeth. "No one's saying you did."

"It's my fault," Jayden said. "I saw Matt in the park and gave him my surprise. You know, from that fairy? Remember when I gave the fairy her purse?"

Anna gripped the back of a kitchen chair. "That's ridiculous. Surprises are supposed to be nice. What's so nice about seeing your father get hurt?"

The boy sneered. "He's not my dad. He's Mum's new boy-friend."

The air seemed to leave the room. Anna felt afraid for her grandson, a child pitted against an indifferent future through no fault of his own. Protectively, she put her hand on the small nape of Jayden's neck. Matt watched her with cold eyes.

After a moment, Anna touched Matt on his shoulder. Matt dropped his head to her hip and sobbed hard. Then, just as suddenly, Matt's tears were over. Wrenching away, he averted his face.

"I'm Nana Anna," she said. "Take a seat, Matt. Would you like some ice cream?"

Matt nodded, snuffling. Jayden, jumping from his chair, lifted his t-shirt and offered its hem. Matt swiped at his eyes. Anna took a tub of ice cream from the freezer, grabbed a bowl and spoon.

"You'll like it here," Jayden said, guiding Matt onto a chair. "We've got special seed in our bird feeder. We'll have parrots that'll sing all day long. Isn't that right?"

"I hope so," Anna said. "If we're lucky, maybe they'll come tomorrow."

The Sequined Shirt

The hills on the horizon shimmered blue. Joanne turned from the highway, through the gates of the caravan park, and drove her car over gravel to where her green tent sat in the dirt. She switched off the engine, snatched her bag of groceries from the passenger seat, and got out. The humid air clung to her like plastic wrap. Cicadas sounded from the trees beyond the chain-link fence. She unzipped the tent flap and slung the bag. Cans rolled across the polyester floor, coming to rest against her backpack.

"Hey there," sang a voice from behind. "Hey, lady."

Joanne braced herself and turned. Coming from one of the residential cabins across the path was a scrawny woman in singlet and shorts with hair that dropped in a thin mousy sheet to her hips. Joanne took a pack of cigarettes from a shirt pocket, pulled out a smoke, lit one. Then the woman was standing in front of her, saying, "I don't believe it. Joanne Donovan? From Stinky's? You remember me, don't you? Crystal?"

"Oh yeah, Crystal, that's right," Joanne said, as it all came back in an unwelcome flood. "Christ, I hardly recognised you. You're skin and bone."

Crystal blushed and said, "How long you been here?"

"Just today."

"Come tonight for a barbie and a proper catch-up, hey? Meet George and my little girl Raelene. Got anybody with you?" Crystal looked over the tent for a clue.

Joanne said, "Thanks for the offer, but I don't have anything to bring."

"Hey, just bring yourself. Come over at six. I'm right there," she said, and pointed. The aluminium cabin, painted white, squatted in the dust like a brick, its meagre veranda lined with pickets.

At five minutes to six, Joanne exited her tent. From various places somewhere in the sprawl of temporary homes, kids squealed and laughed, and different songs played. An elderly man in Y-fronts sitting on the veranda of a cabin gouged a finger enthusiastically into his nostril, oblivious to Joanne's hostile stare as if she were a face on television.

The garden inside Crystal's fence featured dead cigarettes, bottle caps and scrawny dandelion weeds. A few metres away, a three-legged barbecue gave off smoke. Joanne knocked on the wall of the house. Crystal opened the screen door. Joanne proffered her tin can and said, "Baby corn spears."

"Yeah, ta," Crystal said, and took it. "Come on in."

The cabin's interior was overwhelmingly orange with faux wood-grain walls. Linoleum creaked under Joanne's feet. To her left, standing in the tiny kitchen, was a slender girl in a pink top with matching mini-skirt and pink thongs, her hair as lank as Crystal's. The girl suspended her hands over a bowl of iceberg lettuce to regard Joanne with doleful eyes.

Crystal gave the tin to the girl. "Put this in the salad and get us a drink." Then she said to Joanne, "This is my daughter, Raelene. Raelene, say hi to Joanne."

"Hi," Raelene intoned.

Joanne nodded and looked around. She saw everything there was to see within a moment. The remainder of the cabin consisted of a u-shaped bench cramped around a laminated table, two doors facing each other—stuck to one of the doors was a ceramic tile with the painted inscription, "Here 'tis"—and then an open curtain revealing an unmade double bed.

Crystal flourished a packet of Winfield Blues and grinned. "Ciggie?"

Crystal's front teeth, which Joanne remembered as square and oversized like those of a horse, were black and ragged around the edges, and their decay made Joanne feel old. She thought darkly of how life always has its million ways to break you.

Outside, they sat in canvas chairs. Music pulsed in a demented concert from all points of the park. Joanne and Crystal lit their respective cigarettes. Raelene exited the cabin to hand them a tumbler of dark liquid each and Joanne took a sip: bourbon and cola. Raelene went back inside and came out again with a tray of uncooked sausages. She passed the tray to Crystal and returned to the cabin.

Crystal headed to the barbecue. "I'll probably stuff the lot. This is George's and he likes to steer it."

"George your son?"

"De facto: moved in a couple a weeks ago. He went to Geelong this morning but I thought he'd be back by now."

Joanne shrugged. The sausages hit the grill plate with a savage hiss.

The three of them were eating their dinner and swatting at mosquitoes when a white ute rounded the path and coasted towards them, crunching gravel.

"Oh great," Raelene said and rolled her eyes.

"Cut it out," Crystal said. She put down her plate to walk towards the ute and wave. The ute pulled into the space between the cabin and its neighbouring site and the engine stopped.

A man with a beard and a round stomach leaned out of the driver's door, got his feet under him and stood up. He wore a singlet and shorts and had his thinning hair arranged into a plait that dangled to his waist. Crystal tried to embrace him but he was busy scowling at Joanne. Sucking at her teeth, Joanne lounged back in the chair.

Raelene muttered, "Here we go."

Crystal said, "George, you're not going to believe it. This here's Joanne. We worked together yonks ago at a supermarket that smelled so bad us girls used to call it Stinky's. Now she's here in the park with us. See the green tent?"

"Get me a beer, love," George said.

Crystal went into the cabin. George strode towards Joanne with his arms held out from his sides as if his back were much wider than it was. He eased into one of the canvas chairs and ignored Joanne while she smiled at the side of his head. Raelene gave an exaggerated sigh, got up and flounced into the cabin, allowing the door to slam. George didn't seem to notice.

Finally, Joanne said to his profile, "That's some nice pictures."

George looked down to admire the knotted blue tattoos riding the outside of both his calves and said, "Yeah."

"I got a real beauty myself."

"Yeah?"

"Yeah, but it's in no place I'd be game to show you."

George snapped his head around at her. Then he laughed. The side teeth in his upper and lower jaw were missing but unlike Crystal's teeth, which had rotted, George's looked like someone had knocked them out. "You're a right one," he said and winked.

Crystal came out of the cabin with a beer. "Here you go, darl'," she said and sat down.

George took a long pull on the beer and said, "Didn't get the bike."

Joanne said, "What kind you after?"

"Triumph Rocket Three."

"Unusual choice. Silver or black engine?"

They fell into an animated discussion that left Crystal with nothing else to do but clean up. That was, until a woman in a floral dress stomped along the path, her apron of belly fat swaying over her thighs with every knock-kneed step. Crystal froze. Joanne looked at George, who snickered and slurped on his beer.

Panting from exertion, the newcomer stood within shouting distance, put her fists on her prodigious hips and bellowed, "It's Robbie's first performance, you cow. Don't you think it's my place to buy his outfit?"

Crystal flung the paper plates she was holding into the dirt and screeched, "We saw it for eight bucks at the mall. Raelene called Robbie on her mobile and he promised to pay us back."

"That's total bull. You never did."

"We did so. We was doing you and him a favour."

"Oh, yeah? Well, I'm his mum and what he wears for his first dance is up to me—so just you wait. Dog's gonna rip you a new one." The fat woman turned and lumbered down the pebble path, buttocks quaking with the shock of each footfall.

"Is that right? Then give us back the shirt if you don't like it, you bitch," Crystal shrieked, then whirled around to George. "Why didn't you stick up for me?"

George's face darkened momentarily. Anything could happen, Joanne thought.

But George, chuckling, said, "Aw, I'm not getting in the way of any catfight."

Joanne stood up. "I'm off."

No one stopped her. She walked back to her tent and dived inside. It was still light but she jammed in her earplugs anyway, using her backpack as a pillow. Sleep came in minutes. The long drive from Sydney had worn her out.

Somebody grabbed her foot and shook it. She woke up in darkness and couldn't see or hear anything. She dragged out an earplug and sat up, confused. A shape coalesced into Crystal's face.

"You got to help me," Crystal said.

Joanne rubbed her eyes. "What time is it?"

"Dog's gonna kill us."

"Dog? Your old man?"

"No, *Dog*, that fat bitch's bloke, the fat bitch whining about the shirt. He rang just now. Who rings after midnight?"

Joanne turned over and punched at the backpack, trying to shape it again into a serviceable pillow. "Can't your old man deal with it?"

"George pissed off to a mate's joint. I'm all alone. Please, what about my kid? Raelene, she's only twelve."

Five minutes later, Joanne was lying on the cabin's double mattress next to Crystal. Raelene's soft breathing sounded from the middle of the cabin where the bench and table had been converted into a single bed. The streetlight from the highway shone through the window. Joanne pulled the fusty sheet over her head.

Crystal whispered, "Don't you want to know what it's all about?"

"No," Joanne said and fell asleep.

She woke up sometime later with Crystal's hand moving between her thighs. Joanne rolled away.

"What?" Crystal said. "Don't you like girls these days?"

"I want to sleep."

"But I'm scared."

"That's not my business anymore," Joanne said and got up.

"Wait a minute. Where are you going?"

Raelene said in alarm, "Mum, who's that? Mum?"

Joanne flung open the cabin door and strode along the pebble path towards her tent. There was a faint moon. The hills looked as purple as a bruise. Back at the tent, Joanne shucked her boots, sprawled across the air mattress and closed her eyes.

The first thing that broke through her dream was the warbling of a magpie. The second thing was a loud groan and the third was a scream. Joanne opened her eyes to a blare of sunlight filtering through the tent wall. She pulled out her earplugs and tried to focus on her wristwatch. Another scream sounded. Joanne thrashed open the zippered door of her tent.

Across the path was George, plait flailing as he tried to weave from punches being thrown by a skinny man who was naked except for low-riding white chinos. Joanne figured that the skinny man must be Dog, making good on his threat, and that Dog seemed to know his way around a brawl. Dog's fist connected with George's temple. George grunted and staggered. Crystal and Raelene were behind their picket fence. Crystal, intent on the fight, shadow-boxed as Raelene doubled over and screamed again. Neighbours watched from verandas. A couple of kids on bikes were stopped at a distance, exhilarated and frightened, shoving at each other and trying to laugh.

Joanne ducked back into the tent and took a few seconds to think it through. Then she dragged on her jeans and boots and vaulted from the tent at a run. Raelene saw her, raced over and collapsed against her, crying.

"Make them stop," Raelene begged.

Joanne pushed Raelene aside and swung Dog by his arm. He lost balance and crashed into dirt. Joanne drove her shoulder into George and he fell against the fence, crumpling pickets. By the time she turned around, Dog was back on his feet, knuckled fists bunched at his jaw, blue eyes blazing.

Joanne held up one hand and said, "Dog, isn't it? Okay, Dog, listen, I don't want any trouble."

"S'too late for that."

"Fair enough, but there's a little girl here."

"My woman's had it up to *here* with that little girl. She's what started all this. Now I'm gonna finish it."

A quiet voice said, "Get back, Joanne."

Joanne cut her eyes left. In her peripheral vision stood George, panting as blood streamed from his brow. He held a broken picket in both hands.

"George," Joanne said. "Don't do it."

"Come on, George, crack his bloody skull," Crystal whooped from the veranda.

Joanne risked a look over her shoulder, said, "Take Raelene inside, for Christ's sake," and was slammed onto her back.

A lost moment; then she blinked at the sky as white chinos leapt over her. Gasping and retching, she realised that Dog must have kicked her in the guts. She rolled over, sat up and spat dust. Dog and George were grappling about, neither making much progress on the other. Joanne leapt onto them and hurled Dog aside. She landed a punch in George's mouth and ripped the picket from him. She flung it and it hit the side of the cabin with a thud.

Pressure crushed against her windpipe. Joanne used all the strength in her legs to launch herself backwards. She heard the air knock out of Dog as she landed on him. An elbow into his ribs loosened his arm about her neck. She flipped onto her stomach and, on instinct, reached down her leg to grab her knife, only to remember with dismay that it was in the evidence locker of a Sydney police station. Dog, on his feet again, stiffened his hands into claws and circled her.

A loud voice keened, "Dog!"

To Joanne's surprise, Dog actually snapped to attention. The fat woman from yesterday afternoon was standing, arms akimbo, on the path. Behind her skulked a sullen teenaged boy, his hair spiked into a blonde bouffant.

"Dog, you stop that nonsense right now," the fat woman shrilled. "What kind of a low-life bastard strikes a woman, you sorry son of a bitch. I oughta beat you stupid."

"Robbie!" Raelene cried. She ran from the veranda and flung herself into the arms of the boy. He wrapped his arms about her and buried his face in her neck.

The fat woman, incensed, grabbed him by his t-shirt and shook him loose. "Robbie, you keep away from that skank," she said.

Crystal hopped from the veranda and bellowed, "Don't you talk about my daughter like that, you bitch, I'll cut your throat out."

Joanne stood up and slapped the dust from her jeans. Everyone about her was gasping, snarling, wild. "I think I'll be going now," she said. She saluted George, who was sitting on the veranda steps with one hand cupped under his bleeding mouth. She must have hit him harder than she thought.

Shouts issued from the circus behind her. Perhaps another fight had started. Joanne didn't look back. The two kids on bikes gawked as she approached. One gave her the thumbs-up while the other regarded her fearfully. Joanne ignored them and kept walking, aware that she was favouring her right side with each step. The old man in his Y-fronts wasn't picking his nose today, but was staring with his slack mouth gaping so wide she could see his glistening gums.

Joanne sniffed, hawked and spat red onto the path right outside the old man's cabin, but he didn't respond. At her tent, she grabbed her keys, hopped in her car and drove to the nearest pub.

In the pub toilets, she washed her hands and face, raked her fingers through her hair and decided to ignore the bloodstains on her jeans. Whose blood it was she couldn't say. One of her front teeth was loose but there was nothing she could do about that.

She spent the rest of the day drinking, eating, playing the pokies, and chatting to other loners. A few hours after sunset, she returned to her tent to find Crystal waiting. Crystal's eyes were bugged wide.

"What now?" Joanne said with a resigned sigh.

Crystal grabbed at Joanne's waist, hugging her, and said, "Take me with you."

Joanne caught Crystal's wrists and pushed her away. "So you can swap one caravan park for another?"

"But I'm in some real trouble."

"You're always in trouble, you bring it on yourself. Now go, get out of here."

She gave Crystal another nudge. Wailing, Crystal staggered back and hurried into the gloom. Joanne felt a stab but let it ride, because what did it matter anyway?

That night, Joanne was woken by a boom and a demonic crackle that went on and on. She poked her head from the tent and saw Crystal's cabin reaching into the sky with orange flames.

There was more here if she wanted it, but running suited her better. Joanne grabbed her pack, slung it into her car and drove from the park onto the highway, abandoning her tent and leaving the past to burn behind her.

Getting and Giving

It's not like he's my boyfriend, just a bloke from work who comes over for some fun every now and then. Look, I don't have time for all the nonsense of dating and talking, what with night shift at the factory and the driving back and forth to my old Mum's place to look after her.

Things with him suit me well enough. But he's the jealous type, casual though we are. Last week he twisted my arm because I said I liked the look of this particular movie star, and he didn't even have the decency to feel bad about it afterwards. I've plenty more stories like that. For someone who reckoned he didn't give a stuff, he sure cared about being the only cock on the walk, if you get me.

Anyway, to cut a long story short, he pounds and kicks on my front door until I finally open it and there he is, stinking drunk. He says to me, *Maureen, what were you doing with Smithy at meal break last night*, and I say, *what in blazes are you talking about you fool*, because Smithy and I happened to be sitting at the same cafeteria table, and so what of it? Then he goes, *you was laughing with him*, and I says, *Smithy told me a good joke about the foreman, don't you want to hear it?* And he hits me right here, right across the jaw, see the bruise?

Then he drags me to my bedroom, rips the clothes off my back and hops right into it. He's holding me by the throat and sticking himself here, there and everywhere and he doesn't give a shit that I'm crying or begging him to stop, oh no, he just keeps going until he's finished and then there he lies. Snoring on my bloodied sheets with not a care in this world.

I stand in the shower for ages and ages but I can't wash him off me. I figure that maybe if I could get the bastard out of my house, I'd start to feel better about it all, so I go to my room and he's hunkered into my pillow and blissful, like he's going to stay for as long as he pleases.

I get near him and I'm planning on shaking him awake and kicking him out, but then I spot the cricket bat I keep next to the bed for protection. So I pick it up and I think to myself, *okay then, Mr Tough Guy, how are you going to like these apples?*

And that's the last thing I'm going to say until you get me a lawyer and a smoke.

We Have What You Want

The roadhouse sat in the dirt on the side of the highway with nothing around it for fifty kilometres in either direction. Out front of the roadhouse was a tin roof that sheltered twin petrol bowsers, and behind was a bungalow of three motel rooms.

The ute pulled off the highway, coasted next to a bowser and parked. A hand-written note taped to the bowser read, *Relax! We serve you!* The driver of the ute, a boy barely out of his teens, picked at his fingernails and waited. His hand hovered over the horn but then the screen door of the roadhouse flapped open.

The owner was an older man, built wide and square. He walked to the bowsers with his shoulders rolling and his head down as if trudging up a steep hill. He was puffing and blowing by the time he got to the driver's window. "What do you want?"

The driver glanced at the owner's nametag and smiled. "You tell me, Gordon."

"I don't want to play games. Do you want me to fill her up or don't you?"

The driver rubbed at his nose. He had an indented scar where the tip of his nose should have been. "You've got a big sign back there on a sandwich board. Don't you know what it says?"

Gordon straightened up and put his fists on his broad hips.

"We have what you want," the driver said. He drummed his fingers against the steering wheel and laughed. "That's what it says. We have what you want. Well, do you? Do you have what I want?"

Gordon turned and began slogging his way back to the roadhouse. When Gordon was almost at the front door, the driver released his seatbelt and leaned out his ute window. "Fill her up, thanks," he called.

Scowling, Gordon came back to the ute. He slapped open the fuel filling door with the flat of his hand, loud and hard. Then he wrenched off the petrol cap and rammed the bowser nozzle into the tank. When he was finished, he pushed his meaty hand through the open window and said, "Twenty-eight dollars." He had to back-pedal when the driver opened his door and got out.

The driver pointed to the roadhouse. "It says on the window you got meals here. I think I might have me some breakfast."

"Breakfast isn't on today," Gordon said.

"The sign says you have breakfast."

Gordon shook his head and held out his hand. "Twenty-eight dollars."

"I'll have a hamburger," the driver said. "Or a pie. Anything you've got."

Gordon huffed. Then he stumped his heavy legs and rolled his heavy shoulders across the lot to the roadhouse, and the driver ambled along behind him. Gordon flung open the screen door but didn't hold it. The driver caught the door, grinned, and strolled inside.

It was dark compared to the outside glare. Opposite the door was a counter top containing an empty *bain-marie*. Behind the counter ran a long stove and grill. To the driver's right were shelves stacked with canned and packaged goods, and to his left, four tables with plastic chairs.

The driver perused the blackboard menu on the wall. Gordon went behind the counter.

"Twenty-eight dollars," Gordon said. "You can't eat till you pay me for the petrol."

"Okay." The driver pulled a wallet from his jeans pocket and handed over a fifty-dollar note. Gordon opened the register and gave him his change.

"So what do you want?" Gordon said.

The driver smirked. "You tell me."

The back door of the roadhouse opened and a girl struggled

in. She held a mop and bucket, and the bucket slopped water and grey suds. The driver took the bucket for her and put it on the floor. She smiled at him.

"Narelle, get back to the motel rooms," Gordon said.

Narelle leaned the mop handle against the counter. "I've finished in there. I've changed the linen, too."

The driver appraised her. She had a dumpy build and wore her dark blonde hair pulled into a ponytail. Freckles dusted her round cheeks. She couldn't have been more than seventeen years old.

"What are you staring at?" Narelle said.

"All the tasty things on your menu," the driver said, and Narelle giggled behind her hand.

Gordon said, "Do you want to order something or don't you?"

The driver looked at the blackboard menu and rubbed at the stubble on his face. "I'll have the breakfast special."

"I told you before, breakfast isn't on today."

"Mum's gone into town," Narelle said and picked up the mop and bucket. "She does the breakfasts."

"Then I'll have a burger with the lot."

"The stove's not ready," Gordon said.

"I can wait," the driver said. He walked to a table and sat in one of the plastic chairs.

Gordon turned to the stove behind the counter and rattled at the controls. Narelle hefted the mop and bucket through the swing door to the kitchen. Gordon followed her. After a moment they both came out again. Gordon carried a box. He went behind the counter and began unloading onions and bags of lettuce and other foods into the *bain-marie*. Narelle had a feather duster. She flicked it around the shelves and saw the driver was watching her.

"What are you doing out so early, anyway?" she said to him.

"Go finish up the motel rooms," Gordon said.

"Dad, I told you already, they're done." She smiled at the driver. "So where are you going?"

"Melbourne," he said. "For a birthday party."

"I really love parties," she said. "Is it a twenty-first?"

"Actually, it's a ninety-fifth," he said.

Narelle laughed. "Wow, that's pretty old, isn't it?"

Gordon hurled the empty cardboard box to the floor. Narelle rolled her eyes and gave her father a sulky look. Then she sidled her gaze to the driver. "Who's turning ninety-five? Your grandma?"

"My Dad's aunty," the driver said. "Everyone reckons it'll be her last birthday, so we're having a party."

Gordon tossed a handful of onion rings on the grill. The onions hissed and sizzled. He shouldered through the swing door into the kitchen. Narelle put the feather duster on a shelf and pulled a cloth from her apron pocket. She approached the driver and started wiping down one of the nearby tables.

"Where's the party at?" she said.

"The retirement village," the driver said. "She lives in a single room now. She used to have a unit but she can't see or hear that well any more. They had to move her."

"Oh. That's really awful, isn't it?"

"Yep, but it'll get worse. Next stop for her is the nursing home. And then a wooden box."

Gordon came out of the kitchen holding a meat patty wrapped in paper. He tore the paper off the patty and slung the patty onto the stove. "Narelle, go tidy up the kitchen," he said.

She sighed and pulled a face. The driver winked at her. She pocketed her cloth and walked slowly to the kitchen door, knowing that the driver would be watching. She glanced at him with shining eyes and pushed through the swing door.

Gordon shovelled at the onions with tongs and cracked an egg. The driver slumped in his chair and stretched out his long legs. He said to Gordon, "What kind of a birthday present do you buy for a ninety-five-year-old woman who lives in a single room?"

"I wouldn't know," Gordon said.

"It doesn't seem right for anybody to live that long," the driver said. He waited a while and then said in a louder voice, "Well, does it, Gordon? Does it seem right to you?"

"I wouldn't know."

The driver got up and sauntered over to the shelves. "She had a whole life once. She ran a hotel. She had a husband and kids to look after, and friends to visit and things to do every day. Now she's got nothing. She sits in a tiny room by herself and she's got nothing at all."

Gordon opened a bread roll and put the two halves on the grill. He flipped the meat patty, flipped the egg and shoved at the onions again with the tongs.

The driver said, "What do you think about that?"

Gordon turned to him. "When your time's up, it's up. And her time isn't up. That's all."

The driver stopped at a shelf. He lifted cans one at a time and inspected them. Gordon watched him. Narelle came out of the kitchen and headed straight to the shelves. She picked up her feather duster and started flicking it again.

"You can mop the kitchen," Gordon said.

"It's mopped already," she said. Then she said to the driver, "Do you live anywhere around here?"

"We've got a farm."

"What sort of farm?" she said.

"Wheat."

"What kinds of things do you do on a wheat farm?" she said.

The driver shrugged. "Lots of things. You've got to know how to use all sorts of machines. And you've got to hunt."

Narelle's eyes widened. "Hunt?"

"For sure," he said. "We get rabbits. And foxes follow the rabbits. Then there's cockies and galahs. If you don't keep them culled, they take your whole crop."

"Do you have a gun?" she said.

He nodded. "Rifles."

Narelle leaned close and whispered, "Did you get that scar from hunting?"

The driver touched at his nose. Narelle flushed.

"I fell off an ag bike," he said at last. "It rolled on me. I broke my collarbone, too. See?" He pulled aside the neck of his t-shirt to reveal a buckled collarbone. Narelle gasped. The driver smiled and let go of his t-shirt. "The handlebars smashed into my nose," he said and ran a fingertip across the scar. "This is the best the doctors could do."

Gordon slammed the hamburger, wrapped in a bag, onto the counter top. "Five dollars," he said.

The driver approached the counter and took out his wallet. He gave Gordon a note and said, "Could I have it on a plate?"

"You can't stay. That ute is blocking my bowser."

The driver swivelled on one heel and squinted out the roadhouse window. His ute was the only vehicle. "I can't see that it's bothering anybody."

Gordon slapped the hamburger onto a plate and pushed the plate across the counter top.

"And I'd like a coffee, too," the driver said, and sat at one of the tables and unwrapped the hamburger.

Gordon went through the swing doors into the kitchen. Narelle put down the feather duster and took out her cloth and started wiping tables again. Gordon came back with a bag of ground coffee.

"I think it's really nice that you're giving this old lady a party," Narelle said.

"She won't even know we're there," the driver said. "Her mind is slipping on her."

"Oh, that's a shame," she said.

"She'll die soon anyway."

"That's a shame too."

The driver bit into his burger. Gordon clattered with the dials and levers on the coffee machine. Narelle watched the driver as he chewed and she bit at her lips and kept wiping at the same section of tabletop. He lifted a corner of his mouth at her in a half-smile.

"What's your name again?" he said.

"Narelle." She beamed and forgot about the tabletop.

The driver swallowed and said, "Narelle, do you know the government keeps track of how everybody dies?"

"They do?" she said.

"Yep. They have warehouses full of death certificates, and

there's people with computers that work out what kills people the most."

"Heart disease and cancer," Gordon said.

The driver sat up in his chair. "See? Your old man knows what I'm talking about."

"Everybody knows that heart disease and cancer are the biggest killers," Gordon said. "Any idiot knows that."

"Dad," Narelle said. "Don't."

"But what you don't know," the driver said, putting his burger on the plate, "is that the government reckons that most people die before they're supposed to. They call it premature death."

"So what?" Gordon said.

"Think about it," the driver said. "Heart disease, cancer, car accident, boat accident, drowning, drug overdose, everything. Premature." He took a bite of his burger and talked around the mouthful. "But then you've got people like my Dad's aunty who just won't give it up."

Gordon stomped over with the cup of coffee. "Yeah? Well, so what?"

"Daddy," Narelle whined.

"Go on to the motel rooms," Gordon said. "Do as I say. Right now, missy."

Narelle tried to stare down her father, but couldn't. Her mouth twisted a little and she went out the back door. Gordon thumped the cup onto the driver's table. Coffee sloshed into the saucer.

"Two dollars," Gordon said.

The driver strummed his fingers on the tabletop. "The government thinks everyone should be dying of old age. That's a cruel way to go, if you ask me. But if all the other ways to die are premature, then how does anybody get to die at the right time? Tell me that."

Gordon sighed hard. "I wouldn't know. Now I'd like you to pay for your coffee and take your burger and leave."

The driver regarded Gordon carefully. "We have what you want. Your sign says that. Now what I want is an answer."

Gordon didn't move or make a sound. It was if he hadn't heard. Then he picked up the burger and threw it into the driver's

111

lap. The driver jack-knifed in his chair as if stabbed.

Gordon's face turned red and his temples pulsed with blue veins. "You smarmy little bastard," he said, spittle flying from his lips.

The driver started to laugh and didn't stop. Gordon balled his chunky hands into fists. Narelle opened the back door and uttered a shocked little peep.

"Daddy, what's going on?" she said.

"Get outside," Gordon said.

"Tell me, Gordon," the driver said, thumbing away tears of laughter. "When is the right time for somebody to die?"

"All right, goddammit, I'll tell you," Gordon said, his chest heaving as the breath rasped in and out through blue lips. "One day you walk in front of a bus and that's the end of it, and it doesn't matter a stuff what the government thinks because you're dead." He swiped at his brow with the back of his hand. "Happy now? Have I given you what you want?"

"Almost," the driver said. He put the hamburger back on the plate, picked shreds of lettuce and onion from his lap and dropped them onto the mangled burger.

Gordon and the driver stared at each other for a long time. Narelle took a few steps towards the table.

"Dad, why don't you go and lie down?" she said.

Gordon turned his florid face to her. The meat of his jowls shook and when he spoke, his voice was strangled. "You shut your mouth, you little slut."

Narelle flinched, and for a second it looked as if she would start crying. Then she steeled herself, came closer, and put a hand on the driver's shoulder.

"Don't worry about your clothes," she said. "I can wash them for you."

"Want to go to this party, Narelle?" the driver said as he stood. "You can come with me if you like."

Gordon swung his fist with all the weight in his heavy body. The driver took the blow on his chin and crashed backwards through the plastic tables. Narelle screamed. Gordon advanced and stood over the driver.

"Get off my property," he said.

The driver gathered his long legs beneath him and got up. His chin was already turning purple. He bent down and grabbed the hamburger from the floor. He put the burger on the counter top, then reached into his jeans pocket and pulled out some coins. He placed a couple of coins on the counter top. "That's for the coffee," he said.

"Good," Gordon said. "Now piss off."

The driver pushed through the screen door and Gordon watched him walk across the lot to the ute. Then Gordon turned to his daughter.

"Straighten these tables," he said. "And then you'd better go out back before I do something I'll regret."

Narelle, mewling, picked up the scattered tables and chairs one at a time. Gordon stood rigidly and took deep breaths to calm his galloping heart.

The door of the roadhouse swung open, and the driver came in with a rifle in his hand. The driver rammed the tip of the barrel into Gordon's neck and forced him back to the counter top. Narelle dropped the chair she was holding.

"I'm that bus you talked about," the driver said, and his smile didn't reach his eyes. "You just walked in front of me."

Narelle stumbled through the tables and chairs and fell against the back door. It opened and dumped her onto the dirt. She scrabbled and crawled, then pitched herself against the wall of the roadhouse. She screwed her eyes shut and jammed her fingers into her ears until all she could hear was the roar of her own blood.

Baggage

Aphrodite signed the lease and moved into the unit on the same day. She'd abandoned most of her possessions back at the house, and had only what she could fit in the van. The move didn't take long.

First, she set up the single bed from their guestroom. As she wrestled the slats into the steel frame, she wondered if she had the money to buy herself a double bed, then considered if an overweight forty-four-year-old even needed one. She made the bed with its dusty sheets and doona, and looked for her pillow, but she'd forgotten it.

She sat on the mattress and put her face in her hands. After a time, she continued to unpack. When she found one of her coats, she used it to stuff the pillowcase. Her pride at this small flash of ingenuity made her smile.

The meagre unpacking done, Aphrodite went outside.

The block held four units arranged along a driveway. Aphrodite's was the last in the row. Her unit's back yard was just a small square of tiles, but over the fence lay a concreted water channel with grassy banks, gum trees, bottlebrush and rosellas.

She watched parrots flitting from tree to tree until the doorbell sounded. Then she hurried through the laundry and lounge, unable to convince herself that it wasn't Brian until she opened the door and saw with dismay that it definitely wasn't Brian. It was a young woman with freckles. She wore a heavy velvet dress and knitted shawl despite the warm autumn weather.

"Can I help you?" Aphrodite said.

"I'm Jenny from unit two," the woman said, and turned to point up the steep hill of the driveway, as if Aphrodite wouldn't have any bearings. "I didn't know someone was moving in, so all I've got to spare is this."

"Well, thank you," Aphrodite said, taking the jar of instant coffee. "And I mean it. I haven't had time to go grocery shopping yet."

"Really? Then I'll take you right now. Let's get a little something to celebrate while we're there. Do you like wine?"

Damn it, a neighbour from hell. But Aphrodite didn't know where the supermarket was and her friends had somehow been Brian's friends and she didn't have the strength to fight for their loyalty, and she suddenly didn't want to be alone on this first night of all nights so she said, "Okay, thanks. I'm Aphrodite. It's good to meet you."

"Good to meet you too," Jenny said. "I hope we can be friends."

That first night, once the groceries were put away, they opened the chardonnay and sat cross-legged on the carpet of Aphrodite's unfurnished lounge to start their conversation with details of work. When it was her turn, Aphrodite carefully talked around the two-man company she and Brian had started together, which involved computer networks and repairs for businesses. She had done admin, marketing, bookwork and reception. When they started to get busy, they hired someone else, a younger woman, to help part-time. Then Aphrodite didn't have a job or a home or a de facto anymore, because this younger woman had taken it all.

Aphrodite stopped talking. Jenny mentioned that, similarly, she was no longer with her husband but they didn't discuss that either. Instead, they talked about wine, good restaurants, travel, and discovered that both of them had hated Lisbon yet loved Florence. Near the end of the second bottle of wine, they realised it was two in the morning. They said their goodbyes. Aphrodite went to bed, not minding the fusty smell of unwashed sheets or caring that coat buttons jabbed through the pillowcase into her cheek.

The next morning, she met the neighbour from number three,

the unit adjacent to hers. Aphrodite was opening the van when a frenzied barking startled her. Emerging from next door was an English setter dancing on back legs, lips pulled into a snarl, and a bent old woman fighting to hold its leash. The old woman, whose cropped white hair resembled a bathing cap, tittered and said in that whistling pitch peculiar to the very elderly, "Oh, she won't hurt you, will you Lady? Oh no, she's as gentle as a lamb. She won't hurt you. Oh no, she won't."

On most mornings, Aphrodite met Ruth and Lady in the double carport they shared, as if Ruth had been watching for her through the window. Ruth liked to offer news about her grandson, who performed well at primary school and was invariably picked by teachers to be a captain, chess club leader or junior council member. And, *click*, Aphrodite would remember how she'd squandered the last six years of her reproductive life on Brian. Throughout these repetitious conversations with Ruth, Lady would strain at her leash and shiver her drooling jaws and always Ruth would say, always, *Lady won't hurt you, she's as gentle as a lamb*. Aphrodite never believed her.

Aphrodite ended up working part-time for cash at the local dry cleaners. Soon after that, her advertisements in school newsletters got her enough students to tutor in English to cover the rest of her bills. At the start of winter, Aphrodite had money to buy furniture and knick-knacks for the unit. By spring, she stopped expecting a message from Brian on her answering machine.

Summer came. The weather couldn't make up its mind and alternated blazing sunshine with furious rain. The rain came and went and came again. The steamy heat drew thunderstorms.

By New Year's Eve, the relentless wet and humidity had left Aphrodite wrung out and testy. She slumped across the couch and tried to watch television. She cranked the volume but strained to hear the newsreader over the hammering tumult on the roof. The screen showed a four-wheel drive abandoned on a submerged bridge, helicopter shots of burst riverbanks, people waving from rooftops. Aphrodite glanced at the bottom of the flyscreen door where a dark line was spreading.

She ran over. Her slippers sank into a mush of wet carpet. She switched on the outside light and looked through the flyscreen. The carport was awash, her van sunk to its hubcaps. The waterline lapping at the front step surged its languorous beat into her unit.

While Aphrodite chocked rolled towels at the front and back doors, it occurred to her that she was sitting on the bottom of a geographical bowl. The open waterway behind her unit was short, cut off at both ends by a culvert that carried the drain beneath the roads. She could picture, with sudden and awful clarity, the astronomical pressure of pent-up stormwater, collected from every concrete and asphalt surface in the neighbourhood, pounding along underground pipes and spouting unfettered into the open waterway.

The rain on the roof intensified as if a towering thunderhead squatted directly over her unit. Aphrodite grabbed the phone and hesitated, unsure of whom to call. If only Jenny was at home instead of at work.

A splintering, rending sound turned Aphrodite to a window. She saw the back yard fence crumple under the weight of a monstrous wave.

The unit swamped fast. Muddy water, shockingly chill, closed over her legs and raced around the lounge room. The pine table lifted and pirouetted past, her handbag undisturbed on its surface. The tea trolley on casters that held her television and DVD player tilted. The television fizzled, then slid into the water, bellied for a moment, and went under.

Aphrodite was hit by the first panic of possible electrocution. She must get out.

Within the next breath, the water climbed to her waist. Aphrodite lunged towards the screen door. The numerous tides grappled at her legs and pushed her one way, then another. She dropped the phone into the roiling murk. She felt for it with one foot, but couldn't find it. A slipper pulled away. Not wanting to walk lopsided, she shucked the other slipper. Too late, she worried about cutting her feet in the filthy water that seethed with scum and debris.

She clutched the handle of the screen door, and pushed.

Nothing happened. The surge held the door shut.

Fear blanched through her like sheet lightning. She shoved against the door with her whole being and it gave. She tumbled into the river gushing through the carport.

Her van and Ruth's hatchback shifted and fidgeted against each other, water fluxing across their bonnets. Aphrodite made for the higher ground of the driveway, but heard something through the roar of the storm that made her pause, an urgent desperate sound, but she couldn't identify it, couldn't figure where it was coming from. She splashed about, trying to squint through the curtains of rain until, in a rush, she recognised the sound as barking.

She twirled in the water. There was Lady, trapped behind the screen door of Ruth's unit, paddling frantically in the racing churn.

Aphrodite struck out across the carport's lake, taking a wide detour around the jostling vehicles. The handle of the screen door turned but, fearful of Lady, Aphrodite remained outside and yelled for Ruth and kept yelling until the silhouette of a reedy arm waved in the unit's gloom. Lady dunked and resurfaced against the far wall, her sleek head bobbing within a whirlpool.

That decided it. Aphrodite wrenched at the door and waded in.

She found Ruth clinging to the kitchen bench and gathered her up. The old woman muttered "Lady, Lady, Lady," until Aphrodite stumbled through the wash, gripped the dog by her collar, and hauled Ruth and Lady out of the unit, up the hill and clear of the water.

They sank to the driveway, stung by raindrops. Seconds later, the rain cut off. The quiet rang in Aphrodite's ears.

A few minutes more, and the flood receded at an astonishing rate, pulling back into the waterway like an octopus into its cave, sucking and slurping at Aphrodite's van and Ruth's hatchback, dragging both vehicles over the buckled fence and down the grassy bank. Then the flood was finished.

Ruth, trembling, clung to Aphrodite. Lady shivered and twined herself against Aphrodite's legs. The couple from unit number one ventured down the driveway under a shared umbrella, smiling and bowing and shaking their heads and gesturing at the ruins, and offered towels. Aphrodite put one towel on the dog and the other around Ruth, who whimpered with her eyes shut. Then Jenny appeared.

Jenny ushered them into her unit which, being further up the hill, was unmolested but for a damp swatch of carpet at the front door. Ruth refused a hot drink and a change of clothes. Jenny said to her, "Who do you want me to call?"

"Nobody. I've already called my son to tell him I love him."

Ruth's chin wobbled. Aphrodite tightened an arm around her. Lady whined and paced fretfully.

After a time, Ruth's son turned up: a shambling, bald man swathed in corduroy. He carried Ruth to his car. Lady, reluctant to leave Aphrodite at first, went with them once Ruth clucked her tongue.

Jenny said to Aphrodite, "Let's check out your place."

Aphrodite's unit looked like a giant had dragged it through a tar pit: the carpet a dark squelch, the furniture tipped and waterlogged, clothes in the wardrobe and drawers black with silt. The stink of mire made them cough. The pine table, rammed up against the toilet door, still held her handbag, untouched. Aphrodite shouldered it, grateful that she had her keys, wallet, some cash, driver's licence, credit cards and mobile phone. And sunglasses, two tampons. A safety pin.

Aphrodite and Jenny picked their way over the flattened fence and down the embankment to inspect the van. Water tipped out when Aphrodite opened the driver's door, so she closed it again. They peered into the waterway at the wreckage of ordinary lives caught amongst exposed tree roots and shredded banksia: papers, plastic bags, the surprise of a bright orange baseball cap. Aphrodite, amused, pointed down the bank at one of her lost slippers. Jenny began to cry.

Sirens sounded across the neighbourhood. From her unit, Jenny tried to ring emergency services but the lines were engaged. She gave Aphrodite a towel and ushered her into the bathroom. Aphrodite stood under the shower jet for a long time. Afterwards, Jenny lent her underwear, sandals and a kaftan.

They got into Jenny's sedan. Jenny drove up and over the lip of the driveway to the crossover and then braked. "Where do you want to go?"

"I don't know," Aphrodite said. "Does it matter? Let's just see where we end up."

Aphrodite clutched at her handbag, all that remained, and smiled. Jenny smiled too. The light after the storm was yellow and bright so both directions gleamed. Jenny manoeuvred the sedan onto the slick, shining road and they were away.

Muscle Fatigue

He's taller than me by a whisker. Side by side, we stand in the lounge room mirror, him wearing pyjamas, me in a t-shirt and track pants, both with dumbbells in our hands. I'm showing him how to work his shoulders with lateral raises.

Lift your arms horizontal to the floor, elbows bent.

Despite all the food I feed him, the disproportionate amount of meat on every plate, he's thin, fourteen-year-old thin, gangly, a collection of long bones. Next to him in the mirror, I'm all curves. Stupendous bust, wide hips, meaty thighs. It occurs to me that I'm not only middle-aged, but fat. I watch myself as I move the dumbbells through space, my son beside me, solemn, copying me precisely.

Tilt your fists at the top of the motion like you're pouring water.

And he does. His green eyes look through the mirror into mine. I feel like he's asking, *Mum, how come it's you and not Dad teaching me how to weight train?*

Because Dad is gone, I want to say. *He got sick of me and left. We loved each other once, I'm sure of it, yet things happened that I can't explain.* I clench my teeth.

Breathe out with the effort.

It takes a few reps, but finally, we are in sync, my son and I. One-two, one-two. The rhythm is hypnotic. He offers a tentative smile into the mirror. I try to smile back. Up and down, up and down, we lift our arms together like earthbound birds, our feet caught in tar.

Waiting for the Huntsman

The horse didn't move its head, just rolled down its apple-sized eye until the whites showed all the way around and the dark iris had Natalie pinned. She took a step back. Her sandal caught on a tuft of capeweed, and Kate laughed.

"What a baby," Kate said. "Go ahead and pat him, why don't you? Come on, I dare you."

Natalie's hand shook. The horse's flank felt surprisingly hard, like the armchair Mum kept in the hall by the phone table. "There, so what?" Natalie said, backing off.

From the other side of the agistment paddock ambled two girls, both fat and, like Kate, wearing jeans and gumboots. When the two drew near, they sneered at Natalie, who suddenly felt ridiculous in her summer dress with its capped sleeves and lace trim.

One of the fat girls pointed at Natalie and said to Kate, "Gawd, what is *that*?"

"Some relative from the city, I don't know," Kate said. "Her mum's in hospital and we're stuck with her."

Natalie tried on a friendly smile. "Dad's a salesman. He does a lot of travelling. He's in Tasmania at the moment."

But the fat girls ignored her and started speaking to Kate about the riding competition Kate was entering the following day. The horse watched Natalie with its crazed eyes and pulled back its lips to show her its blunt, square teeth. Did horses bite? Were they prone to unpredictable attacks, like elephants? She didn't know, but Mum would. Mum knew just about everything.

Natalie noticed a squat man approaching from the car park. The man wore overalls strained across a paunch that sat round and tight as a basketball. The other girls noticed him too.

"Uh-oh," one of the girls said. "Look out."

"Bye, Kate," the other one said. "See you at the championships, okay?"

Both girls took off. Natalie turned. The man was getting closer.

"Who's that?" Natalie said.

"My old man," Kate said.

"What should I call him? Mr Wallace? Or is he my uncle?"

"Call him whatever you want, dumb arse."

Kate's father walked straight under the horse's chin, his gaze fixed on Natalie and his eyes sunk within dark circles. His face was sunburnt, chapped and whiskery. "You must be young Natasha. How was your ride in on the train?"

"Good thank you, Uncle Henry, but my name's Natalie."

He put his leathery hands on his knees and laughed, and kept laughing. Natalie didn't know why. The sharp desire for home caught in her chest.

This wouldn't be for long, Dad had promised as she cried into his neck at Flinders Street Station, only a week or so and then everything would be back to normal.

At last, Henry stopped laughing and straightened up. As if startled, he noticed the horse and slapped angrily at its withers. The horse shied, apple eye revolving. Natalie braced, ready to run, but the horse steadied itself, stamping its hooves and curling its frothy lips while Henry's expression changed to one of open admiration.

"Look at him, he's just a big kid, that's all he is, just a big kid," Henry said. "He's just a big kid, that's all he is, just a big kid."

Natalie glanced at Kate, who was playing statues, frozen and waiting.

"He's just a big kid," he said, and Natalie thought of her toy robot, unable to stop marching its little tin legs until the key in its back wound down.

"Uncle Henry?"

Henry whirled and stared about blindly for a moment, then

struck out across the paddock towards the car park, gesturing for the girls to follow. He flung open all the car doors, took a rifle from the back seat and put it in the front next to a blue and white esky.

Kate pointed at the esky and said to Natalie, "Have a look in there."

"Why? What's in it?"

"Open it and find out."

Natalie felt her insides clench. She lifted a corner of the lid. On a bag of ice, curled up as if asleep, lay a rabbit with soft ginger fur, a dull eye, and a coin of dried blood on its ribs.

"That's your dinner," Kate said, smirking.

The drive to Kate's house was ten minutes along a ruler-straight road that divided paddocks and green hills, followed by turns through a town with roundabouts, but no traffic lights. The weatherboard house had a pitched tin roof. Kate pointed through the carport—"Go out the back and give Mum a hand"—and went inside the house with Henry and the esky.

Kate's mother, Betsy, was thin and wore her grey hair chopped short. She was behind wire in the chicken coop, mucking out straw into a wheelbarrow while hens clucked at her feet.

Natalie wandered over. "Hello again."

Betsy stopped and leant on her fork. "Right. Have fun with the horses?"

"It was okay."

"I'd ask you to help put this straw on the garden beds, but you're not exactly dressed for it. Didn't your dad pack any clothes you could use?"

"I don't know."

"Well, go on inside. Ask Kate to lend you some jeans."

The house smelt of mothballs. Natalie walked through the kitchen past Henry, who was seated at the table drinking beer from a large bottle, and didn't appear to see her. The house looked to have been cobbled together in unrelated stages, with dead-end passageways, rooms opening into other rooms, and wooden steps in doorways that led up or down depending on the slope of the floor. There were metal horseshoes hammered into walls, horse figurines on the mantle, a velour painting of a galloping horse on a beach with foaming rollers, a clock face that showed a stampeding mob, a brass rubbing of a horse's head.

Natalie wandered into a narrow junk room with stacks of boxes and broken deck chairs. She was about to walk out when she noticed the bookcase. Lining the shelves were dozens of trophies engraved with Kate's name, and a stack of ribbons and pennants. Natalie picked up a framed photograph of Kate on a pony. The girl couldn't have been more than five years old, her chubby face pinched in concentration.

"What are you doing in here?"

Natalie turned. "You must be a fantastic rider."

Kate hesitated, said, "Hey, let me show you something," and opened a cupboard. She brought out, on hangers, white britches and a buttoned red jacket, and from the foot of the cupboard, two boxes that held a black riding hat and a pair of buffed knee-high boots. "I'm in a couple of categories tomorrow: champion rider under thirteen years, and champion local under seventeen. I'll win at least one title, maybe both."

"That's so great. Your parents must be really proud of you."

Kate's face closed up. She rammed the items of clothing back into the cupboard and slammed the door. "Go on, get out," she said.

Natalie retreated to her designated bedroom, a space in the roof accessed via a ladder at the rear of the kitchen. The rafters hunkered so low that she couldn't stand up, and there was only room within the chipboard walls for a double mattress. A window cut into the tin roof looked over the back yard. Outside, Betsy put the rake in the shed, approached the house and walked under Natalie's line of sight. Soon, Natalie could hear her moving about in the kitchen below, humming and clattering pans. Then silence.

Betsy must be skinning and gutting the rabbit, Natalie thought, and remembered the animal's glassy button eye. She grabbed her toy bunny, Violet, from her suitcase at the foot of the mattress and lay down. Her pillow smelt like home.

"**T**ea's ready."

Natalie broke from her doze in alarm. Kate's scowling face peered through the hole in the floor and ducked away. Natalie hid Violet under the clothes in her suitcase, then descended the ladder. Betsy, Henry and Kate were already at the kitchen table. Natalie took her seat. Henry didn't have a plate; he stared at nothing in particular and drank in slow, thoughtful draughts from a large beer bottle. Three empty bottles were lined up on the table in front of him.

"You must be starving, girl," Betsy said. "Tuck in."

The meat on her plate glistened in its gravy but Natalie picked at the beans and mashed potato instead. No one spoke for a time. Then Kate said, "Hey little baby, what about your casserole?"

Natalie speared a chunk of rabbit with her fork and placed it in her mouth. As she chewed, she tried to think of sausages and chops, but the meat stuck in her throat like chaff. She managed to swallow and said, "Has my dad called?"

Betsy said, "Why, did he say he was going to?"

"Maybe he's having so much fun he's forgot about her," Kate said. She grinned at Natalie, and made a point of chomping with her mouth open to show off the rabbit meat gnashing between her teeth.

The attic room didn't have a nightlight. Natalie switched off the lamp and lay on her back, clutching Violet. She heard a noise and sat up. Kate climbed up from the hole in the floor and crawled across the empty side of the mattress, pillow in hand.

"What do you want?" Natalie whispered.

"Shut up. Mum told me to keep you company."

Kate threw herself onto the mattress and wrenched up the sheet. Once Natalie's eyes adjusted to the gloom, she could see something in the rafters, a black shape like an open hand above her face. "Kate, I think there's a spider up there."

"Probably. We get huntsmen all the time."

Natalie, gasping, flung herself into a corner. "Kill it, please kill it."

"What for? Huntsmen eat mozzies. Want to get bitten?"

"I don't care, you have to kill it."

"Aw, shut up, will you? I've got to compete tomorrow."

"It'll drop on me."

"No, it won't. Go to sleep."

Natalie clenched her teeth. Then she heard muted shouting, and scraping noises like furniture getting shoved around. "What's that?" she said.

"Nothing. If Dad comes up here, pretend you're asleep."

Natalie's heart kicked against her ribs. "I want to go home."

"Tough."

Natalie thumbed at tears and stared into the rafters. The space in the roof had its own presence, thick with darkness. The huntsman was watching her, she knew, she could feel its eyes on her. It was waiting for her to drowse off so that it might begin its slow creep down the wall.

The yelling and banging downstairs got louder and closer. *Please get me out of here.* Natalie pressed her face against her toy bunny and waited for a sign from the heavenly Father. None came. She wondered if He was moving in one of His mysterious ways or if she hadn't prayed correctly, but the only person who would know for sure was in a hospital somewhere, and Natalie had no clue how to find her.

Cash Cow

Sarah Ramsey glanced at the wall of perspex that separated her office from the rest of the bank, and saw Mitchell. Unbelievable. What was that son of a bitch doing here? Sarah leapt up, opening her door.

"I told you to leave me alone," she said. She'd kept her voice down, but even so, some of her tellers were looking over, concerned. Taking a breath, pressing a hand against the small of Mitchell's back, Sarah whispered, "Let's talk somewhere else."

He shrugged and sauntered outside with her. They weaved through the traffic snarl to the coffee shop across the road, took a table inside and placed their order.

"Okay, then," Sarah said, arranging her face into a smile. "Here we are."

Forgoing the pleasantries, Mitchell said, "I need you to cash cheques for me. Two right now, and plenty more to come."

"Christ, Mitchell, another scam?"

"Kind of, but it's for public liability insurance this time. The cheques are from national and international corporations, so cashing them shouldn't give you any grief." He leaned over the table and flashed white teeth. "I'll give you eight per cent. Okay, ten per cent of every cheque, how would that be?"

She shook her head. "I'm still paying for helping you the first time."

"This is different. Nothing to do with Victoria Chiang, I swear."

"Screw you."

Sarah went to stand. Mitchell grabbed her arm and forced her to sit down again. He thumbed at his mobile phone, muttered into it, "Coffee shop opposite the bank," and hung up. Sarah couldn't find her voice to speak.

A minute passed.

Mitchell nodded towards the door. Sarah looked around. There stood a tall, pale and thin man of indeterminate age. The man's gaze found Mitchell. Then the man's vacant, milky eyes roamed around the coffee shop, and finally settled on Sarah.

Frightened, turning away, she whispered, "What's this about?"

The tall, pale and thin man rolled his foot on the doorstep and tumbled into a lanky heap, tipping a table on his way down, spilling sugar packets and shattering a cruet set across the tiles. He began to scream and writhe, clawing at his ankle, while customers drew back in alarm.

"Oh God," Sarah said.

Mitchell said through teeth, "That's Edward, my cash cow. Okay, let's go."

He dragged her by the wrist from the coffee shop. She said that they hadn't yet paid for the coffee. Instead of answering, Mitchell manhandled her to a silver sedan parked a few doors down from her branch. With a hand on her head, he shoved her into the passenger seat, then ran around and jumped into the driver's side, slamming the door. The car's interior seemed muffled, sound-proofed.

Sarah said, "I don't get it."

"Okay, listen," Mitchell said. "Edward Dellenbrandt was born with a weird disease. He can't feel any pain. You could smack him with a piece of two-by-four and he'd just laugh and ask you to do it again."

Sarah, despite herself, couldn't stop the tears. "You're making this poor bastard hurt himself for money?"

"No, dopey, he just *pretends* to hurt himself. He does pratfalls. Look, Edward's lived his whole life without knowing what pain even feels like. He's learnt other ways to protect himself from injury, right?" His chest rose and fell. "Answer me. Right?"

"Right."

"Okay, so stop your crying and listen to me. I've got a mate in the insurance business. He tips us off to places that give payouts no questions asked. I've got a mate who's forged a stack of IDs for Edward. And we've got bank accounts. But I'm taking the business to the next level: I need a banker to cash cheques and clean the money. That's you."

He pressed a folded square of paper into her hand. Then he reached over, opened the passenger side door, and pushed her out of the car.

Back in her office, Sarah swivelled her chair so that its back faced the perspex wall. Only then did she open the square of paper. It was two cheques, both from large insurance companies, one made out to *Edward Dell* for three thousand, the other to *Lars Bache* for fifteen.

She locked the cheques in the top drawer of her desk. Until she'd had time to think, she wouldn't make a single move.

Early the next morning, Sarah cashed both cheques. She put the bundled hundred-dollar notes—minus her ten per cent—into the main body of her handbag. Then, she put her share into a business-sized envelope, which she tucked into the zippered section of her handbag. She told the head teller that she had an unexpected meeting with a client.

Sarah drove her rental car to Mitchell's flat. She had to ring the bell five times before he opened the door, bleary-eyed and wearing nothing but boxers.

"Sarah? What time is it?"

"Eight-thirty. You should do the Seafood Chest restaurant in the city. It's owned by an old man named Jakub Pankowski, a client of mine."

"Hey, did you cash my cheques?"

She reached into her bag and handed him the bricks of money. He grabbed them with both hands, face brightening.

Sarah said, "Pankowski just paid fifty grand in cash—out of

his own pocket—to one of his cooks who cut off a finger during a dinner service."

"Cash, you reckon?"

"In small bills. He always pays up and pays up fast because he doesn't want any authorities involved. Ask for twenty-five and you'll get it for sure."

"Seafood Chest? In the city? Okay, good girl."

He leaned over for a kiss but Sarah was already down the stairs.

From Mitchell's, she drove to an up-market strip close to the city. The Quality Jewellery Emporium had bars on the windows and an armed guard at the door, while inside were plush carpets, velvet walls, locked display cases, and plenty of diamonds. The sales assistant, a slender girl with crooked eyes, murmured into the intercom. Sarah had to wait for an hour before the intercom buzzed and the sales assistant ushered her through the rear door, down a corridor and into Victoria Chiang's office.

Instead of a desk, computer and filing cabinets, the windowless room featured a leather suite, sculptures, abstract paintings, and a fully stocked bar. Victoria Chiang had her neat body tucked into an armchair, her dyed red hair glowing like lava in the beam of down-lights. A thickset Chinese man sat in the far corner reading a newspaper. Victoria gestured at the lounge suite.

Sarah sat on its edge, heart flittering, and pulled the envelope from her handbag. "Eighteen hundred dollars," she said, placing the envelope on the coffee table. "Miss Chiang, I'd like to start buying back my car. Do you still have it?"

Victoria Chiang took a cigarette from the packet on the coffee table, and lit it with a gold-coloured lighter. Taking her time, she exhaled a stream of smoke. Finally, she said, "Come back with cash whenever you want."

"Okay, but what about my car?"

Smiling, Victoria Chiang fanned smoke from her nostrils and said, "Say hello to the Pancake for me when you see him. And tell him I want my money."

The Chinese man looked up from his newspaper and pointed at the door.

Sarah obeyed. The velvet-lined door shut soundlessly behind her. The cockeyed sales assistant smiled as Sarah left the premises.

A week later, and Sarah's new place was hard to find, especially in the dark. Mitchell gunned his car up and down a maze of grotty side streets, leaving rubber on every road, until he stumbled upon the correct block of flats, a squat cube of concrete. Sarah's pigeonhole was upstairs, number six. He knocked, and she opened the door straight away.

He pushed past her and said, "Okay, Edward did his thing and now it's gone bad."

"Hang on, what do you mean?"

Irritated, he turned to her, about to give out some hard words, but her t-shirt was cut low and her tracksuit pants were sitting smooth over the curve of her hips and instead, he felt a stirring in his jeans. Maybe he could persuade her into the bedroom for old times' sake.

"Mitchell, what's gone bad?" she said.

He flung himself onto her sofa. "We did the scam on the Seafood Chest like you said, all right? It was perfect. The inside stairs weren't lit, no contrast paint on the steps, a loose rug on the staircase turnaround, and Edward worked it like he'd never worked it before, you know? Brilliant."

"So?"

"So, the owner's a criminal."

"Jakub Pankowski?" Sarah giggled and dropped to the floor like a cat, arranging her slim build cross-legged on the floor opposite him. "Are you mad? Jakub's a great-grandad. He must be in his eighties, at least."

"Oh yeah? Well, let me burst your bubble. This great-grandad of yours is a drug baron."

"A drug baron? Not a red baron?" She laughed again.

Mitchell jumped to his feet and stood over her, flooded with the maddening urge to kick in her sweet face. "Alright then, smart arse, he's a dealer—meth, coke, smack—understand me now? And he doesn't want to give any of his drug money to some retard for falling down his bloody stairs, okay?"

Sarah had stopped laughing. She stood up, edged past Mitchell's heaving ribs, and went into the kitchenette. Mitchell watched her sashaying buttocks and followed her, crowding her against the kitchen bench. He gripped her shoulders and breathed in her scent of shampoo.

Then she said, "So what? Forget about the Seafood Chest. There are plenty of other places to scam."

"Too late," Mitchell said, and pulled away from her. "Edward, the dumb prick, actually broke a bone in his back this time. If it doesn't heal right, he's gonna get the wheelchair and his girlfriend—and who knew this freak even *had* a girlfriend— reckons she's got him a lawyer, and now Edward won't listen to me."

Sarah regarded him with her violet eyes. Then she left the kitchenette to sit on the sofa. He could tell by her steady blink rate that she was thinking. He kept quiet, holding his breath.

Finally, she said, "Don't worry. I'll talk to Pankowski for you."

"What? You can't do that. Pankowski doesn't even know I exist. He thinks Edward's solo." Mitchell tightened his jaw. "Hey, hitting his place was *your* idea. If you snitch on me, I tell on you, and we both end up in the river."

"Christ, will you stop panicking? I won't even bring it up. Pankowski trusts me with his money problems. I'm his bank manager, remember? If he's worried, he'll want to talk about it. And give me Edward's contact details; I'll talk to him too."

Mitchell smiled. "You were always the smart one. Okay, I'll disappear for a while, until you sort this out." He moved to her side, pressed his lips against hers for a chaste kiss, a small taste of her, and whispered, "We're so great together. Why did we ever break up?"

"Because you threw me to Victoria Chiang to save your own pathetic arse."

Mitchell drew back. "Oh, yeah, that's right. Now I remember."

It was late, but Sarah drove her rental towards the city, revving the car twenty kilometres over every speed limit. Mitchell Klems—damn him—was the biggest regret of her life. Six months ago, thinking she was in love, she had pushed aside her doubts and trusted him, just that one time, on a dodgy business deal.

Idiot.

As soon as Mitchell had sacrificed her into Victoria Chiang's debt, Chiang had taken Sarah's car, her house and her savings, and loaned out Sarah's banking services to Jakub "Pancake" Pankowski. Sarah had to clean his drug money through the various accounts of his cash businesses—the Seafood Chest included—and she had to do it for free, risking jail time or death with every transaction.

Sarah pulled up at the Seafood Chest and got out. A genuine anchor from a merchant ship, some two metres high and rusting, was affixed to the restaurant's roof with steel cables. It leant over the footpath at a precarious angle in violation of city council regulations, but a man like Pankowski didn't have to worry about regulations. A light burned behind the frosted window. Pankowski was waiting for her. Sarah braced herself and pushed open the restaurant door.

The Seafood Chest smelled faintly of brine. There was dark carpet, dark walls, a switchbacked staircase towards the rear. A fish net suspended from the ceiling dripped with plastic sea creatures. A discreet cough made her turn to the window. Grey-haired Pankowski was sitting at a table for two, his chair pushed out to allow room for his paunch. Sarah took a seat.

"*Czesc,*" he said quietly.

"Hello, Jakub," she said, and slid her briefcase onto the table. "The transfer agreement is coming along. The Cayman Islands should be another week or two. And I've got some papers for you to sign."

Pankowski sighed and reached over to take her hand in both of his, his eyes filling with tears.

"Jakub, what's the matter?"

"You know me. You are my *przyjaciel*, isn't that true?"

"Yes, Jakub."

"Then you know I keep the right hand hidden from the left hand, always."

"Yes, always."

"So, no names. A boy falls down my stairs and wants money, twenty-five thousand. I ask a friend to find out about this boy. Now I know everything there is to know."

Everything?

Sarah's heart rate climbed. She tried to extricate her hand from Pankowski's bear-like grasp, but when she couldn't, she willed her face into a calm mask.

He said, "My friend knows a person who knows a person who made false papers for this boy. This boy is a con man. He wants to rip me off, *tak*? And now I trust you with a name. I've no proof, but Victoria Chiang sends this boy. We had a deal, and she accuses that I took twenty-five from her unfairly. The boy asks for the same amount. You see the coincidence? Well, I don't believe in coincidence. I want to send a message. The message should be the boy." He gazed morosely at a plastic crab hanging from the fishing net above their heads.

"But has the boy gone to a lawyer?" Sarah said.

The old man shrugged. "I remember some paper…"

"Paper that links you to him? It's not worth it. Just pay him out and forget it."

He nodded and let go of her hand. "I was right to ask you here. *Dziekuje*. My smart bank manager, *nie*?"

Edward Dellenbrandt's eyes were spaced too far apart, glazed and empty like pale buttons, but it was his mouth Sarah couldn't stop staring at—nothing but a slit cut through the meat of his face, a nasty wound with healed edges.

He tittered, scalloping his ruined mouth, and said in his strangely high voice, "I chewed off my lips when I was a baby. My parents found me in the crib with a mouthful of blood, but it was too late by then. I'd already swallowed the lot."

Sarah felt the threat of a feverish swoon and looked down at the plastic tabletop. Edward Dellenbrandt slid his hands across the table into her line of sight. The last knuckle of each finger was gone, the digits ending in blunt, gnarled scars.

He said, "After the lips, I started on my hands. My parents had to tie my wrists to the crib." He chuckled and said, "You want to see my toes?"

"No thanks," she said. "Let's talk about something else."

"Like what?"

It was just after 10am. The fast food restaurant was already crowded. Sarah pushed aside her foam cup of coffee, and said, "Let's talk about your back."

"What for?"

"Didn't you hurt it the other night when you fell down the stairs?"

"Oh, at the Seafood Chest." He rolled his eyes to the ceiling, and then regarded Sarah brightly. "Yes, I've got a little crack in a bone. But Nancy's going to take me trekking through India and find a holy man who'll fix me."

"Nancy? Your girlfriend?"

"As soon as we get the money from the lawyer, we're off."

"The money from falling down at the Seafood Chest?"

Edward nodded and gulped at his hot chocolate.

Sarah said, "Tell the lawyer you don't want to go ahead with the insurance claim."

"Why would I do that?"

"Because the man who owns the Seafood Chest doesn't want to give you any money. He wants to kill you instead."

Edward giggled into the palm of his disfigured hand. "No, he doesn't. I don't even know who he is. I don't even know who you are. Are you my friend?"

"Yes, I am. And I'm telling you the truth."

Edward's button eyes swam with tears and his scarecrow mouth started working and stretching. Then he began to weep in great noisy hiccups. People at other tables looked over, whispering, pointing. "Oh no, what am I going to do?" he said.

"You're going to go see the man and explain everything. Tell him that it was Mitchell all along, and that Mitchell did it because a lady called Victoria Chiang told him to. Understand? This is very important."

"Yes, I understand."

"Victoria Chiang. Can you remember the name?"

"Yes, I can remember. Victoria Chiang."

E dward followed Sarah's instructions to the letter.

His lawyer ran Edward's paperwork through the document shredder and never again thought of the abandoned claim against the Seafood Chest restaurant. Edward went to Jakub and explained the scam. Jakub, who liked to think of himself as a kind-hearted man, took pity and gave Edward, the patsy, ten thousand dollars in cash, instructing him not to share a penny of it with Mitchell or Victoria Chiang. Edward and his girlfriend, Nancy, bought two air tickets to New Delhi and left the country four days later.

While Edward and Nancy were enjoying salted peanuts at thirty-six thousand feet, Jakub Pankowski called his butcher—not the regular one he used for his restaurant but the other one, Vaughan—who turned up half an hour later. One of the waiters escorted Vaughan upstairs to Jakub's private table, where Jakub was waiting for him.

"Packed out," Vaughan said, taking a seat.

Jakub smiled and nodded. It was Saturday night. The Seafood Chest trilled with the conversation and laughter of over one hundred and eighty happy patrons. The waiter returned to the table with a carafe of red and two glasses.

"Get us both the lobster special," Jakub said, and the waiter nodded and retreated.

"Ah, the good life," Vaughan said, and made a show of rubbing his hands together as if he couldn't wait for the plate of food to arrive.

For such a dainty man, Jakub thought, Vaughan had monstrous forearms, each one like a leg of lamb and bunched with tendons and ropy veins. Those tremendously powerful forearms looked like they could manage just about anything, and usually they did.

"Shall we make the arrangements?" Jakub suggested. "Then we can forget about it and enjoy the lobster, *tak*?"

"Sure. Who is it?"

"Victoria Chiang."

Vaughan froze. His black eyebrows twitched. Exhaling in a sudden rush, he said, "You're joking, aren't you? Well, I dunno. It'd be a tough one, a real tough one. Maybe even double-the-money tough, you know?"

"Why don't we make it triple?" Jakub said, pouring the wine. "That's how sick I am of that two-faced *kurwa*."

Dusk: Sarah parked the rental outside her block of flats and started to get out of the car. Mitchell barrelled her back inside with such force that he vaulted her into the passenger seat and bounced her skull on the dashboard.

It took a moment for her head to clear. She touched her fingers to her eyebrow, found blood. Mitchell was right next to her in the driver's seat, the breath whistling in and out of his nose.

He said, "Victoria Chiang is trying to kill me."

After a time, Sarah whispered, "Oh, Mitchell, that's terrible."

"Yeah, isn't it just? Do you know why she's trying to kill me? Because your good mate Pankowski is trying to kill her and she blames me for that, but I dunno why." Mitchell struck Sarah with the flat of his hand, knocking her into the side window. He shouted, "What did you tell Victoria Chiang about me?"

"Nothing, I didn't tell her anything."

"And where's the retard? Where's Edward? Tell me before I break you in half."

"For Christ's sake, I swear I don't know," Sarah said.

She began to cry in earnest. Minutes passed. Sarah stopped weeping. She looked around at Mitchell. He looked as if he were chewing something over in his mind.

"That sly bastard," he said at last. "He wasn't as retarded as he made out. It must've been him, unless he's already in the river."

Mitchell grimaced and rubbed his fingers into his eye sockets, shaking his head gently as if he couldn't quite believe the nightmare he was living. When he finally glanced around at Sarah, she was surprised to see tears on his cheeks. "How did everything go so bad?" he whispered.

Gingerly, Sarah patted Mitchell on the shoulder and said, "Maybe you should go and see Victoria Chiang and get this sorted out."

"Maybe you're right," he said. "What else can I do? Hide for the rest of my life?"

He smiled sadly and opened the driver's side door. Then he hesitated, as if remembering something, and leaned back to smash his fist into her face. Sarah's cheekbone gave way with a loud pop.

Mitchell said, "If this turns out to be your fault, I'll be back to give you some more." He hopped out and slammed the door hard enough to rock the car.

Sarah languished in the rental's passenger seat for another half-hour or so, yawing in and out of consciousness, before a next-door neighbour, leaving home for a mosaic class at the local community centre, saw blood on the car window and peered inside.

The ambulance took Sarah to hospital. During the three-hour wait for the craniofacial surgeon, the attending emergency doctor did his best to convince Sarah to make a report of assault to the police. Sarah maintained that she had incurred her facial injuries in a fall, the attending doctor refused to believe her, and they eventually settled on a sulky silence.

The surgery to realign her cheekbone and screw it into place went as expected. The next morning, coasting on painkillers, Sarah was served a bland breakfast of oatmeal and juice. A newspaper was folded on the tray. Her eye on the affected side was swollen to a weeping slit. So, it was with just one eye that she read of an unidentified male body, missing its head and hands, that had been found late the night before, in a shallow grave along a no-name highway, by a council worker cutting grass.

Despite everything, Sarah cried.

Exactly one week later, sitting at home with a rug over her knees watching the news on television, Sarah learnt that police investigating the murder of jewellery store owner, Victoria Chiang, had attended the Seafood Chest restaurant in the city early that morning before opening hours. The officers had tried to question the eighty-two-year-old owner, but were forced to shoot him dead when he threatened them with a handgun. Sarah grabbed the remote and the footage of the Seafood Chest, with its defiant anchor, shrunk to a dot on the screen and disappeared.

Sarah figured that the police would be surprised by the modest amount of money the drug-dealing Pankowski had left behind. The very next morning, she resigned her job, left her flat, and flew to London. A bank account, flush with ten thousand Australian dollars converted into Euros, was waiting for her.

Dozens of other accounts in dozens of other cities across Europe and Asia were waiting for her, too. Sarah Ramsey was rich in untraceable funds. This knowledge certainly helped to numb any lingering pain and suffering she may have felt, if she were the kind of person to feel any pain and suffering in the first place.

One Grand Plan

The tachometer needle hovered in the red and the engine screamed. Wheat fields flashed by. A tyre strayed onto the gravel at the shoulder, twitching the rear of the car. Daniel adjusted the steering wheel and aimed his Holden sedan down the centre line. There was no oncoming traffic. The two strangers with him were shrieking and cursing. The man with the ruined face, who was sitting in the back of the car, began to wail. At this, the old man in the front passenger seat stopped yelling, but continued to jump about, as if his singlet crawled with fire ants.

"Calm down," Daniel told him.

"Don't tell me to calm down, you little prick." The old man in the passenger seat was small, like a jockey, with the yellow, watery eyes of a drunk. On his stringy biceps were the kind of tattoos familiar to anyone who has done time: faded blue pictures made from a paper clip and ballpoint ink. Daniel had similar tattoos across his back.

"Listen to me," Daniel said. "This is my car, so calm down. You want to get out and walk?"

"You bastard, how am I supposed to walk? Have you seen my leg, for Chrissake?"

The man in the back seat stopped wailing and said, "Please, mate. Oh please, don't kick us out."

"Okay then, just shut up," Daniel said. He didn't look in the rear-view mirror. He didn't want to see the man in the back seat. He said to the old man in the passenger seat, "Quit your flapping and calm down."

The old man stopped jumping about. He clamped his hands on his scrawny knees and squeezed until his knuckles showed white. The man in the back seat wasn't wailing any more. For a time, the only sounds in the car were the hard, frightened gasps of the three men and the screaming of the engine.

The old man in the passenger seat twisted around to peer out the rear window. "They're not coming. Slow down, dickhead, you're close to one-eighty. You'll have the coppers on us next."

Daniel relaxed his foot on the accelerator. The ticking of wooden fence posts eased off. The speedometer dropped to one-sixty, one-twenty, one hundred.

"You know where we are?" Daniel said.

"Nah, dunno this area at all." The old man grimaced. "Those bastards. It hurts like a thirty, or maybe a forty-five."

"What?" Daniel said.

"The bigger the bullet, the more it hurts." The old man smiled, showing rotten teeth and glazed, faraway eyes. "I been shot once with a twenty-two, and hardly felt it. My missus at the time says to me, *jeez, you got blood on your shoulder, darling,* and I says, *huh?* It was nothing." The old man started laughing. "Oh, for Chrissake, I'm bleeding all over your car."

Sweat popped on Daniel's face. The pain in his side twisted and dug in hard. He said to the old man, "Shut up and think. We've got to dump these boxes."

"No, we need a hospital," said the fat, balding man in the back seat, weeping.

Daniel forgot and glanced into the rear-view mirror. The right side of the fat man's face was swollen and had turned purple. A course of dark blood was pumping from his cheekbone, the eye above the hole closed into a plump, black slit. It made Daniel sick to look at it. He said, "How am I supposed to get us to a hospital? I don't even know where we are."

The old man said, "You think any of the other blokes got out?"

Daniel shook his head. "Probably not."

The job had been simple enough: to help a mate's friend-of-a-friend to move house, a morning's work and no questions asked in exchange for one thousand dollars. Daniel had known by the price tag that the job was dodgy, but he'd been laid off from the factory and the rent was due. If he missed one more payment, the landlord would chuck him out.

Dumb.

He had risen while it was still dark, driven five hours from Melbourne to the township, and had turned up at the designated time. The place was a weatherboard located some fifty metres from a strip shopping centre. Daniel had got out of his car and looked up the road to watch ordinary people going about ordinary Saturday morning business at the bakery, dry cleaners, newsagent, and he had found this reassuring. Criminal activity so close to civilians would be crazy. It just wouldn't happen.

Seven other men, all unknown to Daniel, were also on the property. One of the men, a short and stocky bloke with a spread of blue teardrops tattooed around one eye, had used a key to open up a shed at the rear of the property. Inside the shed were scores of plain white boxes sealed with duct tape. "Here's your merchandise," the tattooed man had said, which had made Daniel uneasy. But he'd started to load boxes into his car boot anyway.

Dumb.

"Oh no, oh no, oh no," said the man in the back seat. "It's bad, it's really bad. Audrey? Clayton? Are you there?"

Daniel said to the old man in the passenger seat, "Do you know anybody who could help us without asking any questions? Like a doctor?"

The old man's laugh was harsh and shrill, tipping into hysteria. "Yeah righto, like how am I gonna know any doctors?"

"Or someone that's like a doctor? A veterinarian, maybe."

"A *vet*?"

"Anybody with medical training."

The old man said, "I want a surgeon, a real surgeon at a hospital, not some horse doctor."

"A real surgeon's going to call the cops. Then what?"

"Then nothing, I wouldn't tell 'em nothing."

"Alright then, forget it."

"What, you don't think I can keep my mouth shut? Unreal,

the balls on this bastard, whaddya reckon?" The old man looked around at the fat man. "Hey, mate, whaddya reckon? Mate? Aw, forget it, he's passed out."

Daniel could hear gurgling from the back seat. He looked in the rear-view mirror. The fat man was slumped sideways, his head down.

The road's centre line wavered. Daniel wiped at the sweat blurring his vision. The landscape was changing. The flat expanse of wheat fields was giving way to stony ground. Squatting in the distance was a range of hills, sparsely vegetated: rock faces gleaming white as bone. Weren't there any other towns around here? Daniel's side was throbbing now, knifing into him. He could have felt his side with his fingers or lifted his wet shirt for a peek to see what he was up against, but decided he wouldn't. He kept his eyes on the road's white line.

The old man said, "Those bastards, what do they want with a forty-five? I'm really hurting. Uh-oh, there's blood everywhere down here. I'm going to lose my toes."

"You'll be okay, just relax."

"Where did those bastards come from? Tell me that. One minute we're at the shed and *bam*, next minute those bastards are shooting us. I didn't even hear a car."

Daniel said, "Maybe they were hiding in the house."

"You reckon on a set-up?"

"I don't know what it was."

While leaning over his car boot to fit in another box, Daniel had heard what he thought was a vehicle backfiring. At the weatherboard's front door were two bikies with shaved heads, long beards and handguns. Daniel, for all the iffy things he'd done in his thirty-one years, had never seen a gun fired before. White smoke and a tongue of flame licked out from the barrel each time a gun went off.

Men were scattering, flailing, falling. Daniel scrambled in a crouch to the driver's side of his sedan. Two strangers were vaulting into his car: a small, old bloke, and a fat man spurting blood from a hole in his face. Daniel opened his door. A punch hit him low on his side and burnt through his guts; then a rush of adrenaline flung him into the driver's seat, and he'd twisted the key and floored the accelerator, go, go, *go*.

Now, Daniel said to the old man in the passenger seat, "Look for somewhere to dump the boxes."

"To hell with that, we need a hospital."

Daniel said, "No shit, really? Can you direct me to one? Well, can you? Come on, you stupid arsehole, tell me where there's a hospital and I'll take you to it. Where? Just tell me where."

The old man groaned.

Daniel took a breath, willed his hammering heart to slow down, and tightened his grip on the steering wheel. Surely, his injury wasn't too bad. He'd seen a documentary once about a soldier rescued after being lost in some wilderness somewhere for weeks on end, and the doctors claimed that what had staved off certain death was the soldier's high degree of physical fitness. And Daniel was nothing if not fit: boxing, running, weight training; he could bench over two hundred pounds for sets of six. He was going to be fine. If he could think logically and take this situation step by step, everything would be all right.

Daniel said, "We've got to dump the boxes. It's the only way we can get out of this. We'll say we were bystanders walking by when the shooting started, and we got hit and we panicked and drove off. That'll work."

"Who gives a rat's arse about any of that? I don't see coppers."

"Listen to me, the car's shot up, we're shot up. There's a dead body in the back."

"He's not dead, he's sleeping." Then the old man said, softly, "Hey, you got blood."

"I know."

"That's a gut shot. Let me drive."

"No. Look for somewhere we can dump the boxes."

"Hey you, back there. Keep a lookout, would you, mate? Mate? You know, he doesn't look right."

The pain in Daniel's side was spreading. He hoped that doctors would be able to fix him. He hoped that nothing vital had been messed up too much.

The old man said, "Do you think those bikies are coming after us?"

"If they're not dead, then yeah, they're coming after us."

The old man dropped his chin to his skinny chest. His lips quivered. "Oh Christ, I can't believe this shit. Oh, Jesus bloody Christ almighty—"

"Shut up."

"You shut up, you prick," the old man shouted.

The old man looked terrible. His face was blanched, his glassy eyes sunk into their sockets. It scared Daniel to look at him, so he watched the road. There was nothing about but paddocks, and the mountain ranges far off in the distance. Daniel felt light-headed and feverish. Then the realisation came to him: pain and fear had clouded his judgement; he could stop and dump the boxes anywhere he damn well pleased. *Shit*.

Over the next rise in the road appeared a wheat silo, a concrete tower shaped like a giant aerosol can, with a railway line running alongside, and a rusted shack nearby. No sign of life. Daniel pulled in. The tyres crunched over gravel. He put the car behind the silo, cut the engine and palmed the keys. It was quiet. There was no sound at all from the fat man in the back.

The old man said, "You dumping the boxes here?"

"Yeah. Now give me a hand."

"I'm not going anywhere. I can't do nothing on this foot, you don't understand." The old man started crying and turned his head away, shoulders trembling.

Daniel glanced into the back. The fat, balding man had toppled over, now partly wedged in the footwell behind the passenger seat. He was the stillest thing that Daniel had ever seen. The left arm was extended. The hand wore a wedding ring. *Too bad for you*, Daniel thought, and felt exhausted.

He pulled the lever under the dashboard to pop the boot. He opened his door and began to ease himself out of the car. It felt like someone was levering between his ribs with red-hot chisels. A fresh spill of warm blood flowered across the waistband of his jeans. He had to walk doubled over. By the time he got to the back of the car, he was streaming with sweat.

He propped himself against the car and held on with one hand. With the other hand, he awkwardly hauled out a box and let it drop to the ground. He kicked it away. It tumbled across the gravel. He had to stop and catch his breath. Then he started work on getting another box out of the boot.

"Get out here and help me," Daniel called. The old man didn't reply. The box slipped out of Daniel's hand and fell back into the boot. Daniel lost his footing, slid down, and sat down hard.

A car approached, slowing down. Daniel held onto the boot of the sedan and dragged himself upright. He was dizzy. He swiped his forearm across his face to clear the sweat, blinked hard, but couldn't see well enough to identify the vehicle. Maybe it was a nosy civilian, which was the best-case scenario. Daniel would try out his cover story of being an innocent bystander shot by mistake — which might fly — and then the civilian would take him to hospital or call for an ambulance.

Or maybe it was the police in an unmarked car, and he'd be facing more jail-time. He'd be cuffed to his hospital bed and read his rights, while the medical staff prepped him for emergency surgery.

Or it could be the bikies. Daniel thought about that and what it would mean.

He considered shouting a warning to the old man but couldn't find the breath, so he sat down again in the gravel behind his sedan. The car pulled off the road, coasted towards him. The car's grille was dull silver and studded with dead bugs. The pain in Daniel's side felt as big and tight as a football, but so what? The pain didn't matter now. Only the car mattered. The car rolled closer, stopped.

Daniel braced himself. The car's engine cut out. He would know what was going to happen to him very soon. He fixed his gaze on the toes of his boots, noting the blood spatters, living the last diamond-bright seconds as they passed. The car doors opened.

Daniel took a breath to still his flittering heart and waited for whatever was coming next.

Free Lunch

The couple, smiling and nodding at other guests, walked through the house like they were walking a red carpet. They headed to the buffet table in the middle of the lounge and started eating. I heard the husband say, "What's your uncle's name?" And the wife replied, "Norman."

Norman was across the room. The husband called over the murmur of the crowd, "Norman, any Shiraz?"

I approached the couple and hissed, "You weren't at the crematorium."

The wife, my own sister, said around a mouthful of chicken, "So? It was Norman's second marriage anyway. It's not like we knew her."

Paramour

It was early on a Friday evening and the lights were still up high. Janice again frowned at her watch and craned her neck, as if waiting on a tardy friend, in case anyone in the club had noticed her sitting by herself at the bar, nursing a glass of merlot. Most of the other patrons—in couples or groups—were fresh-faced and slim, not middle-aged and dowdy, soft in the belly. The thought of actually approaching someone and trying to strike up a conversation was paralysing.

A quarter-hour passed. More people came into the club, which sat between a burger shack and an ice cream parlour in the restaurant precinct that abutted Janice's local shopping centre. The lights dimmed and the wailing techno-jazz got louder.

While getting ready at home, Janice had mentally rehearsed the cool and confident demeanour that had once come so naturally when, as a young woman, she had drawn men as surely as strewing bread in a lake brings ducks. But that was a long time ago: about twenty years, twenty pounds and three children ago. A whole cheating husband ago. Peter was probably making love to his new girlfriend right now and, please God, having a heart attack.

The bartender, a kid with orange hair and freckles, thrust a glass of red at her and said, "One merlot."

"Sorry. I didn't order it."

"Yeah, I know, but it's already paid for. Do you want it or not?"

She blinked at him, electrified, frozen. It took her a couple of seconds to find her voice and even then, she was stammering.

"No. Wait, yes. Hang on, who bought it for me?"

The kid grinned, showing gapped teeth. "He told me to tell you you'd find out when you accepted the drink."

She looked around at young men, handsome men, older men, fat men, men sitting at tables in the half-dark, and who could tell? What she did next could change everything or nothing. The pressure of the decision made her nauseated. Then she considered how Peter might react if he were to find out she'd had drinks with a stranger—Peter, who thought her dull, nagging, *matronly*—and she snatched the glass and drank.

He stood up from a table in the far corner, a tall, heavy-set man in dark trousers with a glossy shirt stretched over his paunch. Janice pulled her mouth into a smile and reminded herself, *I'm damaged goods too.*

As he walked over, she was nakedly aware of her belly fat, sitting in her lap like a sleeping puppy, and she pulled up tall in her chair and sucked in her stomach. Then the stranger was standing next to her at the bar.

"This is an odd way to meet, don't you think?" he said, eyes green as grass. "If we end up as a couple, promise me we'll give another version of how we got together."

"Okay. What about saying we met through mutual friends?"

"Yeah, that'd be good. But are you from around here? You never know, we probably have friends in common anyway. The old 'six degrees of separation' thing."

He grinned again, white teeth in a tanned face. Back in the day, he would have been the high school jock who kicked the footy at lunchtime, while the girls watched him from the sidelines.

"I'm Janice." She held out her hand and he took it.

"Mike. And someone's going to take my table if I'm not careful. Would you like to join me? Or do you want to keep waiting for your friend? Either way, the drink's yours."

She took her wine glass and stood up. Mike led her back to his table, tucked the chair beneath her, and took his seat opposite. He picked up his drink. They fell into an easy conversation. Mike, divorced, a sales rep for a company that made corporate promotional products like hats or magnets or pens, had just come back from a conference in Athens. They compared lively notes, since Janice had backpacked through Greece about a quarter-century ago. According to Mike, Athens was essentially the same as she remembered—the stink of two-stroke fuel that blanketed the intersections, the ouzo taverns tucked into side streets, the cake and boiled eggs for breakfast. How wonderful that nothing fundamental had changed, that she could jet to Athens tomorrow and still find her way.

Janice offered to buy the next round of drinks, but Mike insisted. She watched him leave the table. With a casual grace, he lounged at the bar, resting his weight on one long leg. Janice made a mental note to phone Peter first thing tomorrow to let him know she wasn't so matronly after all.

Mike sat down with the drinks and said, "We should go dancing."

"Dancing? Where?"

"Just opposite us. The Irish pub has live music."

Janice, on route to one of the shopping centre car parks, had walked past the Irish tavern countless times, with its faux-Tudor, white-walled façade and black trim, but had never gone in. She wiggled her feet, puffy toes protesting against the fit of her high-heels. After standing all day behind the checkout, dancing was the last thing her legs could handle.

"That sounds great," she said. "I haven't been dancing in years."

"All right then, let's go."

The tartness of the merlot burned her tongue. She put her empty wine glass on the table at the same time as Mike slammed down his tumbler. *Snap!* They both laughed and stood up. Mike put out his hand. Janice took it.

The air outside was humid. Patrons milled back and forth across the cobbled walkway of the restaurant precinct. Mike led her through the crowded pub to its bar. The blat of electric guitars rattled her teeth. He leaned into her ear, shouted if she wanted another merlot, and she nodded. She stood by his side, waiting, looking around at the young girls and boys clotting the place, jamming the dance floor.

Ten minutes to eleven. If she were at home right now, she'd

be on the couch in her slippers, drinking cocoa and watching her favourite cop show, flipping the remote to the cookery channel at every ad break, her cat Marmalade by her side, her teenaged children asleep…

Mike turned from the bar with drinks in hand. With a nod of his head, he gestured *over there*. She followed him to a chest-high round table cluttered with empty beer glasses, and said, "I'll be right back."

It was cool inside the ladies' room. She went to the toilet, washed her hands, reapplied her lipstick, tried to fluff her wilting curls. Then she regarded herself in the mirror. How far was she going to take this with Mike? She would give him her phone number at least, but what was the protocol for dating these days, at their age, with failed marriages in their wake? She didn't know.

Back at the table, Mike urged her to drink up and she did. He took her arm and they weaved through the mob to the dance floor, a square of hot heaving bodies, flailing elbows, open whooping throats. Janice began to dance in a creaky step-touch fashion, but he clamped his hands on her backside and drew her against him and, *ohmygod*, started doing some kind of dirty dancing. He smiled, twinkled his grass-green eyes at her, teeth fluorescent white under the strobe lights. Janice broke away and hurried back to their table. A group of young men were clustered around it. She stumbled past the table and went outside.

"Janice, are you okay?" Mike said, close to her. "Do you want me to take you home?"

"No, thank you, I'm fine."

Her battered silver hatchback was not fifty metres away. Janice took a step and the world tipped. She staggered against a concrete flower box .

"Hey, let me help you," Mike said. He drew her arm over his shoulders, and clamped his other hand around her waist, supporting her against him.

"This is so embarrassing," she said.

Mike walked her away from the restaurant precinct. Janice had the sensation that her legs had lost their bones and her feet were trailing along behind. Her mind slewed around, loose and easy, a kite on the breeze.

She must have blanked out for a time, because now she was inside an unfamiliar car that was hurtling along an unfamiliar road. Mike was at the wheel.

"Are you taking me home?" she said, but she couldn't recall telling him her address. Consciousness winked in and out like a stuporous eye, now open, now closed. Then a jolt: *where was her clutch bag?* She said into the ether, "I want to go home," and heard, through a funnel, a tinny voice that said, "We *are* home."

Janice realised she was in a car, and the car had stopped. She turned and saw Mike in the driver's seat. "Mike? What's going on?"

He got out of the car. Janice looked through the windscreen and saw a house lit up like a furnace, orange lights burning around the closed curtains. It would be hot in there, steamy. Drawing breath would be a suffocating impossibility.

Her car door opened. Janice looked around. Mike leaned into the car and grabbed at her. Then everything fell away.

White Powder

Most of the passengers boarding the plane were sunburnt backpackers wearing singlets and braided cotton wristbands. Sixty-something-year-old businesswoman, Lorraine Cornell, knew she looked out of place but didn't care. She checked her ticket number and stopped. In the aisle seat was a woman in a crumpled linen pants suit, an outfit far too heavy, Lorraine thought, for the muggy Bangkok climate, but maybe it was to anticipate Melbourne's winter chill some ten hours away.

Lorraine said, "Excuse me, I have the window seat."

The woman put aside her magazine. "No worries," she said, and stepped into the aisle to allow Lorraine through. The woman sat down and jerked a thumb at Lorraine's handbag. "You want to put that in the overhead locker?"

"No."

"I'll do it for you, save you getting up again."

"Thank you, no."

"Okay then. If that's the way you want to play it."

Play it? What could the woman possibly mean by that? Lorraine turned to the window to gaze at the steel and glass terminal of Suvarnabhumi Airport. There was nothing to worry about, she reminded herself. Her suitcase had already passed unmolested through security.

The woman said, "I'm Kylie, by the way."

"Lorraine."

"Did you have a good business trip?"

Lorraine smiled politely. "What makes you think I was in Thailand on business?"

"Oh, come on, you're not a tourist by any stretch, you're import-export, right? Or am I right?"

Kylie was watching her with bright eyes. Lorraine glanced around. All the passengers were seated. Aircrew were marching along the aisles and testing the locked hatch on each overhead locker.

Finally, Lorraine said, "Import."

"Of what?"

"Knick-knacks, artwork, clothing. That sort of thing."

"Wholesale or retail?"

"If you're from the Australian Trade Commission," Lorraine said, attempting to joke, "I've already filled out my paperwork."

"Forget it. I can't imagine you shipping any suspect Buddha statues."

"You sound like you work in airport security."

"Aw, does it show that much? Yeah, I'm a Fed. Good thing I'm not a poker player."

"Yes, quite," Lorraine said, as her mouth dried up. She stared unseeing out the window as the plane took off and Bangkok fell away.

The seating arrangement had to be a coincidence, she thought. Everything was all right. Lorraine's hands clamped into fists. How would her supplier Jutharat cope? By shutting up, that's how. But while the crew distributed the lunch trays, Kylie kept craning her neck around the cabin until Lorraine just had to ask what she was doing.

"Checking to see who's skipping the food," Kylie said.

"Why?"

"Because they've probably swallowed condoms full of heroin. We get drug mules on every flight from the Golden Triangle. It's Australia's weak customs barrier that's to blame. There's too many holes in the fence. Did you know we open and search just one x-rayed bag in every hundred and fifty?"

Lorraine thought, *just one*? Surely that was good news…wasn't it? Or maybe not. Maybe people like Kylie nominated the bags to be searched, which could shorten the odds. Lorraine forced her mouth into a smile and said, "No, I had no idea."

"Us jacks use what's known in the biz as 'profiling'. We look for certain things, like the solo eighteen-year-old that won't eat, and carries hand luggage but no suitcase. He or she is the first person I take aside once we hit Melbourne. The second person is the one hiding in plain sight. You know, the unassuming grandparent, the mature businessman. Or woman."

Their seat assignments weren't bad luck; she was under surveillance. A flush crept over Lorraine's cheeks. "That sounds like just about everybody on this plane."

"It pays to have a suspicious mind."

Lorraine tried a gracious laugh, and then turned to face the window. How on earth could she get rid of the heroin mid-flight? Her suitcase was locked inside the belly of the plane but she had to dump the stuff somehow. Prison was unthinkable. The noise of the engines swallowed up her involuntary groan. She wanted to drop her face to her hands, but didn't.

So here it was at last, what she'd worried about and dreamt about ever since becoming business partners with Jutharat: what he liked to call *The Test*. He talked about it often, particularly after a few lagers. He would press upon her that when *The Test* came, she must be colder than a bottle of beer, and she always promised that, for fifteen grand a throw, she could be the ice queen under any circumstances. Well, now *The Test* was here and she was perspiring through her dress.

"You okay, Lorraine?"

"I think I'm airsick. Excuse me. I must get to the bathroom."

Lorraine staggered down the aisle, closed the toilet's accordion door and shot the bolt home. Lights came on above the mirror. God, she looked scared. She ran the tap and began splashing water over her face. Surely, if the Federal Police had her under surveillance, they'd have arrested her by now, which meant that sitting next to Kylie was a coincidence. Unless they were planning to arrest her on Australian soil to avoid the Thai death penalty. So what was it: coincidence or set-up? Jutharat would know.

Could she risk using her mobile?

Lorraine dried her face on paper towels, rummaged through her handbag, took out her phone and hesitated. What if the aircrew could detect illegal onboard calls? If the seating arrangement was nothing more than bad luck, then ringing Jutharat would draw attention. She regarded her reflection for a long time. Then she dropped the phone back into her bag and zipped it shut.

Lorraine joined the queue for Tullamarine's Immigration Hall. The air was cool and scented with lavender. After a few minutes, a man in a suit approached a girl up ahead in the queue, a young girl wearing a t-shirt and board shorts. The man was built like a buffalo: long delicate legs, and a huge head with fleshy jowls. After a brief exchange that Lorraine couldn't hear, the man escorted the girl away. They exited through a grey door with a keypad lock. Lorraine peered around. Behind about a dozen passengers stood Kylie. Their eyes met. Lorraine looked away.

When her turn came at last, the immigration official spent far too long comparing her face to her passport photo. Lorraine knew she was pale and sweaty. Taking a punt, she said, "I'm so glad to be on the ground. It's shameful, but I'll admit it anyway. I have a terrible fear of flying."

"Is that right?"

"My therapist is very proud of me. This was my first trip without sedatives, and I don't know whom to call first, my therapist or my grandkids. What do you think?"

The immigration official stamped her passport.

Lorraine rushed through the clots of passengers towards Baggage Reclaim. The carousel was already operating. She broke into a run to take a spot next to the opening in the wall. Suitcase after suitcase trundled through the opening but none was hers. *God, if you let me out of this…* Minutes passed. The crowd thinned as passengers took luggage from the conveyor belt.

A voice said, "I wonder if your bag will turn up," and it was Kylie next to her.

Lorraine said, "Why wouldn't it?"

"Because we've got sniffer dogs back there."

Lorraine scanned the hall for the nearest toilet. She had to get rid of the stuff before Customs and Excise Control. Then the breath died in her throat. Across the carousel stood the buffalo-shaped man who had earlier taken the backpacker, and he seemed to be staring at her. Lorraine fumbled in her bag for her prescription glasses. Yes, Buffalo Man was definitely staring at her.

And then, sweet Jesus, from the opening in the wall appeared Lorraine's hard-shell suitcase. She snatched it up and lugged it across the hall, the case bumping and bruising her leg. No one stopped her. Once inside the ladies' restroom, she ducked into the disabled cubicle and turned the latch. There was no bench. She flung the case to the tiled floor, got to her knees and unfastened the case. After shoving aside some clothing, she unzipped the toiletry bag and seized the talcum powder and the foot powder.

The lids wouldn't screw off.

Lorraine pulled at each lid. Then she bashed the containers against the floor, hoping to split the packaging. Gasping, she sat back on her haunches. *Damn.* Maybe the bottles were small enough to flush. She grabbed the foot powder and stood up.

The swing door to the ladies' restroom hissed open and closed. Footsteps clicked across the tiles and stopped outside the cubicle. Lorraine froze.

"I know you're in there," Kylie said. "Open up."

Lorraine held her breath for a long moment, paralysed. Then fresh panic hit, and she worked feverishly on one of the bottles, her fingernails breaking against the lid. A creak sounded and she glanced up.

The door latch was turning all by itself.

She watched its slow progress in horror. Of course, latches on public toilet cubicles open from the outside in case of emergencies. Lorraine understood with awful clarity that her life would now end in prison.

Kylie pushed open the door.

It was over in seconds.

Kylie advanced and Lorraine shoved her. Kylie toppled back

through the doorway and smacked her head against a porcelain sink on her way down. By the time Buffalo Man was inside the ladies' restroom with his gun drawn, Lorraine, trembling, was standing over Kylie's body and watching a puddle of blood spread across the floor.

Behind the grey door with the keypad lock was an office featuring a table and two chairs. Lorraine occupied one chair. A man came in and sat opposite. He was bald, and wearing a shirt and tie. Lorraine couldn't meet his unblinking gaze, so she focused on her hands clasped tightly together in her lap. She needed to urinate but didn't dare say anything.

"Sergeant O'Sullivan," he introduced himself. "You're very clever," he continued. "Six hundred grams in one bottle, four hundred in the other. Shrink-wrap to fool the dogs and clear plastic so the powder shows up white on x-ray. But the real kicker is the reservoir in each lid. Genuine talcum powder and genuine foot powder. Nice."

The door opened and Buffalo Man strode in. He shut the door and sat on the edge of the table, dangling one spindly leg. There was a smear of blood across his shirt.

Lorraine whispered to him, "Is she all right?"

Buffalo Man said, "I don't get it. You should be retired and looking after tomato plants."

"I needed the money."

"Don't we all?" O'Sullivan said. "Now explain your relationship with Caitlyn Rowe."

"Who?"

"The woman whose head you just smashed in."

"You mean Kylie? But she fell. I swear it wasn't my fault."

O'Sullivan shrugged. "Okay, let's call her Kylie. She uses a lot of aliases."

"In her undercover work?"

"Aha," O'Sullivan said, and laughed. "She told you she was a copper? So that's why you spooked."

Through a film of tears, Lorraine looked helplessly from one man to the other, and waited.

O'Sullivan leaned back and put his hands behind his head. "Caitlyn Rowe is a con woman who poses as authority figures to hustle people. One of her favourite scams in airports is getting passengers to hand over their passports so she can sell them on the black market. We were watching her, not you. You could have waltzed through customs and straight out the door."

Lorraine's vision pinned. Buffalo Man caught her before she slid off the chair. O'Sullivan took a pair of handcuffs from his pocket.

Rooftop

Nina did a slow turn on the rooftop to gaze at the surrounding skyscrapers, and then she thumbed her mobile phone and waited. The breeze whipped her hair about her face.

He answered after three rings. "Mark Atwood."

"I think I can see the ocean from here," she said.

"Nina?"

She squinted, and lifted a hand to shade her eyes. "Oh, wait. The ocean would be south, right? The trouble is I'm not sure which way I'm facing. Maybe that's a lake. Is there a lake anywhere near the city? I can't seem to recall."

"Everything's all right, Nina. Just let me speak to one of the nurses."

"Mark, I really am in the city. Truly."

"How did you get there?"

"Taxi."

She could hear him breathing, a slow and steady in and out, the rhythm of it like a pulse of tide against the shore. Her eyes closed. A fragment of memory rose up: water foaming at her feet, Mark jogging towards her across the beach, his trouser legs rolled to his knees.

Mark said, "The medications can get you a little spacey."

Nina's eyes snapped open. "I didn't take any meds today."

"Why's that?"

"You know why."

"I need to speak to one of the nurses. I mean it, Nina. Come on, now."

"Fine, don't believe me, I don't care. But get this," she said, and moved towards the edge. "I'm on top of a building that's made of foam. You know that stuff, like a takeaway coffee cup?"

"Polystyrene?"

"Yeah, that's it, polystyrene," she said, and laughed. "I swear I'm not making this up. These bricks at the front of the building are scooped out and filled with what looks like popcorn, but it's really polystyrene balls, hundreds and hundreds of them. The building's falling apart."

"No, that's just the façade."

"Who in their right mind would make a building out of polystyrene?" She grabbed at white pellets and trickled them through her fingers. The wind flung the pellets over the brink. "It's a miracle the building's still standing."

"No, the building would be made of regular bricks and mortar; it's only the façade that's made of polystyrene."

"The façade?"

"The detailing, the sculpted mouldings. They make them out of polystyrene because cement would be too heavy. What's the building called? Give me the address and I'll come and get you."

"Polystyrene is a silly choice. It's falling to bits."

"The damage is probably from cockatoos."

"Huh?"

"Cockatoos. A flock of them probably goes to that rooftop every day and chews the hell out of the façade."

"They eat the foam?"

"No, just wreck it."

Nina's grip tightened on the phone. "Why? Why would they want to do that?"

"I don't know."

"That's crazy. Why chew something if you're not going to eat it?"

"Please, don't get upset. We can talk about it in the car."

She leaned against the parapet. The rooftop was grimy, crowded with ventilation shafts and air-conditioning units, and everywhere, tiny pieces of polystyrene stirring in the breeze.

She laughed. "You should see this, Mark. It's like a giant bag of popcorn exploded up here."

"Nina, listen to me. Take the lift to the ground floor and wait for me in the reception area. Can you do that? Now tell me the address."

"But you'll drive me back to the hospice."

"That's the best place for you right now."

"No," she said. Far away beyond the buildings, sunlight glittered on water, either the ocean or a man-made lake, she couldn't tell. "Here is the best place right now. We talked about this sort of thing, remember? Months ago. We talked about it."

Mark didn't speak for a time. Then he said, "Please, Nina."

"It's okay."

"Please."

"I've got to go."

"Wait a minute, let's talk about it again, pros and cons. Nina? Answer me. We can make another list. Nina?"

She laid the phone on the parapet. Soon a crowd would gather below, with people running over from all points of the street.

Lopping and Removal
in Three Parts

Our story starts like this:

John, after slogging for some twenty years as an accountant, set up his dream business—tree lopping and removals—against the wishes of his wife, Ellen. She fretted about losing their beautiful home and investments, and having to live in the Land Cruiser. But John's business instincts were right, and for a brief and beautiful time John and Ellen enjoyed the happiest and richest years of their married life. Ellen indulged in restaurants and shoes, while their two grown children had extra mortgage payments and college fees respectively.

Then things changed. John's desires for the unsavoury took all the money.

What a shame.

That version of the story was exactly 100 words. The next version expands upon the particular details surrounding the end of John's golden financial era:

In the grip of a mid-life crisis, John throws in his accountancy career for a tree lopping and removals business. The Australian drought gives him and his team of lumberjacks no end of suburban ghost gums to cut down and chip, before the limbs can drop and crush passers-by. Money flows. Within a couple of years, however, John's exponentially increased whoring, gambling and meth-amphetamine usage undermine his business until finally, today, it ends.

Bankcards are refused. Wife demands explanation. Humiliation is complete.

John, feeling ridiculous in his customary wool and cashmere, is pinned by Ellen's glare against the metre-wide hearth that forms the centrepiece of their three-storey home. He says, "It'll be okay, darling, I promise, I'll get us out of this," but the whole time he's confessing his agonising failures to his wife of twenty-three years, John is thinking about his favourite girl, Candy. He presses fingertips into his eyelids, willing the fog to clear. He has to focus on turning this disaster around. He's got to forget his dreams that never eventuated, and his kids that smirk at him, and his loneliness with Ellen, and the feel of Candy's PVC cowboy chaps, and *concentrate*.

Ellen flees the room. John longs for a hit, goes to the kitchen and settles for whisky. Through the window, flowers in his professionally landscaped back yard drowse under the birch tree. He paid for it all but doesn't know the names of any of the blossoming plants. This seems significant. He takes another drink while Ellen sobs and smashes belongings upstairs.

Concentrate. The flowers are purple and yellow.

I have to concentrate.

He could sell the house, the Land Cruiser, the caravan, investment property. Not enough. Well, what about bankruptcy? That would make financial sense, but no. *No.* Death would be better than that. Then suicide occurs to him as a reasonably attractive option. John rolls the whisky around in his mouth, tasting it for a while, and hits upon a wonderful realisation.

He takes the stairs two at a time. Ellen is in the master bedroom standing round-shouldered and hiccupping in the midst of ruin. His smile infuriates her. "You bastard! I gave up everything for you!"

John ponders momentarily the mystery of what in hell she could have given up, then approaches, crunching in handmade shoes over the broken mirror, jewellery box, lamps. He hardly notices when she slaps him. He says, "We'll fake my death and collect the insurance."

Two weeks later, Ellen tells police that John didn't return from his dip in the sea. His memorial is apparently well attended. Only Ellen knows that John is living in their 24ft caravan in the back yard. The caravan is a prison that suffocates him, and guilt over his children's grief chokes him, but the debts are clear, his business is thriving again, the house is safe. Ellen has her restaurants and shoes.

And a lover. The pain of it almost kills him. Ellen is sleeping with one of John's lumberjacks.

What a shame.
That version of the story was exactly 500 words. The next version expands upon the particular details surrounding the aftermath of John's faked death:

Ellen balanced the tray on one hand and went to knock. She stepped back as the caravan door was flung open. He stood in the doorway in his Y-fronts, unshaven and red-eyed. "Hello, John," she said. "I've got your breakfast."

"Oh yeah? Well, I don't want it," he said, sneering. "I don't want anything from you. *Slut*. You scrubber. Is he up there? He was my best lumberjack, goddamn it. Answer me, why don't you? Have you got Brandon up there in my bed?"

She said, "You're drunk again. Maybe I should limit your whisky."

"No, wait, there's no need for that. Please, darling. I've got nothing else."

"Then don't bait me." She held out the tray. On it sat a cup of flat white coffee, cutlery, a bowl of dry cereal, a jug of milk, two pieces of toasted bread and a pat of butter smeared on a square of greaseproof paper. John stared at the food. "Take it," Ellen said. "I don't have all day."

"Why not? Is Brandon up there?"

Ellen made a move and John snatched at the tray. He put it on the caravan's table and said, "Listen, I just want you to know, I've been thinking."

Ellen narrowed her eyes. "About what?"

"This. All of this," he said, gesturing behind him, and then he sobbed. "I can't do it anymore."

"What do you mean?"

"I mean I'm going to confess to the police."

Ellen didn't answer for a time. She said, "If you do, then we both go to jail for insurance fraud. John, the whole world thinks you're dead."

"So? I'm in jail anyway. No, it's worse than that, I'm in hell. Jail would be a relief." His mouth wobbled into a smile and fresh tears shimmered in his eyes. "We're a team, aren't we? Husband and wife for twenty-five years, we can make this right, we can undo everything we've done, you see? I don't need meth anymore. I could run my tree lopping and removal business again, I swear. And I want to see the kids, Ellen. Please, love. You understand, don't you?"

Ellen nodded. "I'll come back in a while and we'll talk about it some more."

She squared her shoulders and walked across the yard to the back door. Once hidden inside the house, she sagged against the kitchen table, trembling. She forced herself to calm down. For God's sake, she was a business mogul, with dozens of men in her employ, a turnover worth millions. She could handle this bump along the road.

In the living room, Brandon was slumped on the couch in his boxer shorts playing a shoot-'em-up game on the Xbox 360. He held the control pad in both hands, and each frenzied finger-tap on the buttons shivered the meat in his shoulders and chest, and clenched his abdominal muscles drum-tight. It wasn't that Brandon was brawny, just young—barely out of his teens, in fact—and bereft of body fat.

"Brandon," she said at last, and he looked up with chocolate eyes. She smiled and said, "I need your help."

He tossed the control pad to the couch and came over, running his hands down her body. He smelt like fresh bread. They kissed, and it was a long, hard and deep kiss that stirred the seat of her pants and thumped her heart against her ribs. (Admittedly, Brandon was inexperienced and overeager—he had a problem with premature ejaculation and actually wasn't that good at foreplay or oral sex—but it didn't matter, because his unflinching adoration wiped away twenty or more years of joyless living. John wasn't the only one who could benefit from a little candy.)

"Babe," she said, "we've got an awful problem. Help me. Help Mama fix it."

And he did. Never underestimate a young man's infatuation with an older woman, particularly a rich one who looks good for her age. Brandon strangled John and fed his corpse through the wood chipper, aiming the crimson spray at the flowerbeds in Ellen's back yard.

John's legacy is an exceptionally vibrant display of irises the following autumn, with the purple and yellow petals so intense that Ellen has to keep the kitchen blinds drawn to stave off migraines. Brandon is also gone. In an unfortunate chainsaw accident, he severed the femoral artery in his thigh and bled out within minutes, while attempting to cut down the birch tree in Ellen's back yard. Ellen lives alone and enjoys restaurants and shoes.

What a shame.
That version of the story was exactly 750 words. So what happens next? A few notes:

Ellen's involvement in either John's or Brandon's death (or why not both?) is discovered and she is sent to prison. Or she lives a good life with a new lover, but falls prey to dementia in later years and is sent by her uncaring children to a nursing home where she is alternately abused and neglected. Or her new lover betrays her by seducing her daughter and Ellen never sees either of them again. Or her son discovers her convoluted and decidedly evil plot and goes mad or turns to drugs like his father or runs off with Ellen's new lover or starts sleeping with his sister, any of which could break Ellen's heart so thoroughly that her chosen recourse is suicide, or whatever.

Possible complications abound. Suffice to say that the story of John and Ellen and their cast of minor characters could keep extrapolating cause and effect for version after version, but for the purposes of verisimilitude, each version must end in tears.

Family Business

It was after midnight on a Tuesday. Roads were deserted. The Holden Calais VT pulled into the supermarket car park and did a slow couple of laps. Built on a hillside, the back end of the supermarket formed a roof over a garage, which was fenced, accessible via an open gate. The Holden nosed into a corner parking space near the street. From there, the two occupants could watch both the front doors of the supermarket and the underground garage at the same time.

The middle-aged driver, Mimi, switched off the engine. It made ticking noises as it cooled. The radio kept playing softly. The young man in the front passenger seat, Damien, flicked through the stations until Mimi snapped off the radio. Damien removed his latex gloves and ran his palms along his jeans as if his hands were sweaty. Then he sat forward, craning to look up through the windscreen at the floodlights and streetlights overhead, and said, "Any CCTV?"

"Contessa says there isn't."

"We're doing it here?"

"The staff members park in the underground bit, so that'll be the best spot. The manager is always the last one to leave. Locking up a supermarket takes a while, I guess."

"So what time is he coming out?"

Mimi checked her watch. "Should be in the next ten minutes. He's white, fat, and balding."

"I hope to God I never go bald," Damien said. "What's it about?"

"He borrowed ten grand off Contessa with a fee of two. He

was meant to pay it back in a month, except he didn't. Now he owes sixteen."

"Sixteen?" Damien said. "You mean twelve."

"You're forgetting the fine."

"Oh, yeah."

Mimi took a stick of gum from her handbag and chewed on it. Time passed. An old woman in uniform exited the supermarket, got into her vehicle, and drove away.

Damien said, "I wouldn't mind having a set of wheels like this."

"If you save your money, then yeah, you could afford a nice car someday."

"Someday? Yeah, right. Like in a million years." Damien cracked his knuckles. "Instead of dumping it when we're done, ask Contessa if I can have it."

"Have it? It's a stolen car, Damien, have you lost your mind? And hey, if you're going to start touching everything, put your gloves back on."

"The seats are leather, not vinyl. You can feel the difference."

"Okay, wipe it down."

"Now that's luxury. There's leather on the console, too."

Mimi spat her gum through the open window. "Did you hear me?"

"Okay, keep your shirt on." Damien took a handkerchief from his jeans pocket and began to scrub along the dashboard. "So, what does Contessa want?"

"Nose, front teeth, one arm."

"Front teeth, that's it? No jaw?"

"She didn't ask for that."

Damien sat back, pouted. "What if I get the jaw?"

"Just try your best, that's all anyone can ask. Did you warm up?"

Sighing, he crammed the handkerchief into his jeans pocket.

"Damien?" Mimi said.

"It's not like I'll be doing a spinning back-kick or anything. A couple of chops here and there, okay? Relax."

"Fine, but if you pull a muscle, don't come whining to me."

He gazed out the window and didn't answer. A few minutes

later, a couple of girls in uniform, laughing, ran out of the front doors of the supermarket. After they drove away, the only car left was the one parked underground: the manager's vehicle.

Mimi said, "Do a warm-up now."

"Aw, Mum…"

"Do a little one right here. Some stretches or something."

"I'm not a little kid anymore."

"Eighteen is still a kid."

"Oh, yeah? Then I should go home and leave you to do the job yourself."

She switched on the radio. An Eagles song was playing. She switched off the radio and said, "You pull a muscle, you can't teach a class, that's all I'm saying."

"I won't pull a muscle."

"You teaching tomorrow?"

"Yeah."

"Ask the bloke when he plans on giving you a full-time position."

Damien began tapping a beat on his knee. "I'm thinking of opening my own dojo anyway. Me and Tim have been talking about it."

"Which one's Tim?" she said. "The one with the ears?"

"Nah, with the tatts on his neck."

"The dumb one?" Exasperated, she threw her hands in the air. "Don't get mixed up with anything that Tim's doing. You've got to keep away from people like that, big dreamers with no brains. How's he going to fund this dojo anyway? With drugs, I bet. You wait and see; he'll have the bright idea of selling meth. And then, bang, he's in jail and so are you. Don't get involved in any of his illegal business."

Damien laughed. "Aw, you're such a hypocrite, Mum. What about the illegal business we're gonna do right now?"

Stung, she turned to him, opened her mouth to reply. Damien sat bolt upright in his seat and pointed at the windscreen.

"Hey," he said, "is that the manager?"

A stout man in grey trousers, white shirt and tie, balding, was walking away from the supermarket double-doors with his face down, keys in one hand, a briefcase swinging from the other.

"Okay, get ready, here we go," Mimi said.

She started the car. The man had turned the corner of the building and was heading towards the underground garage. Mimi edged the Holden in a crawl after him. Meanwhile, Damien looked about, checking the empty surrounds.

"By the way," Mimi said, "this discussion isn't over."

"You just don't like Tim because of that crack he made about the sausage."

"He's got a mouth on him like a sewer, that kid."

Mimi braked. The entrance to the underground garage was a few metres away. The supermarket manager, Cameron McGrath, weakly lit by lamps fixed at intervals along the brick wall, was approaching a lone vehicle. Damien snapped on his gloves.

"See if you can sneak up on him," Mimi said. "I'll block the exit."

Damien jumped out of the car and slammed the door. The manager turned at the sound and hesitated, looking unsure, as Damien approached.

"G'day, mate," Damien said. "How's it going?"

Mimi pulled into the mouth of the underground garage and killed the engine, leaving the headlights on. Then she got out.

The manager looked at them, blinking owlishly. A little way from the manager, perhaps spitting distance, Damien stopped and put his hands on his hips. This particular stance made him look even wider across the shoulders.

"You know why we're here?" Mimi said.

"I can guess," the manager said, blanching. "Look, I don't have any money on me, no cash. I've got credit cards, but they're maxed out."

Damien said, "Step away from the car. Drop your keys."

"You want my car? Here, you can have it."

The manager lobbed the keys underhand to Damien, who slapped them away. They hit the concrete floor with a metallic tinkle, bouncing once.

"A four-cylinder hatchback?' Damien said. "Aw, come off it, mate. It's a chick's car."

"Yes, but it's cheap to run."

Mimi picked up the keys. "Okay, shut up about the car, the both of you. We're here about the money."

"I can't open the safe once I've locked up. An alarm will go off at the security company."

Mimi said, "Do you see us wearing balaclavas?"

"Pardon?"

"Are we standing here with shotguns?' she said. When the manager continued to look perplexed, she added in a loud voice, "This isn't a supermarket robbery. This is about the money you owe."

The manager let out a huge breath of relief. Then he leaned over, put his hands on his knees, and actually laughed. Mimi and Damien exchanged glances.

Straightening up, the manager said, "You really had me going there. Are you relatives of hers? Wait, I don't care who you are. I'll just tell you exactly what I told her: talk to my lawyer."

"Your lawyer?" Mimi said.

"And if she wants the money that badly, the bitch can come get it herself."

"Whoa," Damien said, taking a step back. "Mum, the nuts on this guy."

"Trust me," she said, "he'd never trash-talk like this to Contessa's face."

"Contessa?" the manager said. "Is that what she's calling herself these days? God, as if *Annabelle* wasn't twee enough."

"Annabelle?" Mimi said. "Who's that?"

"Why, my ex-wife, of course."

Mimi and Damien looked at each other again.

"Chuck us your wallet," Mimi said.

He did. Damien opened it up, took out the driver's licence, handed it to Mimi.

"Jeremy Halliday?" she said.

"That's me."

"Uh-oh," Damien said. "Where's Cameron McGrath?"

"The manager? Sick. I'm the assistant manager. You're after Cameron?"

Damien broke out into a guffaw. "Mate, you almost got your head kicked in by mistake."

Jeremy laughed too, but it wobbled. He said, "I'll buy a Tatts ticket."

Damien threw back the wallet.

Flinching, Jeremy caught it in both flapping hands. "Thank you," he said, and slid the wallet into his pocket. "I think I'll be going now."

Damien wagged a finger. "Don't mention us to anybody, okay? We've seen your driver's licence, we know where you live. And don't give Cameron the heads-up, right?"

"Right." Jeremy's face shone pale and sweaty. "I'll need my keys."

Mimi said, "You owe your ex-wife Annabelle some money?"

"Yes. Well, she believes I do, anyway."

"For what?"

"Child support."

Mimi's mouth tightened. "So why aren't you paying it?"

"She moved to Sydney to live with her parents." Jeremy shrugged, tried to smile. "Look, if I have to get on a plane to see my own son, I'm not paying a cent."

Mimi turned the keys over in her hand, as if studying them. "Maybe she had to move back in with her parents because she's broke. And she's broke because you wouldn't give her any money."

"I don't know. Her problems aren't of any interest to me."

Damien said, "That's harsh. You want your kid to grow up poor?"

Jeremy didn't answer. He looked from Mimi to Damien and back again.

"You know, funny story," Mimi said, pocketing Jeremy's keys. "Our lives would've turned out different if I'd had child support."

Damien took off his watch and gave it to her.

Jeremy's eyes bulged. "Hold on. What are you doing?"

"A favour for Annabelle," Mimi said.

"Good God, what for? You don't even know her. She's a bitch."

"Nah," Damien said, jogging on the spot, rolling his head from side to side to loosen his neck. "This one's for your kid."

"But you're getting paid to beat up Cameron, aren't you? Not me. There's no money in it. You won't get paid. There's nothing in it for you. What's in it for you? Nothing, I tell you, nothing."

Swinging his arms back and forth, Damien said to his mother, "Nose, front teeth, one arm?"

"And jaw too, why not?" Standing up on tiptoe, she kissed her son on the side of his unshaven face and whispered, "Now be a good boy, and don't pull a muscle."

Burnover

The hills were on fire. Mandy stood on the road and watched the smoke boil in the distance. Then she crossed the front yard and went back inside her house. The television showed footage of bushfires in the faraway east and north of the state, hundreds of kilometres away. Mandy thumbed the remote. When there was nothing on the fire in the nearby hills, she wandered for a few minutes without purpose throughout the rooms of her home, only to sit again, helplessly, in front of the television. What else could she do?

The doorbell rang. It was Grigori, the middle-aged neighbour from across the street, holding a bowl covered in foil.

"Salad. For your lunch," he said. Grigori was from somewhere in Eastern Europe—Belarus, or maybe Azerbaijan—and he spoke with a heavy accent. Sidestepping Mandy, he strode to the kitchen, slapped the bowl onto the bench and smiled, showing his long teeth. "No word from husband? Too bad. You are used to that, however."

Mandy nodded. What she wanted to say was *No; I'm not used to it at all*. Where is the danger when he stands on a footpath and aims a hose at a single burning building? Joe and his crew attended more car accidents than fires. They often whiled away shifts kicking a footy in the station's car park. *Joe is no different to an accountant or a bank clerk*, Mandy would say to the ghouls who cornered her at parties or barbecues or functions, *he goes to work and then he comes home.*

"Joe, he has fight bushfires before?"

"Please, I'm very tired." Mandy shuffled to the front door and opened it.

Once Grigori had gone, Mandy binned the salad and perched on the edge of the couch. The television ran images of blazing forests, reddened skies and gutted houses. Mandy lay down, intending to just rest for a minute. Instead, she fell asleep.

She dreamed of the hill fires again. This time, Joe and his crewmates Mal and Andrew were skidding down an embankment while the leaf litter around them erupted into sparks. They sprinted for the truck. The wall of flames reached the lip of the embankment and paused, as if reluctant to run downhill. Joe opened the truck door and leapt inside. Mal and Andrew vaulted on top of him. In the mad struggle of bodies, the door remained open. Mal threw out an arm and wrenched the door shut. Joe cranked the ignition. The engine turned over, stalled. Each man dug underneath a woollen blanket.

Mandy thrashed awake, sweating. The television was still ticking over its horrors. She went to the kitchen, poured herself a wine, gulped it, held the cold glass to her cheek. These past few days, she'd had all sorts of feverish dreams and could only remember snippets—horses crowded by flames, trees on a hilltop burning in a row like candles—but this was her first dream about Joe. The panic felt sticky in her mouth. She took another slug of wine.

Truck burnover. She'd seen the training DVD. Joe had brought it home at the start of the week when his station signed up for the hill fires.

Mandy closed her eyes and, despite herself, gave the dream its proper ending. The fire runs over the truck. The tyres blow out. The rubber seals around the doors and windows start to spit and fill the cabin with fumes. The men cough, hack and retch. Still the flames beat at every window. The fire won't pass. It will hunker down until the truck and the men trapped inside are reduced to carbon.

Mandy switched off the television and returned to the kitchen. From her seat at the table, she had a clear line of sight to the front door. One of the fire chiefs would come, or a police officer, counsellor, perhaps a psychologist. It could even be a priest. She wasn't sure how the fire brigade handled such things, but someone would come. Joe's shift should have finished hours ago.

Daylight faded and went out. In the dark, Mandy kept staring at the door.

Finally, the doorbell rang. And rang again and again. An insistent knocking started up. Mandy put her hands on the kitchen table and pushed herself upright.

"Please go away," she said, but her voice didn't carry and the knocking kept on.

She cracked the door a few inches. An outside light shone across the road at Grigori's place. She could see Grigori on his porch, craning, hoping to get a better look at Mandy's visitor. Mandy flung open the door. The hulking shape was black. For a crazed moment, she thought a demon had come to tell her.

"A couple of the boys dropped me off," Joe said. "Sorry I didn't ring."

She kissed him and tasted fire. In the bathroom, she peeled his uniform and dropped each fouled item into the tub. He offered neither resistance nor help; just stared blankly at nothing, shivering a little. Then she sighted the mirror. She hadn't felt the soot on her skin but now that she saw it there, smudged like countless fingerprints, she could feel it working its way inside her, its soft creep staining her somewhere deep down. She ran the shower.

Joe slumped in the stall with his arms dangling between his legs. Mandy knelt and reached in to wash him. He seemed to doze for a while.

"Andrew's home," he said at last. "Mal is in hospital. He burnt his hand on the truck door."

The trembling started in her legs and quavered like a long note through every muscle. She crawled into the shower. Her dress soaked against her, tight as a caul.

"I'm frightened," she said.

Joe opened his arms. She twined herself around him and hung on.

When she heard the doorbell, Mandy knew it would be Grigori, holding in his manicured hands another salad or maybe a flask of soup this time, his sharp face sniffing for the ash in Mandy's bones. Mandy clung to Joe and waited.

The doorbell rang a few more times and stopped.

Party Animals

"Can you see the dam, Preston? There by the fence?"
I nod, but I can't focus. I've been drinking the entire week, and with the full sun striking the veranda, it's all I can do to keep my eyes open. I'm sprawled in a deck chair. Rob and his wife, Julia, are propped together in the aluminium loveseat, which he tries to swing and she fights to keep steady.

"Well, someone at the party might take an unscheduled swim in that dam, if you follow me," Rob says, and gulps at his scotch. "A particular woman could get chucked in head first."

Julia slaps at his leg. "Stop it. I've warned her, you know. Bronwyn knows we've invited Graham."

I smile. Bronwyn came for dinner last night. During the meal, Rob tried and failed to beat her in an argument about women's sports. Similarly, I tried and failed to persuade her to sleep with me.

I say, "Do you think they'll fight?"

"Of course," Rob says. "They haven't spoken since their falling out. She'll end up in the dam, I just know it. Christ, I hope she does, anyway."

"That's enough. Now what do you guys want for dinner?"

"Preston, you're the guest. What'll it be?"

I'm too hammered so I just shrug. Rob laughs. Julia goes inside. Dinner is beef satay and bottles of red. We eat, drink and talk. When the meal is done, Julia finishes her wine in a long swallow and says, "Graham's problem is that he still loves her."

"No, he doesn't," Rob says, then looks at me and freezes like he knows I'm about to contradict him, which I do.

Graham and I once shared a flat. He told me everything about his relationship with Bronwyn, why they had broken up, how they were trying to stay friends. When sober, Graham liked to rant about Bronwyn's faults, but talking about her when drunk reduced him to a wretched, almost catatonic state. He loved her with the kind of awful intensity that threatens to last a lifetime, but as Rob points out, how could I know that for sure? Graham and I are no longer friends. One day, we argued about something—a late bill, dirty dishes, whatever—and both moved out. Soon after, I heard that he and Bronwyn weren't speaking to each other either.

"He's going to love her forever," Julia says miserably.

"You want them to fight," Rob says, eyes shining, "don't you?"

"Yep. I hope we have to call the cops."

Rob leans over and plants a loud kiss on her cheek. I think about cutting my holiday short and going home to dry out.

"She'll win," I say.

Rob pokes out his slim hand. "Want to bet?"

"All right, put me down for fifty."

We shake on it. Rob leaps up, grabs the phone from the kitchen and shouts, "Let's get a book rolling."

Julia whoops and giggles. Rob retreats to another room. The bottle runs out and Julia opens another. I make a mental note to stay sober on Saturday night so I can talk to Bronwyn without slurring. Julia and I polish off the bottle. Meanwhile, she's yabbering about how she *likes* Bronwyn in many ways, but *dislikes* her in other ways, on and on. I'm barely listening. Barely conscious.

Rob finally comes back and says, "We've got hundreds on it."

"We'd better not lose, hubby dearest."

"You know me, Julia. When was the last time I ever lost anything?"

Yesterday at dinner, I recall, *when you lost that argument about women's sports.* I think of Bronwyn's lovely mouth and say, "I don't want to bet anymore."

"Too late," Rob says, and raises his glass. "It's already in the book."

"Have another drink," Julia says. She slops wine into my glass and over the table and her laugh wails on and on.

"To Bronwyn and Graham," Rob says.

I can hardly see his face. The last of the daylight has slipped away without us noticing. We drink. Then I'm hanging my head over the toilet. I make my excuses and go to bed. The guestroom is airless. I'm too drunk to work the window latch. Before I pass out, I can hear Rob and Julia cackling and braying in the lounge.

In the morning, I take the train home.

I miss the party, but nothing happened between Bronwyn and Graham. Apparently, neither of them showed up. I'll never know for sure, though, because Rob was too insulted by my early departure to ever speak to me again.

Later, I hear from somebody else that Rob and Julia sold the farm and bought a city townhouse, but I hang out with a new crowd these days and can't confirm the rumour.

Flashpoint

Rebecca shakes the last drops of petrol over the chair cushions. The petrol container is red with a yellow spout, cheerfully coloured, like a preschooler's toy. The radio is playing. Rebecca puts the empty container on the kitchen bench and rinses her hands under the tap, rubbing her thumbs over the places where petrol spatters burn so cold they feel hot. She dries her hands on a floral tea towel and looks around. She hasn't been here for years. Nothing much has changed: floral oven mitts, floral apron, "Mum's Restaurant" ceramic tile hanging next to the microwave.

The petrol fumes are making Rebecca dizzy. She hurries into the living room and hauls open a window. Directly across the road is a park, the kind with benches and iron sculptures and topiary. The backdrop is Melbourne's city skyline. This fourth-floor apartment enjoys an outlook that is undeniably pretty, but when her parents sold the family home to buy this three-bedroom condo, and Dad kept saying *the price is high but the view is worth it*, Rebecca knew that he was actually paying to leave the skeletons behind.

With the breeze on her back, she sits cross-legged in the window seat and checks her watch. Nearly 6:30am. Half an hour until the breakfast program on 47.8 BUCK FM, hosted by none other than Luke "The Duke" Miller.

She calls the station, says to the receptionist, "I've got hostages. Let me speak to the station manager now or everybody dies."

The astounded receptionist transfers her call to the office manager. Rebecca explains the situation again to the office manager, then to a news director, and next to a producer. Finally, she's put through to the stammering, flabbergasted station manager. She tells him exactly what she wants: *Luke "The Duke" Miller*.

All to herself.

The manager agrees and puts her on hold. What she hears through the phone is the same live broadcast that's coming out of the stereo in the living room, but several seconds earlier, as if she's occupying a vast, echoing space. Not long now until the Duke is on-air. When it is 7:00am and time, the broadcast switches to adverts, one after another. Rebecca waits, keeps waiting, and checks her watch. Duke's program should have started nine minutes ago. She bites her nails, already gnawed down to bleeding quicks. It's probably chaos at the radio station. The staff doesn't know what to do. Now ten minutes ago. Eleven minutes.

The program's theme music jolts Rebecca out of her reverie. She fumbles in her jeans pocket for the sheet of foolscap paper, folded untidily. She opens it with one hand, smooths it out on her leg and scans her notes, handwritten in round letters, the dot over each "i" a tiny circle. Live radio with two million listeners. Rebecca hasn't got any spit to swallow.

Duke speaks at last, but it's not his usual banter. He says, "Listeners, you're with The Duke and this is a very different program of *What Pisses You Off*; one guest and that's it, so don't call in, the switchboard won't answer. Our guest is on the line now. Her name is Rebecca. Uh, Rebecca, are you there?"

"Yeah," she says, and flushes. "Duke, I'm here."

After a beat, he says, "Is this for real?"

"Well, shit yeah, it's for real."

"Watch your language, or I'll cut you off. Look, my boss has called the cops already. If you're just trying to punk me, you'd better come clean. This isn't funny. In fact, it's pathetic."

"Pathetic?" Her grip tightens on the phone. "My parents are in the master bedroom. Their apartment is soaked in petrol. I have a cigarette lighter. Okay? I'm not mucking around."

"All right, take it easy."

"I've got rules." She reads off her notes. "If anyone storms the door, everything goes up. If you stop talking to me, or someone else tries to talk to me, or we go off-air, everything goes up. No ad breaks, or everything goes up. Got it? I want everyone to know what happened to me."

Duke says, "Fine, I'm listening. We're all listening."

She closes her eyes.

A long time ago, so long ago that it seems like she's remembering someone else's life, Rebecca was a girl who lived with her parents and older brother in a red clinker brick house. Life was soccer practice, flute recitals, ballet classes, lamb roast on Sundays, a television with a 70cm screen housed within a faux-walnut case.

The first time, she was seven years old, camping alone in the back yard in the pup tent that Santa had brought. Her best-loved doll crooked in one arm, a red torch with a weak yellow light nearby, a Barbie comic. The door zipper scritched and she sat up, thin bare legs, shortie pyjamas.

It's me, Pumpkin. Move over.

Aw, Daddy, I'm not scared, I promise. Please? I don't want to go back inside.

Shh. Turn off your torch. Let's play a game.

The next morning, Mother was sitting at the kitchen table and eating toast and smiling at her. *Hey, Princess, did you have fun, would you like some breakfast?* And Daddy, walking out of the hallway, remarked to Mother, *Why don't you make pancakes?* And Mother made pancakes like Daddy had instructed. Then the family was at the table and eating and grinning and chatting, while each of Rebecca's bites got stuck in her throat.

At twelve, it stopped. By then, Rebecca was already swapping sex for beer and cigarettes with the older boys in the neighbourhood. At fourteen, her family moved into this three-bedroom apartment. At fifteen, she ran away.

For a while, she lived with friends, or squatted, or freecamped. Then she discovered seasonal work, and learned to roam the country following the weather: spring in Darwin to pick mangoes, summer in Western Australia for strawberries, autumn in Shepparton for pears, winter in southern Queensland for pineapples. Her daily routine winnowed into a simple equation of boots, gloves, and sunscreen lotion. Christmas Eve two years ago, while sleeping on a beach up north, she met Stella, a prostitute with a drug habit and the same kind of bad memories.

Rebecca fled the beach that night.

She took a bus, a train, and hitched rides the last stretch all the way across Australia back to this shitty three-bedroom apartment, and knocked on the door in time for Christmas dinner, to say: *Let me tell you why I turned out so rotten*.

There were tears at first, shouting and mayhem, Daddy the eye of the family storm. Rebecca kept waiting for Mother and Brother to turn to her, remorseful and tender. Instead, as the hours went by, they began to calm down and consider their options. Brother said, *He's always been a good father to me*. Mother said, *I'm too old to start again*. Rebecca, dazed, stumbled out the door. No one came after her.

Life went on in a distorted jangle.

A month ago, at a party in a squat, she'd bumped into Stella again. This time, both of them were prostitutes with drug habits.

"Oh my God," Duke says.

Rebecca opens her eyes. Did she tell everything to Duke? She can't remember. She feels sick, and she can't remember.

"You want revenge?" he said. "Is that it?"

"I don't know. I want it to end."

"Then give yourself up."

"That's not what I meant." Rebecca turns to look out the window. One marked police car and one fire engine are parked on the twin-carriage road below. A couple of police officers are slouched next to the car with their hands on their hips. One of the firemen is out of the truck and sitting on a bench, legs crossed.

"Listen," Duke says, "I've got a police negotiator right next to me."

A strong female voice breaks in. "Rebecca? My name is Valerie.

I'm a police officer. We need to sort this out."

"Duke, have you forgotten my rules?"

His voice hisses. "Oh shit, for the love of... Look, I don't want to get blamed, all right? If this goes bad, it's not fair to put it on me. Can you hear me back there? Nod if you can hear me."

"Huh?" Rebecca says.

"Give me something in writing, indemnity or whatever. I'm not trained for this. Hey, wait a minute." His voice breaks. "Jerry!"

"Who's Jerry?" she says.

"My producer. I don't believe it, he left the control room. He's pissed off on me, that son of a bitch. Shit." He panted for a time. "Listen, Rebecca, the police negotiator has gone. She's left the booth. That wasn't my choice, okay?"

Rebecca looks out the window. There's a black van sitting behind the fire truck. In the park are six officers in black helmets and black vests, and each officer carries what appears to be a submachine gun, a ridiculously massive weapon, something out of an action movie. One black-suited officer is talking to the uniformed cops. The others are gazing up at the building, perhaps gazing straight at her.

She ducks down, lying along the window seat, breathless, out of sight, and whispers, "Jeez, I think they want to shoot me."

"Can you blame them?" Duke says. "You've got your hostages, you've got everyone's attention, but you haven't given any demands. So what is it? Money? Jail time for your dad? A book deal?"

She lets out a nervous, seesawing giggle.

He sighs. "Okay, let me speak to your parents."

"What for?"

"The cops keep passing notes into the booth. They've found your brother. He confirms some of your story, but they can't find your parents."

"They're here in the master bedroom."

"Then let me have one word with them, okay? I've got cops and producers and studio bosses, you name it, breathing down my neck. I'm in a tough spot."

"Not as tough as mine." Rebecca swings her legs to sit up,

and looks out the window at the street. "Too bad you can't see this, Duke, it's a real circus."

"Yeah, I know, I'm online. There's uploads already."

"No kidding? Maybe I'll go viral. It'll be my birthday present."

"Your what?"

"My present. It's my birthday today."

After a while, he says, "Many happy returns."

"Thank you, Duke. That means a lot."

"If you come out, I could buy you a drink to celebrate." She doesn't reply. "Let me tell you something," Duke continues, dropping his voice as if whispering in private. "The cops don't think you've got any petrol up there."

"Well, there's five litres of it."

"No one can find a receipt. There's not a service station within fifty kays of you that sold a can of petrol to a woman today. What do you say to that?"

"Maybe I didn't go to a service station."

He makes a huffing sound, as if annoyed. "You realise the cops are eavesdropping, right? Convince them. Tell them where you got the petrol. Or put your parents on the line. This is your last chance."

Her mind is adrift, snagging on memories. "My last what?"

"I'm watching it live on my laptop. Put your hands out the window and surrender, would you, please? Do it now. A heap of armed cops have gone inside the building."

She knew it would come to this, but the news shocks her anyway. She stands up. Rhythmic booming starts to shake the walls, no doubt the concussion of steel-capped boots reverberating up the stairwell. She drops the phone.

The sudden *one-two* hammering on the apartment's front door is loud but measured, regular as a pulse. Rebecca claps her hands over her ears. It's a pair of sledgehammers in tandem, she tells herself; nothing but sledgehammers. The door explodes from its hinges, crashing into the shelving unit and toppling the stereo and speakers, shattering Mother's collection of hand-painted floral teacups. Rebecca flinches, braces herself. Seconds pass.

Nothing happens.

She opens her eyes to stare at the ruined doorway. Both stereo speakers are face-down on the floor. Even so, she can hear Duke on the radio, pleading, saying her name over and over, his voice a small, welcome comfort.

The doorway remains empty.

Can the cops smell the petrol? Surely, yes, the whole place reeks. Maybe they're debating what to do. Maybe they're getting ready to throw in a canister of tear gas. Rebecca wonders if such a canister would carry a spark, and if so, whether the spark might be enough to tempt the apartment into flames.

Gruff voices shout, "Police; don't move."

"Back off," she calls. "I don't want to hurt you guys, okay?"

No answer. From around the broken doorjamb peeks the muzzle of a black gun followed by a black visor and many more visors; then riot shields, more guns. Milling together, the officers hesitate in the doorway.

Rebecca takes the cigarette lighter from her pocket, and holds it up, shaking her head at them. The officers charge across the living room anyway. She closes her eyes, flicks the wheel, drops the lighter.

The price is high but the view is worth it.

Fortune Teller

Cotton shirt, linen trousers, no tie or jacket, clean-shaven. I gestured towards a chair and he took it. I sat down opposite. The passage of our bodies through the air flickered at the candlelight in my consulting room, releasing a fresh scent of sandalwood. My new client didn't speak. I stared at him, blinking slowly, gently, until he dropped his shoulders and relaxed.

It is important to set the mood.

He was handsome, Caucasian, just a few years past his prime, the square jaw softening into jowls, and wrinkles starting to gather around his eyes. I smiled. For male clients, I always wear red lipstick. This colour works better than plum or pink. I took his left hand in both of mine and turned it over. No stains from ink, paint, grease; no calluses, scars or recent injuries from work tools.

You have to know your demographics.

"The spirits tell me that you make your living from your intellect," I began.

He didn't argue. His ring-finger bore a circle of pale skin.

"You have lost a loved one," I continued. "That loss has been recent."

He nodded, but didn't say anything. Usually, a client will give me valuable information at this point: yes, *my wife died* or yes, *my husband left me*.

I rubbed my fingertips into his palm. Male clients are distracted by touch. Not so much the females. For older women, it's all about evoking memories or dreams of motherhood, so I tend to wear pigtails, and pencil a smattering of freckles across my nose. For younger women, I scrape my hair into a bun and go without makeup. That's because younger women are competitive, insecure; bitchy.

Trust me. If you want to make money in this line of business, you need to understand your client.

I traced the bumps of his knuckles, thumbed the back of his hand. "This loss has affected you deeply. To the world, you show a stoic face. It's only when you're alone that you feel that you can grieve. Why is that?"

"Because she made a fool of me."

"My guides say that she loved you very much."

"Then why did Mother cut me out of her will?"

Oh, it's a great feeling when you score this early in a reading. It tells you that the rest of the session will be a doddle, your chance to hook the client for years to come. Most of my long-termers are convinced that I speak to their deceased loved ones. Let me be frank: I have paid off my mortgage, secured eight rental properties, bought many cars, and enjoyed tours throughout Europe and Asia on my uncanny ability to channel the dead.

"Your mother admires your independence," I said. "She didn't leave you anything in her will because she wants you to keep to your path."

"No," he said, and pulled his hand free from mine. "Mother was duped."

"Duped?"

"By a charlatan."

An important note: if you suspect you're being called out, keep your mouth shut. Just wait. Usually, the client will calm down and apologise.

This time, however, my client drew a knife. The blade was thin, its tip honed to a needle, the kind of knife that was made to slip easily between ribs. He raised the knife.

"Mother thought you could talk to Dad," he said. "She gave you every cent." He stood up.

My consulting room is in my own house. Unfortunately, my house is in the hills, set amongst a hectare of natural bushland. If

I screamed, no one would hear me. Then again, if this particular client screamed, no one would hear him either. I know this from experience. My hectare occasionally comes in handy.

"I'm going to kill you," he whispered.

I shook my head. "Not if I kill you first."

He laughed. I lifted the gun, pointed the muzzle at his chin. He stopped laughing. I racked the slide. His face turned grey. He dropped the knife. I shot him anyway. Understand? Sure you do.

Now, close your eyes.

Okay, here's the final lesson: you can't work the shadows without picking up a little darkness in your soul along the way.

Hot Dog Van

One of the staff, an old man, led Senior Sergeant Adam Powell through the green grocery. The old man lifted his feet high with each step, as if walking through a field of long grass, rather than across a bare concrete floor, and Adam wondered why. Degenerative disease? War wound? There was something reminiscent of a prancing show pony in that gait, Adam mused with a smirk. Or perhaps the bloke used to be in a marching band. That thought made Adam snigger out loud. For a moment, he wished that his crew was here so they could trade quips, have some laughs, but no one on the police force could ever know about this visit of Adam's. Just being here might be enough to trigger an investigation against him.

"Right in here, if you please," the old man said, stopping to gesture towards a kitchenette at the back of the green grocery. "She won't be long. Could I interest you in a cup of coffee while you wait?"

Adam glanced around the kitchenette, took in the peeling linoleum, the bare bulb that hung over the chipped laminate table and vinyl chairs. "No thanks. I don't want to get food poisoning."

The old man gave a puzzled smile. "Food poisoning?"

"Ah, don't worry about it," Adam said, waving him away.

The old man nodded and returned to the front of the green grocery, high-stepping all the way, to resume unloading a box of parsnips from a cart.

Adam dragged out a chair and sat down. The ashtray in the

centre of the table overflowed with dead cigarettes. So Bethany Bonner owned this place? It didn't seem likely; then again, a shitty cash business was the perfect front. She apparently had a string of cash businesses throughout Melbourne: seafood wholesalers, fish and chipperies, florists, you name it; any business that could write off perishables, no questions asked, was the kind of business she liked to own. Around the traps, Bethany Bonner was known by her initials, BB. Some people, although not to her face, called her BB Gun. *Ha, very funny*, Adam thought, frowning. He had already decided to address her as Bethany rather than Mrs Bonner, since an easy familiarity would suggest an equal footing.

He checked his watch. She was late. A mutual associate, the SP bookie who had set up this meeting as a favour to Adam, had stressed the importance of getting the upper hand in negotiations. Shit. Now Adam would look inexperienced, over-eager; he should have waited longer in the car park. Sweat beaded his upper lip, despite the autumn breeze fanning through the open back door. *Be careful*, the bookie had warned. *Bethany is a snake.* Adam thought about his twenty-eight years on the force; twenty-eight tough years of law and order and breaking heads, and thought, *No worries: I'm a mongoose.*

"Senior Sergeant Powell?"

Adam stood up, turned around. A dumpy, middle-aged woman in a blue paisley dress and flat sandals was framed within the back door. He had expected something different: a worldly, cosmopolitan woman, meticulously coiffed, elegant, rake-thinned from gym sessions, tight-skinned from plastic surgery. A cliché, he realised. "Mrs Bonner?" he said, extending one hand.

She took it. Her face was round and full, chipmunk-cheeked, with no hint of makeup. This took him aback. The infamous BB Gun, multi-millionaire, looked like a suburban mum. That dress must be straight off the rack from a Target store.

"Please take a seat," she said, taking one herself.

He sat down again. "Thanks for agreeing to meet with me."

"Of course. I'm always happy to help the police in any way I can."

Startled, he said, "Hang on, what did the bookie tell you? I'm not here in any, uh, official capacity."

"Yes, I know." She removed a pack of cigarettes from the pocket of her dress, tapped one out, and proffered the pack.

"I quit four years ago," he said. "Thanks anyway."

She lit up and exhaled over one shoulder, to keep the smoke away. Then she said, "Please tell me your problem, in as much detail as you can."

He shifted around in his chair. Now that the moment was here, he didn't quite know how to proceed. The possibility that the room may contain a hidden microphone rippled a flitter of panic along his nerves.

"In your own time," she said, drawing again on the cigarette.

"Okay, well, it's about my brother-in-law, Charlie. Me and him own a hot dog van that makes about ten grand a week."

"Just from hot dogs? My goodness."

"I know. Crazy money, right? Charlie operates every night. We've got four clubs we look after, on a rotation, so he parks outside one club per night. Get me?"

"Yes."

"We've got no competition. I chased off the other food vendors months ago."

"Chased them off how?"

"Oh, in various ways."

Bethany offered a demure smile. "Any of them legal?"

Adam hesitated, uncomfortable. Was she mocking him? He thought again about a hidden microphone. Finally, he said, "I'm taking a big chance."

"Yes, you are. I'm sorry. Now isn't the time for me to be making silly jokes. Please forgive me."

"Sure. Look, I'm sorry too. It's just that I'm… I'm a little on edge."

"I understand. Everything you discuss with me is confidential. You have my word. Please continue."

He took a deep breath and inadvertently sucked in her cigarette smoke. Instantly, the familiar craving for nicotine knocked and scratched at the back of his throat, the roof of his mouth. A dart would be fantastic right about now.

Placing an elbow on the table and leaning forward, dropping his voice, he said, "I want to take the hot dog business in a new direction. Actually, it was Charlie that gave me the idea. Every Sunday afternoon when he comes over for lunch with me and the wife, he whinges about the customers. Lots of night clubbers buy a hot dog then ask him for drugs, usually speed. I figure it's so they can keep dancing."

"Oh, dear." She shook her head, crushing out her cigarette. "I'm afraid our bookie friend has given you the wrong impression. My organisation specialises in a totally different type of merchandise."

Namely heroin, Adam thought, but said, "That's not why I'm here. I've got my supplier already. Well, for ecstasy and base, at least. There are kinks to iron out, but I reckon I've got an importer for crystal meth, too."

"I see. And how much are you hoping to shift per week?"

"About half a kilo. Enough to bring in maybe twenty to thirty grand, depending on the product range. But that's just the beginning. Once I've got the cash flow, I'll buy more hot dog vans."

"Impressive. So how may I help you?"

This was the most difficult part, the actual request. He'd rehearsed it many times, most recently in the bathroom mirror this morning while shaving. *It's not that I'm a cruel man* was his opening line, with plenty more to follow; he decided to drop the palaver and come straight to the point. Adam cleared his throat. "It's Charlie."

"Your brother-in-law? What about him?"

"He won't do it. Flat-out refuses. In fact, he won't even discuss it with me."

"That's a shame."

"And I need the money. I've got a kid in university, and two more in the last years of high school, and they want to go to university as well. The youngest is aiming to be a surgeon. That kind of education's not cheap."

She laughed politely. "And your fondness for horseracing

wouldn't help either. You're not very good at picking the winners, are you?"

Adam sat back in his chair. If Bethany knew about his gambling problem, she would also know that he had only one child: a grown son who worked in retail selling new and used computer games. A mix of embarrassment and outrage burned a deeper flush of blood into Adam's face.

Meanwhile, Bethany lit another cigarette.

"Let's get back to Charlie," she said. "If he doesn't want to expand the current business, so what? Go buy yourself another hot dog van. Branch out on your own."

"I would, but things are more complicated than that. Charlie was pissed off at first. Now he's holding it over me. He's threatening to tell Esther unless I give him a bigger cut of the profits."

"Esther?"

"His sister. My wife."

Bethany flicked cigarette ash. "Well, that is a sticky situation."

"You've no idea. Police officers have to get permission to own businesses. All of my sideline ventures are in Esther's name, including my fifty per cent share in this hot dog van. If Esther walks out—and she would, she's a good Catholic girl—I'd be destitute."

"And in jail?"

"Esther wouldn't go that far."

"Are you sure? An angry wife is capable of unexpected things."

The rumours about Bethany Bonner's husband came to mind; Alrigo, missing now for six years, presumed dead. With the back of one hand, Adam wiped sweat from his forehead. "Let's get down to brass tacks," he said.

"All right. Fifty thousand."

"*Fifty?* Jesus, I was told thirty."

"In cash, up front."

"All of it?" Perspiration was seeping through his business shirt; he could feel it under his arms. "What about half now, half later?"

She stood.

Clattering the chair, he stood too, saying in a rush, "Okay, fifty up front. Christ, I'll need a few days. How do we formalise this? Do we sign something or what?"

She smiled gently, courteously, and walked out the back door. Adam, hands on hips, felt shaken; even more so when, unexpectedly, the old man high-stepped from the green grocery into the kitchenette a few seconds later.

"Shit, where did you come from?" Adam demanded, turning on him.

"Please follow me, sir."

"Were you listening the whole time?"

The old man grinned, and gestured the way out with a sweep of his arm.

Brushing past, Adam muttered, "Goddamned cripple," which was a dumb thing to say to one of Bethany Bonner's employees, but screw it. The prick was probably deaf anyway.

Within days of the meeting, Adam dropped off the money in a shoebox to the green grocery. Also in the box, a dossier on Charlie: photographs, address, car registration, habits, interests. (There wasn't much to report. Charlie was a bachelor without children. His will stated that, upon his death, the bulk of his assets would go to Esther, including his share of the hot dog business. Adam knew this, being executor of Charlie's will.) The old man at the green grocery took the shoebox and told Adam to be patient; the matter would be taken care of shortly. No worries, Adam agreed.

But then nothing happened.

The rest of the week passed with excruciating slowness, as did the week after that. Esther couldn't stand Adam's grouchiness and kept shouting at him. Adam blamed a bad case at work. Plenty of after-dinner whisky sodas hardly soothed his nerves.

Christ, how long was this going to take? Every time the phone rang, he jumped. And in the middle of every night, when he woke up and couldn't go back to sleep, he felt convinced that Bethany Bonner had scammed him, pure and simple. No doubt she was laughing about the rip-off, the easiest fifty grand she'd ever made. The thought of it caused Adam to grind his teeth.

One morning, about three weeks after delivering the money, while Adam was getting ready for work, Esther took a phone call. Her anguished scream made him drop his tie and sprint to the kitchen. Tears were already coursing down her cheeks. She held the handset like a cold compress to her forehead.

"Honey, what is it?" he said, his heart in his throat.

"It's Charlie."

"Charlie? Is he...okay?"

She shook her head.

"Dead?"

She nodded. Unexpectedly, Adam's eyes filled too, but his were tears of relief. Esther wasn't to know that. They clung to each other and cried.

Adam made the arrangements. The funeral took place the following Tuesday. Apparently, Charlie, a hobbyist woodworker who churned out quaint, old-fashioned toys like train engines and pull-along chickens, had been working alone in his shed when he must have slipped with his saw and cut a brachial artery, which bled him out within a minute. People at the wake kept saying to each other, *at least he died doing what he loved*, but Adam knew better. A couple of thugs must have cornered Charlie in the shed. One must have held him, while the other worked the saw. Jesus, it didn't bear thinking about. Adam drank far too much at the wake. Esther didn't even get angry. She assumed he was grief-stricken.

On a wet and stormy night after Charlie's funeral, Adam drove home from work to find an unfamiliar car in his driveway that blocked access to the garage. Shit. Now he had to park on the street. By the time he got through the front door, he was fuming and soaked.

"Esther," he yelled, throwing his keys onto the sideboard. "My car's out in the goddamned rain. Esther?"

"We're in here," called an unfamiliar voice.

Adam headed to the formal lounge, a room that Esther reserved for dinner parties or people she wanted to impress. Could he smell cigarettes? He spotted Esther through the open doorway. She was sitting in the leather armchair, her back stiffly upright, eyes wide and frightened. His pulse had already quickened by the time he stepped in.

Bethany Bonner and the old man from the green grocery were sitting in the leather three-seater couch. A cigarette, no doubt Bethany's, smouldered in a saucer on the coffee table.

"Adam, what's going on?" Esther said.

Stunned, he couldn't think of a single thing to say.

"Oh, good, you're home." Bethany lifted an open bottle of champagne in Adam's direction, and then said to the old man, "Could you please get us another glass, Uncle Henry?"

The bloke Adam had called a cripple—Bethany Bonner's frigging *uncle*, no less—high-stepped across the lounge to the buffet, where he opened one of the doors and helped himself to a champagne flute.

Esther, her voice a notch higher, said, "Adam, for God's sake. What exactly is going on here?"

The old man held the glass while Bethany poured. When the old man gave him the drink, Adam numbly took it. He still couldn't think of anything to say.

Bethany raised her champagne. "To us. And to our new business relationship; may it be long and fruitful."

"Business relationship?" Adam said.

"Of course." She sipped her drink and smiled at him. "Congratulations on your imminent retirement from the police force. I'm very happy that you'll be running my fleet of hot dog vans for me. Very happy indeed."

Broken Things

The weatherboard house was built into a hillside. Craig, on crutches, had to negotiate the steep asphalt path from the carport to the front door. Dad trotted down the slope with their suitcases, and then strolled back up a minute later to put his hands on his hips and shake his head over Craig's slow descent. Dad's scrutiny made Craig feel like a kid again instead of a man in his twenties, and the feeling irritated him.

At last, Craig stood inside the old house. The kitchen was unchanged as far as he could remember, except for a fish tank the size of a wide-screen TV that sat on a cabinet near the back door. Craig used his good foot to drag out a chair from the kitchen table.

Dad said, "Bet you never pictured being under my roof again."

Craig lowered himself into the chair and said, "Where do you want these?"

Dad took the crutches and propped them against the wall nearest the tank. Two angelfish darted from the greenery and flitted against the glass with the intensity of moths hammering a bright window.

Dad laughed. "See that, mate? Reckon they missed me or what?"

Dad squatted in front of the tank, his nose at the glass. More fish rose from hidden places in dark foliage. Craig looked at the flashes of colours, stripes and scales, but mostly looked at Dad. He had aged plenty. Chapped, whiskery skin hung from his face as if his skull had shrunk. They hadn't seen each other in eleven years. The car trip from the hospital in Adelaide to this house on Melbourne's outskirts had taken the best part of a day, and yet they'd hardly spoken. *Well,* Craig thought, *some things don't change.* Then he said, "I didn't know you liked fish."

The doorbell sounded. Dad checked his watch. "That'll be Amy. She must've been watching for the car."

"Amy?"

Dad headed to the front door. "The foster kid from over the road. She's at my aquarist hobby group. A good kid, you'll like her."

"What hobby group? Dad? Don't let her in."

Craig pressed his fingertips into his eye sockets. The world burst into red blotches. When he opened his eyes again, he saw a thin girl of about twelve standing at the fish tank with her back to him. She wore a grey school uniform. Her lank, home-cut hair was the colour of cheese.

"You better check ammonia and nitrite," she said to Dad. "A storm yesterday knocked out the power. We only got it back this morning."

Dad made an exasperated sound. "Christ, that'd be right. Gone for just two bloody days, now look at Sweetie's tail, would you? She's got it clamped." He flung open the doors of the cabinet below the tank and took out a box. The box held white plastic bottles and test tubes.

"I'll do ammonia," Amy said, and turned to grab one of the bottles. Craig noticed that her eyes were blue, and recalled those other blue eyes: those round and startled ones.

"Dad," Craig said, "my crutches."

"Here you go, mate."

Craig left the kitchen. It was quiet in the lounge room. He half-sat, half-lay across the couch and listened to the ticking of the wall clock. Amy came in after a while and squatted next to him. She gave off a sour, loamy smell like wet dirt. She rested her hand on his cast.

"Don't touch it," he said.

"I broke my arm once. Crashed my scooter into a wall."

"Remove your hand."

Amy stood up. "I've still got the cast, everybody signed it. Why hasn't anybody signed yours?"

He turned his face and closed his eyes. When he at last looked around, Amy was gone. He could hear the clock but couldn't see it. The shadows in the lounge room had deepened and were pushing against him. "Dad," he called out.

Dad came in, wiping his hands on a towel. "We got to get to the aquarium shop before it shuts. Come on, I'm not leaving you to mope."

The aquarium shop was long and narrow. Lighted tanks lay along both walls. The tanks, burbling and droning, were full of dark shapes. Craig stayed by the front door and leaned on his crutches, breathing hard, while the cast dragged on him like a shark trying to pull him under.

After a few minutes, Dad emerged from an aisle with a teen-aged boy. The suggestion of a goatee beard struggled from the boy's chin. Half his work-shirt hung loose from his trousers like he didn't care for the job anyway, and his lopsided nametag announced him as *Toby, Fish World Customer Consultant.*

"This is my son, Craig," Dad said.

"Yeah?" Toby said.

"He has to stay with me for a while. Road accident."

"Really?" Toby said, and winked at Craig.

"You don't know the half of it," Dad said. "Busted nearly every bone in his body, didn't you, mate? Riding his motorbike, minding his own business, and t-boned a woman coming out of a side street. Bang." Dad speared his hand flat through the air and whistled to demonstrate Craig's trajectory. "Straight over the top of her car."

And hit the road like a stone skipping across water, Craig thought. Bounce, bounce, bounce, then stillness, three-quarter moon coolly overhead, sirens.

"Wow," Toby said, and grinned.

Back in Dad's kitchen, Craig sat at the table while Dad siphoned water from the fish tank into a sixty-litre plastic drum. The water level fell away and plants sucked their leaves against the glass. Dad had bought a bottle from the aquarium shop and Craig picked it up from the table and read the packaging. *Releases vast quantities of nitrifying bacteria into the water to reduce the risk of fish loss.* Craig put down the bottle and said, "Toby's an arsehole."

"He knows his fish."

"Yeah, well, he's still an arsehole."

"I've already told you once. Now don't start with me, by God."

"Okay, okay, forget it." Then Craig said, "I'm gonna go home anyway."

"To Adelaide? Ha! What for? You can't teach at the karate club, so how do you plan on earning a wage and paying your rent? You don't even have a car, and even if you did, how the blazes are you gonna drive it with your leg the way it is? And not one of your so-called mates gives a rat's. So where does that leave you? Exactly nowhere but here, and don't think I like it any better than you do."

Craig clamped his jaw and, despite himself, recalled the physiotherapist from his two months in hospital; Millie, the bitch with the doughy face, and fat, callused hands. She had come to his ward every day to make him wave his arms, touch his toes and squeeze a tennis ball, goading him to stand and walk and stretch and strive, and he had hated her and her loud, relentless cheeriness. Throughout every painful exercise he had insisted that, given time, he would recover like nothing had ever happened and go back to karate, weights and running while Millie doggedly maintained that some things, once broken, could never heal and he was one of them. Now he understood what she had meant. He understood so well, so completely, that it weighted his guts.

Craig said, "I'll catch a train home on Monday."

Dad, who had been lugging the sixty-litre drum to the kitchen sink, thumped the drum to the floor. "Yeah? And then what? Live on the streets like a bum? Now give me a bloody hand with this water change."

That night, Craig went to bed in his old room. The wooden bed-head still bore gummy traces of the dinosaur stickers that he'd applied some twenty years ago, and the familiar paint chips in the wall next to his pillow disturbed him. With his eyes shut tight he was seven again, the bright kid who had a knack for sports and a mother who loved him and was still alive. He fell asleep imagining her cool hand on his forehead and his future beckoning large and sure. Then he woke up, a figure looming over him.

"You were yelling," Dad said. He was wearing pyjama bottoms and nothing else, his chest flabby as if someone had let out the air.

Craig said. "Get out of here, let me sleep."

Dad left the room and shut the door. Craig fell back onto the bed. His leg rang with a clenched ache that never stopped no matter how many pills he swallowed. He blamed it on the bone tissue forced to grow torturously like a vine around the screws, bolts and wires that now held his leg together. But sometimes, like now, he recognised the pain as the phantom wail of his kneecap that had shattered so thoroughly that the surgeon had simply given up on it and tossed every last little fragment—more than sixty in all, according to a theatre nurse—into a medical waste bin.

He got up. In the kitchen, he closed the door to the hallway and switched on the tank lights. Fish stirred out of plants and rose from the gravel, coasting in the warm water. Craig got a chair and sat down. A silver angelfish, no bigger than a ten-cent coin, struggled past, its tail furled to a point instead of fanned like the other fish. It swam back and forth in a hitching motion and gulped strenuously at the water.

The hall door opened. Dad sat down at the table.

Craig pointed at the tank. "Is that Sweetie, the one with the tail? What's wrong with her?"

"Poisoned. The blackout stopped the pump. That dropped the oxygen in the water and killed off the good bacteria."

Craig didn't understand, but let it go. "The other fish seem okay."

"They're bigger. They've got what's known as *constitution*." Then Dad said, "It's three in the morning, mate."

"I keep seeing her eyes. Just before I hit her door, she looked at me."

Dad got up, reached over the hood of the tank and switched off the lights. Sweetie disappeared into the sudden black.

After breakfast, Craig sat at the table with coffee while Dad prepared another water change for the fish tank. He put the sixty-litre drum and siphon on the kitchen floor, opened the lid of the tank and said through his teeth, "Bugger it."

"Is she dead?"

"Near enough."

Craig grabbed his crutches and stumped over to the tank. Sweetie bobbed in the gentle current on her side, fins slack, wide eyes clouded.

"Blast it. Come here, Sweetie." Dad slid his hand into the tank and scooped her out. The fish lay motionless in Dad's palm, glossy as a drop of sap. Craig went out the back door to the balcony, took a seat on one of the benches and leaned against the house.

The yard below was a sea of eucalyptus trees. A stiff wind shimmered millions of wet leaves. The rain came and went and came again. Then Amy was on the balcony and glaring at him, her squinty eyes red-rimmed.

"What?" he snapped.

"Nothing. Sweetie's dead. You don't even care."

"Shouldn't you be at school?"

"It's Saturday."

Craig sat up and said, "Jesus, why are you always here? Haven't you got somewhere to go?"

She kicked a sneaker-shod foot at his cast, too far away to connect, but before he could stop himself, Craig flinched and jarred his knee. Crackles of white pain sliced through his leg and bit into his ankle. The agony concussed in waves, yet he was aware of Amy observing him, unmoved. As soon as he was able, he grabbed a crutch and swung it. Amy skipped out of the way.

He blushed and hurled the crutch to the balcony floor. "Piss off."

"You piss off, you cripple." Sneering, she added, "You murderer."

Craig's heart dropped, swung and clattered against his ribs. He finally said, "She ran the stop sign, not me."

"So what? She had a baby in the back, didn't she? Now it's got to grow up without a mum." Amy's face collapsed for a moment into a sobbing grimace. Then she set her jaw and stabbed a middle finger at him. He struggled to stand up, lunging for his crutches, but she had already slammed the back door behind her.

When he finished crying, Craig slid off the chair, bore his weight on his good leg and leaned over to gather both crutches. It took him some time to descend the balcony's slick wooden steps. At last he stood on the foaming wet mush of the back yard. Rain peppered his face and saturated his jumper. He picked his way through the trees down to the rear of the back yard. Over a low chicken-wire fence ploughed the brown murmur of the Yarra River, its surface jumping with countless strikes of rain. He stepped over the fence.

The cold water poured into his cast and soothed his skin. The relief urged him to stride further into the flow. When the river was waist-high, he allowed it to wrench the crutches from his grip and hurl them out of sight. Wading was difficult now without the crutches to stabilise him. He took a couple more steps. The river pushed him over and swirled him in circles, dunking him, pitching him downstream so fast that Dad's back yard flurried out of sight in an instant, gone forever.

Tearing along felt like a thrilling ride until the plaster cast, heavy and sodden, pulled him under. The river drove itself into his nose and throat. It occurred to him that he didn't have the strength to make it to the bank, even if salvation was what he wanted. The horror of it made him thrash and shriek for a few seconds until he could steel himself. He clumsily flipped onto his back, spitting out river. Branches flashed by overhead. The rushing water cradled him. Sticks and leaves churned furiously alongside as if racing him to the finish line, but he knew he would get there first.

The blue eyes came to mind. He apologised again for the millionth time. This time, his apology would really mean something.

Crazy Town is a Happy Place

Dr Vivienne Leach walked into reception. Sitting in the waiting area were Dr Paholski and the journalist. As Vivienne approached, they both stood up.

The journalist turned out to be a young girl in a summer dress, cardigan and flat lace-up shoes, no makeup, ginger hair pulled back from her freckled face in scores of stiff, wiry plaits. The kind of principled little girl who wouldn't shave her armpits, Vivienne decided, and probably smoked weed every Saturday night just to be subversive. Vivienne gave a practised and professional smile. The girl responded by lifting one side of her mouth.

"Vivienne, meet Daisy, the writer I was telling you about," Dr Paholski said. "Daisy is putting together a profile on Krantzen Town for an online newspaper."

"Pleased to meet you," Vivienne said.

Turning to Daisy, Dr Paholski continued, "Dr Vivienne Leach is one of our pioneers. Back in the day, she and four other geriatricians took over this place when it was nothing but a foreclosed retirement village. They created Kranzten Town from scratch."

"Based on the original Dutch model, the Hogewey care facility," Vivienne said. "Let's give credit where credit is due."

Daisy said, "Yeah, okay, can we get going? I'm running to deadline."

Vivienne frowned. Damn these obligations to the press. But Krantzen Town needed good PR; needed more benefactors if it was to flourish. Vivienne held up a forefinger—*wait one second*—and

223

approached the reception desk. The nametag on the receptionist's jacket read "Naomi".

"Naomi, excuse me," Vivienne said. "Any messages?"

"Sorry, Dr Leach. Still no word from your husband. I'll page when he calls."

Vivienne nodded, smiled. Hopefully, Hugh would remember to pick up the champagne flutes. She turned from the reception desk. Dr Paholski was gone. Presumably, he'd left for the specialist suites while her back was turned, noiseless as usual on his crepe-soled shoes. Meanwhile, Daisy stood in the middle of the rug with both hands clasping an oversized, garish carpet bag; the hippy version, Vivienne supposed, of a briefcase or satchel. Oh yes, this was going to be a tiresome few hours.

"Ready?" Daisy said.

Vivienne ran a hand through her bobbed hair, straightened her glasses, tugged at the hem of her white coat. Daisy would ask about the movie star, no doubt. Every journalist did. It was the ghoulish side of human nature: that desire to goggle in fascination at the mighty after they have fallen.

"Let's commence," Vivienne said.

They walked through the double doors of the main building and out into the weak sunshine of a Melbourne spring day. The grounds were manicured. The breeze carried the cloying smell of jasmine. Vivienne cut left at the driveway's turnaround. Daisy followed.

"I don't want to waste your time or mine," Vivienne said, over her shoulder. "How much do you know already?"

"About Crazy Town? That it costs each patient about sixty grand a year."

Vivienne stopped walking and spun around. "Hold it right there. We don't call this Crazy Town, and neither will you."

Daisy faltered and she blinked like an owl.

"It's *Kranzten* Town," Vivienne continued, "named after the first benefactor, Norbert Krantzen. Haven't you heard about him?"

"Yeah, the millionaire with the crazy wife."

Vivienne narrowed her eyes. "No one here is crazy. Our patients have dementia. Do you understand what that is? It's a term for the symptoms of various mental conditions like stroke, acquired brain injury, Alzheimer's disease. A person with dementia loses memory, intellect, rationality, social skills; physical functioning too as the condition progresses. But they're not crazy. Is that clear?"

"Well, sure. Okay."

"Are we clear, absolutely crystal clear? If not, this interview is over right now."

Daisy shrugged, blushed, smirked. "Jesus, I'm sorry. It's just that everybody calls this place Crazy Town."

"No one here calls it that."

Daisy lowered her gaze to the footpath, suitably chastened. Vivienne felt a sudden pang for this ugly little goose with her graceless demeanour, flat chest, the rash of acne across her cheeks.

"Shall we press on?" Vivienne said.

The girl nodded, shrugged half-heartedly. Vivienne strode ahead. Daisy hurried to catch up.

Small, well-kept brick houses lined both sides of the road. Each house had its own garden bed, at this time of year a colourful riot of flowering magnolia, camellia, marigold, geranium, freesia, and some others that Vivienne couldn't name. There were no fences dividing the properties, only a rolling green lawn as immaculate as any golf course.

"Krantzen Town kept the set-up of the original retirement village," Vivienne said. "Many patients are functional enough to live in the free-standing units, the homes you see here."

A distant male voice shouted, "Morning, Dr Leach."

Vivienne stopped and turned. One of the gardeners waved at her from a front yard. She waved back.

"Oh shit, is he a patient?" Daisy said.

"No. He's on staff. It takes a full-time team of gardeners and maintenance men to keep Kranzten Town looking as beautiful as it does."

She waited for Daisy to acknowledge this truth, to compliment Kranzten Town with perhaps an admiring smile or nod, but the girl just hefted her carpet bag from one hand to the other, and shot a worried glance at the gardener. Vivienne resumed walking. Daisy kept pace.

"The patients who struggle with day-to-day functioning live in our communal houses that have five or six bedrooms and shared living areas," Vivienne said. After a time, she added, "Aren't you taking notes?"

"It's more of a first-person kind of article."

They walked in silence for a time. The footpath went over a little rise and cut to the right. The side wall of the pub came into view.

"Apart from the hospital and medical suites," Vivienne said, "we have an onsite supermarket, and a High Street with a pub, hairdressers, newsagent, town hall, movie theatre, and café. The patients don't realise they're patients at all. They think they're living in a village."

"What about the carers?" Daisy said. "How do you hide them?"

"Depending on the patient, the carers are thought of as servants, members of the extended family, friends, perhaps neighbours. Most of the patients think I'm their GP, which I suppose I am, in a way. A few of them believe I'm a relative, usually their daughter or sister."

"And you don't correct them?"

"Of course not."

Daisy whistled through her teeth. "So, everybody here lives a lie?"

Foolish girl, Vivienne wanted to say. Everybody lives some kind of lie, not just the residents of Krantzen Town. But Daisy would learn that herself one day. It was one of the many painful realisations that came with experience, hindsight, wisdom, age, after life had kicked the stuffing out of you a few dozen times.

Instead, Vivienne said, "It's the illusion that keeps them well. It's called *reminiscence therapy*. Our patients take very little medication. Some patients don't need medication at all."

"But morally? Come on, doesn't it disgust you?"

Vivienne gave a derisive snort. "You've obviously never been to a regular nursing ward for dementia patients. Everyone over-medicated to the point of stupor, almost comatose, forced to wear nappies, lined up in wheelchairs around a television all day, every day, strapped into their beds at night, trapped behind locked doors. It's a horrible way to end one's life. Here, our patients are happy. They live in the past where their minds wish to be, back when they were whole and had full cognitive function. That's why we don't have mirrors in Krantzen Town. It's important not to break the illusion."

"I suppose the movie star still thinks he's a movie star."

Vivienne stopped walking, ready to give this ignorant little girl a dressing down, a lecture about privacy, the importance of doctor-patient confidentiality, but then she noticed something. The breeze carried more than just the fragrance of jasmine. A tiny cloud of pollen had swirled by on a current, barely visible, fine as a puff of talcum powder. If her son had forgotten to fill his antihistamine prescription, he'd be coughing and sneezing for the duration of his engagement party tomorrow tonight.

"Dr Leach?" Daisy said.

"My apologies, I was thinking about something else."

"That's okay. So...the movie star?"

Vivienne pointed at a Japanese maple on the nature strip. "Do you see that?"

"The tree? Well, yeah, sure I do. I'm not blind."

Vivienne approached the maple, gestured for Daisy to come closer, then pointed again into the branches. "See the camera?" Vivienne said.

"Oh my God, yeah. Oh wow, it's tiny."

Vivienne kept walking. Daisy fell in beside her. "We have hidden cameras everywhere to monitor the safety of our patients," Vivienne said. "Except for the front gate, there are no locks in Kranzten Town."

"No one ever tries to leave?"

"Our patients prefer the familiarity of staying at home. They don't need much in the way of outdoor life. Our High Street is enough for them. And here we are."

The road was a dead end, the shops of the High Street arranged around the cul-de-sac. It was an eye-catching shopping centre.

Each red-brick terraced building was fashioned in the Georgian style with sash windows, decorative ironwork, panelled doors. A carer walked the footpaths, masquerading as a fellow shopper. A handful of elderly patients tottered about. Most of the patients showed the same empty, grinning face, the same aimless wandering.

Daisy hesitated, drew back.

"Come along," Vivienne said. "It's quite all right."

Every patient was out alone, walking singly, none in pairs or groups. Some carried shopping bags. Vivienne smiled or nodded to each patient, and received cheerful greetings in return.

"Oh my God," Daisy said. "They don't sound crazy at all."

"That's because they're not crazy. They have dementia."

"What I mean is that you'd never know there's anything wrong with them. They're like old people you'd see anywhere, like grandparents, you know? Like normal people."

"Thank you. We work hard to keep our patients happy. But don't be fooled. Everyone you see is severely and untreatably demented with zero chance of recovery. There's no way out of Kranzten Town. Once you're here, you leave in a coffin."

Daisy shivered. "Oh, Jesus."

"There are worse ways to die, believe me." Vivienne held open the door of the pub, and said, "After you."

They went in. The pub was the most impressive building in the whole of High Street with its panelled ceilings, red wooden floors, and leather armchairs. But Daisy didn't appear to notice. Vivienne gestured towards a table. They both sat down.

Daisy said, "The booze in here. Is it real?"

"As real as we are."

"So, if I wanted an alcoholic drink, I could have one?"

"Now? At ten in the morning? Well, yes, of course. And so could every patient here; at least, the ambulatory ones. Actually, the problem we have is getting the patient to consume the drink once they've ordered it. Typically, they forget and start to leave. The staff members have to remind the patient to stay." Vivienne pointed towards the chandelier. "See the camera up there by the light fitting? Go ahead and wave to the clinic doctors."

Instead, Daisy pressed fingertips against her closed eyelids.

"Hello, Dr Leach," the waitress said, coming over from behind the bar. "How are you today?"

Daisy started.

"Please try to relax," Vivienne said. "Our waitress is a member of staff, just like the gardener. Remember? Everything is all right."

"Can I get you girls a drink?" the waitress said. "Tea? Coffee?"

"Bourbon and coke," Daisy whispered.

Vivienne gave a rueful smile. Most journalists fell to pieces on this tour. Particularly the young ones. It was never easy to be confronted with the frailties of being human, to see evidence first-hand of the terrible cost that everyone ultimately had to bear if they lived for long enough, even when the evidence was as palatable and friendly as Krantzen Town. Lots of places were worse. Palliative care for cancer patients was worse, for example. Vivienne thought about mentioning this to Daisy. However, the girl seemed too shaken.

"Dr Leach?" the waitress said. "The usual orange juice?"

"Yes, please."

"And how are the plans for the engagement party?"

"Under control for the most part. Hugh is meant to be hiring the champagne glasses today, but he's getting rather forgetful in his old age."

The waitress laughed. "Uh-oh, look out. You've got to be careful saying that kind of thing around here."

"Oh my God,' Daisy said, blanching.

The waitress headed back to the bar.

A wedge of gentle sunshine slid along the wall as the pub door opened. Mr Eastford wandered in, a snow-haired and frail old man who favoured one leg as he bent over a walking stick. Perfect.

"Come and join us, Mr Eastford," Vivienne called.

"What are you doing?" Daisy hissed.

"You need an interview with a patient to round out your article," Vivienne said. "Mr Eastford, this is Daisy, a journalist. She's writing about Krantzen Town."

"Good day," the old man said, easing himself into a chair, gazing at Daisy with shining eyes. "Are you my wife?"

Daisy stared imploringly, beseechingly, at Vivienne.

"Why don't you tell us about yourself, Mr Eastford?" Vivienne said.

"Oh, there's nothing much to tell. I'm a plumber with my own business, thirty-six years old, married, three kids." He turned to Daisy. "Are you my wife?"

Daisy held her hands over her nose and mouth, breathing hard. She looked pale, as if getting ready to faint. Concerned, Vivienne gestured for the waitress. The waitress hurried over, placed the drinks on the table, and took the old man by the elbow.

"Mr Eastford," the waitress said. "Please come over here with me."

"No worries," he said, and stood up. "Are you my wife?"

"Right this way, Mr Eastford," the waitress said, with a nod at Vivienne, steering the old man away. "Come along now. Let's go."

Daisy whispered, "Is the movie star like that?"

"Have some of your bourbon," Vivienne said. "It'll calm you down."

"Stop changing the subject."

Vivienne sighed. "If you're expecting collusion for some kind of exposé, I'm afraid you're going to be disappointed. All patients here are protected, especially the high-profile ones. We will not allow them to be humiliated by tabloid magazines."

"I don't understand. They told me you'd talk about the movie star."

Vivienne said, "Let's visit the town hall. We have music recitals there. Some of our more cognisant patients sometimes hold plays or poetry readings."

"But he's dead."

"Who's dead?"

"The movie star." Daisy hugged the carpet bag to her chest. "I was supposed to talk to you about the movie star," she said, voice rising. "That's what they told me."

The waitress came over. "Dr Leach, is everything okay?"

"I'm not sure," Vivienne said. "Daisy seems overwhelmed. She could be having some kind of delusional episode."

Daisy turned to the waitress. "I did what I was told and it didn't work. Get me out of here."

"Okay, let's go," the waitress said, taking the girl by the arm. "I'll escort you to the main building. Dr Leach, please stay here and finish your drink."

"Your son's engagement party happened twenty years ago," Daisy said. "He's married with teenage kids. They visit and you don't even know who they are."

"Stop it, that's enough," the waitress said, waving at the chandelier.

At the camera, Vivienne realised. As if signalling for help.

"You're a patient," Daisy continued. "You live the same day over and over. Is any of this getting through? Hubby isn't picking up champagne glasses; he's in a hospice dying from prostate cancer."

"Shut up," the waitress shouted. "You signed papers. You're breaching terms of agreement."

"Aw, screw that shit," Daisy wailed. "I quit, I can't do it."

A chasm opened up in Vivienne's stomach. Daisy wasn't a journalist, she was a trainee carer. A trainee carer for... Vivienne lifted her hands. Wrinkled, covered in age spots. They weren't the hands of a fifty-year-old, more like those of a seventy-year-old.

Oh, dear Lord.

Realisation hit in a wave of panic. She closed her eyes against the onslaught. The immensity of the wave bore down, crushing and suffocating, closing over her head like black water. She had been scared of the ocean ever since she was a little girl; scared of its enormity, its unknown depths and currents, the relentless dark, the hidden creatures lurking within. And now the ocean pulled her under. She was drowning. Teeth were coming for her.

"Dr Leach," said a stern voice.

Swimming frantically towards the light, she snapped open her eyes. Daisy had been right. There was nothing worse than this. Vivienne fought for her husband and son, for her faceless grandchildren, for the other children she may have had, the daughters or sons she couldn't remember. She fought for those she had always loved but had somehow lost.

"Dr Leach," said the voice again.

Shadows crouched at the edge of her vision. In the dead centre of it all appeared Dr Paholski's blue eyes, bristling eyebrows, meaty nose. Her attention gradually brought his entire face into focus. As usual, she hadn't heard his approach. Those crepe-soled shoes of his were so quiet, so stealthy.

"Can you hear me?" Dr Paholski said.

Vivienne couldn't speak. Her heart was caroming too hard against her ribs.

"Here," Dr Paholski said. "Have some of your orange juice."

He pressed a glass into her hand. She was sitting in a chair in the pub. Dr Paholski was on one side of her, the waitress on the other. Poor old Mr Eastford was sitting by the window, nodding his snowy head over a forgotten pint of strawberry milk. Vivienne ran a hand across her face, realised she was sweating.

Dear Lord.

Now this was important.

Something was important.

She glanced around at the shadows in the corners of her eyes, tried to snatch at them as they streaked away, like the ghostly remnants of a dream.

"Drink up," Dr Paholski said.

She did as she was told. The juice ran icy cold down her throat. She put the empty glass on the table. Time passed. Her heart rate began to slow. Feeling returned to her hands and feet. Mr Eastford looked over, his head nodding like a doll.

"You had a dizzy spell," Dr Paholski said. "But you've recovered now."

"We're so glad," the waitress said.

"Thank you," Vivienne said. "Thank you for helping me."

"I hope you'll be okay for the engagement party tomorrow tonight," the waitress said.

"After what I've spent on catering?" Vivienne managed a smile. "I'd better be."

Toby Mulligan

Dizzy and hot, Diane stood up from her computer and left the study, her skin prickling and itching beneath the dressing gown. Her slippers whisked over the kitchen tiles. This end of the house still smelled of pancakes and caramelised strawberries, the breakfast they always had on Saturdays. Diane put a wrist to her forehead. God, she was sweating. In the lounge room, Harper was lying on the rug in front of the space heater, kicking her legs and playing on her iPad, while Adrian watched car racing on TV.

When she stopped in the doorway and didn't speak, Adrian looked at her.

"Di, what's the matter?" he said.

She tried to smile. "You'll never guess what I just read in the paper."

Adrian muted the TV. She went over and perched on the arm of the couch. He held out his hand but she didn't take it. If she did, she would cry. It occurred to her that she might cry anyway. The intensity of her grief felt shocking. She had believed herself to be made of sterner stuff, yet here she was, a child again. A lost, forlorn, helpless child.

"There's a pet cemetery in Melbourne," she said. "It's closing down."

"A pet cemetery? Sorry, I don't follow."

The sob swelled and ached in her throat. She swallowed. Her cheeks burned like a fever. Adrian got up, gathered her to him and sat her down on the couch beside him.

"Tell me," he murmured into her hair. "What's happened?"

233

She swallowed again. No use. She closed her eyes and the tears spilled over. "It's about my dog, Toby. They buried him in a cemetery but I never knew where. I assumed there were dozens of pet cemeteries but there's just one, you see? Just this one and no other. And it's closing."

"Everything's all right," he said.

"I remember they showed me a Polaroid of his grave. A metal plaque on the ground." She wiped away tears and perspiration. "I want his plaque. It has to be there. We have to get Toby's plaque before it's thrown away."

And before *they* get to it first. She didn't say this aloud. Probably didn't need to; Adrian knew about her past, about her childhood. Panic clamoured inside her like a trapped bird.

Adrian stroked her hair, kissed the side of her head. "Okay. We'll visit the cemetery."

She stood up. "Then let's get dressed."

"You mean now? You want to drive to Melbourne right now?"

"I've called the cemetery number and it's disconnected." There was an edge to her voice and she took a breath. "For all we know, the plaques are being chucked into a skip."

Harper, who had come over silently, pressed against Diane and wrapped her arms about Diane's hips. Diane clutched at her daughter, felt Adrian's palm against the small of her back. Fresh tears. Thank God for her little family. *Thank God.*

"Don't be upset, Mummy," Harper said. "You've found your dog. You should be happy."

"Yes," Diane said. "Yes, I should be."

Middle of July, the dead centre of winter. Coats and hats in the back of the station wagon. A hammer and chisel too— Adrian's idea—just in case the plaque had been cemented into the gravestone. She was grateful for her husband's practicality. But once the plaques were retrieved by families or thrown away, what would the council do with the interred bodies of dogs, cats, horses, birds, lizards? Concrete over the top of them and build high-rise apartments? The newspaper article hadn't explained this critical point. What would happen to Toby's body?

Diane usually enjoyed this two-hour drive to the city along the

South Gippsland Highway, with its long stretches of paddocks dotted with cows or sheep, the occasional peek of water from Bass Strait and Port Phillip Bay whenever the road veered towards the coast. Now, hunched in the front passenger seat, she bit her nails. Oh, she could do with a drink.

"Let's play *I Spy*," Harper said.

"Not at the moment, sweetie," Adrian said. "Mummy needs a bit of peace and quiet."

"Is she thinking about Toby?"

"That's right."

"Mummy, are you thinking about Toby?"

Diane glanced around and arranged her lips into a smile. "Yes, I am."

"He was a good dog," Harper said with a nod, for Diane had told her a few stories.

Diane's chin trembled. "Yes, very true," she said, and turned her face to the side window to hide the glisten of unshed tears.

Damn it, was she going to teeter on the brink of tears all bloody day?

The problem, this goddamned vexing problem, was that every memory of Toby was entangled with memories of that house, those people. After running away at sixteen, Diane had slammed the door on that part of her life and refused to give it air. She'd had to forget. By necessity, she'd had to forget Toby as well.

Toby. A stout Golden Labrador.

Pink tongue covered in black spots.

A patch of fur on his back as wiry and dry as broom bristles, no matter how often Diane brushed it.

Puppies had been put in a sack and thrown into the creek, so the old story went. Someone working at a service station had rescued the litter. The Father, taking his car to this particular servo to fill up on petrol, had decided on a whim to take one of the puppies.

Was the story true? Diane didn't know.

What did it matter? She and Toby had grown up together.

The house had backed on to that creek. The two of them used to ramble for hours. Sometimes, they would sit under a tree. They had a favourite tree, a gum with a smooth bark, which she could lean against without fear of camouflaged spiders. Diane used to sing to him, silly songs that she made up, and he would thump his tail on the ground. They would cross the creek at its shallower parts—Diane using stepping stones and logs, Toby splashing through chest-high without a care—and climb the other bank to lie in a field of wild buttercups. She would gaze at the clouds and tell Toby about the various shapes. If she put out her hand, Toby licked her palm.

But long ago, authorities concreted over the creek to make a freeway. Everything there was gone.

"You okay?"

Diane jumped and looked around. Adrian took his eyes off the road to gaze at her for a moment.

"I'm fine," she said. "Or maybe not."

"Yeah, I know."

She bit at her thumbnail. "What if we can't find his plaque?"

"Well, at least he'll know we tried."

She had to turn her face again. Agnostic, she never gave much thought to heaven, but if she happened to die tomorrow, she hoped Toby would be waiting for her. There would be no one else. If Toby wasn't in heaven, she would enter the place alone. The dreaded sensation flooded through her again: that of a lost, forlorn, helpless child. *Stop, stop, stop. I'm thirty-eight years old,* she told herself. *I am a good wife, good mother. The past is done.*

But if she wanted Toby back, she *couldn't* stop.

He used to sleep outside, on the front step. In the mornings when they let him in, he would run through the house to find her. They played the *Snuffle Game*, a kind of playful wrestle that always ended with her lying on her back and his front paws pinning her to the floor by her hair. He would lick her face while she screamed with laughter.

That house. The off-white carpet, brown wallpaper, stink of cigarette smoke—

"Don't think about them," Adrian said, as if reading her mind. "Just think about Toby."

Rain started up. The windscreen wipers came on.

"Did we bring umbrellas, Mummy?"

Shit. "No, we didn't," Diane said. "Sorry. Mummy forgot."

Adrian said, "It might not be raining in Melbourne. We're still an hour away."

"Oh, it doesn't matter to me," Harper said. "I don't mind getting rained on for Toby."

Diane's heart cramped a little. Twisting in the seat, she said, "Harper, I told you about that time when Toby saved my life, didn't I?"

"From the other dogs?" Harper nodded vigorously. "Yeah. Let's play *I Spy.*"

"Not yet, sweetie," Adrian said. "Di, we've got to stop somewhere for lunch."

"Can it be quick?"

"How about sausage rolls from a bakery? We can eat in the car." He patted Diane's thigh and put his hand back on the steering wheel. "So, how big is this cemetery?"

"I don't know. Not that big, by the look of the photo. Maybe the size of a house block? It's been around since the 1950s."

"There might be a map," he said. "Well, here's hoping, anyway."

"It'll be like a treasure hunt," Harper said. "And Toby's the treasure."

Diane closed her eyes for a moment. "Put the radio on. Christ, I need a distraction."

"Aw, can't we play *I Spy*?" Harper whined. "Daddy promised."

"Okay." Diane sighed, put her hand on the nape of Adrian's neck. Her muscles ached from tension. She felt very tired. "You go first, Harper."

"No, this can't be right," Diane said.

"GPS reckons different," Adrian said. "We're almost there."

He was threading the car along a street pocked with traffic islands and speed humps, crowded on both sides by two-storey houses and landscaped gardens.

"Why would anyone build a pet cemetery in the middle of suburbia?" Diane said.

"Back in the fifties, this whole area would have been empty fields."

"Oh yes, of course." She slumped back in the seat. "Things always change."

"Are we there yet?" And then Harper squealed, "Daddy, there it is!"

He braked. "Are you sure?"

"I can read, can't I? Turn around, Daddy. Turn the car around!"

He did. The sign read PET MEMORIAL GARDENS. Adrian parked on the other side of the road and cut the engine. Diane's stomach flipped. Ever since her husband had mentioned it, she'd been worrying about overlooking Toby's plaque. She imagined herself as if in a movie, giving up and returning to the car, only for the camera to zoom in on the plaque not a metre away, the cinematic score swelling into its sad refrain...

Oh please, she thought. *Just let me have this. Please let me have this one, small thing.*

They got out of the car. The wind had a cold bite. They pulled on coats and beanies. Harper, in the middle, held both their hands while they crossed the road. Diane had expected some kind of grand entrance, perhaps a pair of giant metal gates, but it was a scrubby dirt track leading into an overgrown paddock with trees, weeds, and hundreds of plaques.

"Looks like nobody's been here in years," Adrian said. "Where's the gardener?"

"I guess there isn't one," Diane said. "Toby's full name is on the plaque: *Toby Mulligan.*"

Harper scampered ahead, stopping to lean over the plaques. "Mitzi," she read. "Blackie. Gus. Pumpkin." She turned to them. "Why would you call your pet a pumpkin?"

Adrian wandered off, looking this way and that. Diane knew he was sizing up the place, devising a plan. Meanwhile, she had frozen to the spot. When Harper had let go of her hand, Diane had experienced a kind of paralysis, a heart rate so high she feared a panic attack. Adrian came back, frowning. It took the air out of her, the strength.

"What is it?" she said. "What's wrong?"

"This place is massive," he said, and pointed behind him. "It goes all the way out the back, maybe another two or three house blocks. Honey, there's probably thousands of graves here."

Her chest ached. "We'll never find him, will we?"

"How do you spell Toby?" Harper called.

Could it be…? Could her daughter have actually…? Diane's heart lurched.

Harper continued, "Does it end in 'i' and 'e'?"

"No," Diane called, exhaling in a long, shaky rush. "In a 'y'."

"Gee, there's so many animals named Prince," Harper yelled. "I've found three already."

Adrian took Diane's hand. "What year did Toby die?"

"Oh, I'm not sure. Early nineties. Maybe '93 or '94? I can't remember."

He had been hit by a car. The driver had read the address on Toby's collar and brought him home. *I'm sorry. He stepped right out in front of me. I couldn't stop in time.* Toby lying on his side in the back yard, in the dark, on one of his blankets. He seemed asleep. They wouldn't let Diane touch him. She wanted to rub his soft ears between her fingertips one last time but they wouldn't let her.

"All right," Adrian said, hefting the hammer and chisel in his fist. "The graves are laid out in decades, more or less." He shouted to Harper, "Look for dates that are nineteen-ninety-something, okay sweetie?"

"Okay, Daddy."

Diane stood and watched them. Harper darted from one plaque to another at random. Adrian marched in lines. He must be checking and extrapolating, making educated guesses like the mathematician he was. He taught *Methods* to seniors in high school. If there was a pattern in this overgrown mess, he would find it. And Diane would…

Try to move?

Take a step?

Instead, she gazed down.

Cass 2003–2014. Thanks for all the joy you gave.

Knuckles Lansky. Our gorgeous little girl. Rest in peace.

Mandy 2000–2008. In loving memory.

Tears blurred her vision. So much loss here. So much pain. She nudged a plaque with her toe and it shifted with a gritty, grating sound. No need for the hammer and chisel.

She turned and yelled, "Adrian! The plaques are sitting loose on top of the cement blocks!"

He waved in return and kept searching. She pushed the plaque back into position. The freezing wind picked up her hair and whipped it about her face. She closed her eyes. Focus. She had to focus for Toby.

She began to walk along the ragged rows, scanning for dates. Some of the graves had a photograph of the pet above the epitaph. Adrian was right: in the main, the graves were laid out in decades. But every now and then, a pet from a completely different decade would appear. They seemed to be birds, mostly, or hamsters: animals small enough to be slotted randomly into an empty spot. So, theoretically, Toby could be anywhere. Literally *anywhere*.

Why didn't this bloody place have a map?

She kept an eye on Harper. Still darting. The girl was a bundle of energy. Harper had never questioned the lack of family on Diane's side. Perhaps it was because Adrian's family was so ridiculously large that birthdays and Christmases felt full to Harper. Parents, siblings, aunts, uncles, cousins; even his grandparents were still alive, for Christ's sake. Or maybe she understood and quietly accepted that Diane was alone. Possibly. One day, Diane would tell her the truth. But later. When Harper would be old enough, mature enough, to process the information.

Chloe. Beloved Dalmatian.

Mr Sox. 1971–1982. Best cat ever.

Tibsy. Sadly missed. 1970–1978.

After leaving home, Diane had decided never to marry and never to have kids. No, not *decided*, exactly… She had known in her heart that these options were closed to her. She'd had flings, boyfriends, nothing serious. And then, at 26, she had met Adrian at a party. And two years later, had married him. One year after that, conceived Harper. It felt like a miracle.

Harper came running over, cheeks red and chapped.

"Sweetie," Diane said. "Are you getting too cold?"

"There's graves buried under dirt and leaves."

"What? You mean the graves are buried? Well, of course they're buried, sweetie."

"No, buried under the trees," Harper said, and took her hand. "Come and look."

At the foot of a eucalypt, years and years had covered the graves and their plaques in detritus, the earth itself swallowing them up. Oh, shit. Toby could be hidden *anywhere*. Panting, Diane scraped and kicked the dirt aside. Here was another row of plaques.

Buster O'Connell 1962.

Lizzie, my special mate, till we meet again.

Brutus 1959–1964. Forever in our hearts.

"I'm off to tell Daddy," Harper said, and sprinted away.

Diane checked her watch. Shit, they'd been here some two hours already. Where in God's name were the plaques for the nineties? She staggered about, moving in pointless circles. Over the far side of the cemetery, Adrian and Harper consulted. Tears rose. What had Diane ever done to deserve them? She glanced up. Grey clouds knitted together, threatening hail. They couldn't stay out here much longer. She crossed to another section.

Ben 1998–2001.

Rusty. Pawprints on my heart.

In loving memory of Martha Van Fleet, the cutest budgie, 1995–1999.

Wrong section. Shit, why didn't the layout of this place make any sense?

She remembered when she had told Harper about Toby's heroic act. Diane had had too much to drink that day. They'd been at a barbecue, a soiree at the house of one of Adrian's workmates, and there had been a Golden Labrador. Diane had spent most of the time drinking and patting Goldie, crooning and whispering to the dog. At home, hammered, she had told Harper the story.

It went like this.

The Mother used to pick up Diane from primary school, walking Toby on a leash. The Mother had a friend, a cheery and fat old woman, whose son was a bully. In fact, he liked to bully Diane. This meant that Diane walked far ahead of them, alone, singing to herself. Composing made-up songs which she would sing later to Toby while they sat under a tree.

Beware, beware, it's Mole
And he lives in a hole,
But he's never found
Because he lives underground…

The way home passed a slate and tile business, enclosed with cyclone fencing, protected by German Shepherds, a couple of dumb dogs that blustered at the gate and barked for no good reason. This one day, this singular and crystal-clear day, the gate stood open.

The German Shepherds bolted at her. Slavering, growling, snouts pulled back.

For a split second, Diane considered fleeing. To where? The dogs were too fast. She dropped her school bag and faced them. *So, this is it.* Here was Fate. In a way, she didn't care. She didn't matter anyway.

Toby flew at those dogs like a bat out of hell.

All teeth, all snarls, hackles raised. Snapping, gnashing at ears and cheeks, ripping and tearing, a whirling dervish, shaking the German Shepherds as they yelped and yowled.

Never before, *never*, had she seen this side of portly, docile Toby.

And when the German Shepherds, whimpering, turned tail and limped back through the open gate, Toby became himself again, grinning his doggy smile, polka-dot tongue lolling. He hobbled over to her. Blood. Blood over his face and back. The German Shepherds had bitten him. Toby didn't mind. His tail wagged. Diane dropped to her knees and hugged him, crying into his fur. (Later, she found out that the Mother's friend, the cheery and fat old woman with the bully for a son, had unclipped Toby's leash the moment the German Shepherds had run loose.) Toby strutted the rest of the way home. There was no other way to describe it. *Strutted.* Diane made him a medal out of cardboard and he seemed to like it, even though she knew Toby couldn't read.

"How do you spell Toby again?" Harper called.

Adrian answered, "With a 'y' on the end."

Diane shook herself, checked her watch. Four hours. Shit, they'd been here *four hours*. The light was fading. Her fingers were numb from the cold.

Lassie. If I could have saved you, you would have lived forever.

Love you Bear! 1982–1990.

Ellie Packer. My faithful companion. Died 12 November 1988.

She strained to remember the black-and-white Polaroid of Toby's plaque. His full name, *Toby Mulligan*, and a date. Diane couldn't recall the details. The Mother had put the Polaroid in front of her for only a couple of seconds. When Diane had reached out for it, to touch it, the Mother had whisked the photograph away. So, the Parents had given him a proper burial in a proper cemetery, not just a hole dug in the back yard, and Diane had been grateful. The Father and Mother had loved Toby too, but that dog had given his whole heart to Diane.

Spurred, she kicked at the dirt under so many gums. Her leg muscles burned. After a while, Adrian came over. Diane saw defeat in his shoulders. The movie reel flashed before her eyes: the giving up, the camera focusing on Toby's plaque as the heroine walks away…

"I don't think he's here," Adrian said. "I've checked systematically."

She looked around. Dusk was falling. Harper came over, pale and pinched.

"I need the toilet," Harper said.

Diane's throat ached. So, there would be no fairy-tale ending. *Where are you?* she had begged Toby, again and again. He hadn't answered. Maybe that, in itself, was an answer. Maybe it meant that her shitty childhood could lie dormant in her mind again. Yes, that made sense. It made perfect sense, yet Diane still felt dejected, gutted, exhausted.

"Let's go home," she said.

"Hang on a minute," Adrian said, and turned to Harper. "Can you hang on, sweetie?"

"Um, I guess…"

"Forget it," Diane said. "We tried, didn't we? Toby knows we tried."

Adrian wanted to keep looking. That was one of the things she loved about him: that tenacious attitude. *Never say die.* Harper slipped her hand inside Diane's.

"I'm sorry, sweetie," Diane said. "You must be worn out."

"Mummy, I tried to find Toby for you but I just couldn't."

"That's okay. Adrian? Come on. It's cold and getting dark."

He was doubled over beneath some kind of waxy-leafed bush. "I've found him."

"What?"

"I've found him."

Diane's heart stopped. "No. You haven't."

Adrian glanced around, his face alive. "Toby Mulligan? That's his name, right?"

It was too much to expect. This was a mistake. A cruel mistake. A lifting of hope and a dashing of hope. Diane's mouth dried out. Harper let go of Diane's hand and scampered over.

"Oh Daddy, is it really Toby?"

"Toby Mulligan. Yeah, he's here. This is him. Jesus Christ, I've *found* him."

"No." A sob broke from Diane. "No, you haven't."

Adrian ducked from beneath the shrub, grabbed her hand and hauled her over. "Look."

The weathered plaque, about the size of a book, was brown with raised lettering.

> *Toby Mulligan*
> *Our friend*
> *2–4–93*

Diane's sob came out in a rush. "Toby," she croaked. "Oh my God. Oh, Toby."

Adrian picked up the plaque and gave it to her. She clutched it to her chest and wept.

"Good job, Daddy," Harper said, and hugged Adrian. "You did it. You did it!"

"What about his body?" Diane whispered.

Adrian shook his head and laughed. "Nah, I'm not digging him up. No way."

Harper wrapped her arms about Diane's hips. "Toby knows you love him. We've been searching for him all the live-long day. That's proof enough for him, isn't it, Mummy?"

"You're right," Diane said, and managed a smile through her tears. "Yes, that's enough. It's enough for both of us."

Last Visit to Samuel P. Garfield

The Supermax Prison was located between the city and a large town some ninety minutes' drive away. Kilometres of empty paddocks surrounded the prison. That morning, someone had stolen a bulldozer from a roadside construction site and driven it through one of the prison's brick walls. A number of inmates — those who had instigated a riot in anticipation of the bulldozer's appearance — escaped. They had associates waiting in cars to pick them up. Other inmates saw the sudden hole in the wall and took their chances, running out on foot.

Belinda considered these facts as she now knew them. Earlier, when she had driven her battered sedan along the highway towards the town, past the roadwork area and prison, she had seen nothing out of the ordinary. But then again, preoccupied with her thoughts, she wasn't taking much notice. Instead, she had been thinking, *If I get a speeding ticket, too bad*.

Her father, seventy-eight-year old Samuel P. Garfield, was in the town hospital, dying at last. A long time ago, exactly one week prior to his thirty-ninth birthday, a massive heart attack had required the surgical implantation of four coronary stents. From that point on, Samuel expected to die at any moment and lived like there was no tomorrow, his interpretation of that adage being: consequences don't matter. Belinda had been ten when Samuel let go of the lawnmower and dropped, clutching his chest. She still remembered how he used to be. But her brother had been too young. All Todd knew was the deadbeat dad, the drunk. So, Todd didn't love Samuel. Felt obliged to him, perhaps, but hadn't loved him for a while. Belinda had never given up hope that Samuel's old personality might somehow resurrect itself.

Well, too late for that. Samuel was lying in a hospital bed, too weak for surgery, beyond salvation. Apparently, he wouldn't last the day.

Belinda was still about fifteen minutes away. If she hurried, she could make it in five. She pressed the accelerator.

The heart attack had struck overnight. When Todd called her at work, he'd said that Samuel's heart muscle had sustained so much damage that it now resembled a burnt steak. Belinda couldn't believe an emergency doctor would talk in such a crude way, but her brother had been adamant. "That's what she told me," Todd said. "I swear to God. As shrivelled as a burnt steak."

Yellowing paddocks lined both sides of the road. The factories on the outskirts of town would be visible soon, over the next few crests. Belinda glanced again at her empty fuel gauge. The car had been running on fumes for the last half hour. Could she reach the hospital without refuelling? Should she take the risk? Up ahead was a service station. It would be just her luck to be filling her car as Samuel took his last breath.

She almost didn't turn in, and then changed her mind.

At the bowser, while the meter ticked, she took her phone from the top pocket of her shirt. A text from her supervisor at the supermarket: *How long will you be? No one can cover your shift. Urgent!!!* Belinda deleted the message, pressing harder than necessary. Let the deli customers wait for their salami and potato salad, for their honey leg ham and skinless goddamned franks.

She heard running feet, two pairs, slapping against the concrete forecourt of the service station, and looked around. The first man was big, some kind of Islander. His mouth hung open and she could hear him wheezing. The other was short and bald. They both wore green trousers and green t-shirts, like hospital scrubs. The Islander pointed at her and both men ran with renewed vigour. Belinda stepped back from her car and put up both hands as if in surrender.

The Islander pulled the nozzle from her tank and threw it to the ground. A drizzle of petrol glugged across the concrete.

"What are you doing?" Belinda said.

The Islander opened the driver's door. "Get the bitch's keys," he said.

The short man shoved her. She fell against the bowser and straightened up. The short man held out his palm and when she didn't respond, he slapped her across the face. The Islander grabbed her arm and shook her. She could feel her middle-age spread jiggling beneath her work shirt, rubbing against the band of her trousers.

"Stop it," she said. "Let go of me."

"Give us ya keys, ya dumb bitch," the Islander said, but let go.

The short man made an impatient huffing sound and reached into her trouser pockets. His fingers felt hot and damp through the pocket linings. He tossed her keys to the Islander and raced around the front of the car. Both of them jumped in. Belinda realised that her handbag was on the passenger seat.

"My bag," she shouted. "Hey, wait a second, that's my car." She hit at the driver's side window. "That's my car!"

The Islander started the engine. She watched her old sedan peel out of the service station. The fuel cap was still open. When the car drove off the kerb and bounced onto the road, skidding, a small amount of petrol lapped out.

Belinda pressed a hand to her face where the short man had hit her.

For a moment, she couldn't decide what to do.

She looked around the service station forecourt. There was only a dual-cab ute parked in one of the bays. Nobody was in it. Movement caught her eye. Sprinting through the dry grass of the paddock on the other side of the road, parallel to the highway, was another man in a green outfit, legs striding. Followed by another man. And another. A siren started up in the distance, the kind with an old-fashioned yawning sound, like an air-raid siren.

Belinda veered towards the glass doors of the service station's building, arms held out as if blind. The automatic doors opened. The air wafted cool over her burning face. A slow and melancholy Cyndi Lauper song murmured from the ceiling speakers. Belinda made it past the bank of fridges, past the magazine racks, intermittently holding onto shelves so that she wouldn't lose her balance. It felt as if she were pitching about on a boat in rough chop. She had never fainted before. This is what coming close to fainting must feel like, she decided.

Up ahead, behind the counter, she could just see the attendant's face. He was an older man with heavy jowls and a high forehead crowned with tufts of white hair sticking out at crazy angles. She groped her way nearer to him.

"Please help," she called out. "My car's been stolen. I've been attacked."

The attendant didn't respond. He watched her approach, his eyes wide, jaw slack. Heavily, she leaned her forearms on the counter. The attendant was slouched in a swivel chair. He wasn't looking at her after all. Frowning, his gaze was fixed at the other end of the store. His nametag read CLIVE.

"Clive, did you hear me?" she said. "They stole my car and my handbag. They hit me across the face."

"I reckon he's having a heart attack," said a voice.

She spun around.

Back there by the fridges stood a man, perhaps in his thirties, with pale skin and long arms hanging loose at his sides. Very tall and thin, he wore jeans and a blue checked shirt. His wavy, collar-length hair was an intense orange, the colour of carrots. Belinda hadn't seen him when she'd come inside. The shelving was chest-high on her and she was only five feet tall. So, the man had been squatting down? Hiding? Or, she reasoned, he had just now entered the store. She looked out the floor-to-ceiling windows. No vehicles apart from the ute. He must have walked here.

The red-haired man said, "It's a heart attack."

"Heart attack?" she said, and remembered Samuel P. Garfield.

Red lifted one arm in a lazy, casual gesture. "Well, shit. Have a squiz at the poor bastard. Wouldn't you reckon? Either that or a stroke."

She looked at Clive. His gaze crawled across the distance to meet her eyes. He panted shallow breaths. The skin around his mouth appeared waxy and yellow.

"Are you all right?" she said. "Do you feel unwell?"

Clive kept panting.

"It's a heart attack for sure," said the other man, very close, right at her ear, and Belinda jumped. Red had approached, cat-footed, and now stood by her elbow.

"Have you called an ambulance?" she said.

Red shrugged. "The emergency lines are gonna be swamped."

His eyelashes were so pale as to be non-existent, his irises a washed-out shade of green. Belinda regarded Clive, thought of Samuel P. Garfield dying in his bed waiting on her last goodbye, and pulled out her phone.

"It's no use," Red said.

She dialled triple zero. A recorded female voice, bright and warm, said, "All our emergency operators are busy. Please hold the line—" Belinda hung up.

"My father—" she began.

"There's been a breakout," Red said.

"What?"

"A breakout." Red lifted his apathetic arm to indicate the window. "Up the road at the Supermax. A bunch of prisoners got out."

She thought of the short man who had slapped her, the Islander who had shaken her, their green uniforms, the other men running pell-mell through the dry grass.

"Got out how?" she said.

Red shrugged. "Somebody drove a bulldozer through the wall, so I heard."

"Heard how?"

With a half-smile, Red indicated the ceiling. "From the radio."

Above, Cyndi Lauper crooned on. Belinda gazed around the mart and spotted the dual-cab ute through the window.

"Is that your ute?" she said.

"Nah," Red said. "I got carjacked too."

She turned to the attendant. "Clive, is it yours? We need your car keys. To get you to hospital, we need your keys."

Clive kept staring. A line of spittle bubbled at his mouth.

"Waste of time," Red said.

Belinda put both hands to her temples. More sirens screamed.

A whisk of police cars flew past, lights red and blue, red and blue, red and blue.

"Oh my God," Belinda said. "What are we doing to do?"

"It's not my ute," Clive whispered.

Belinda jolted. His unexpected response felt like a dash of cold water. "You must have a car," she said. "How else did you get to work? Are you parked around the back?"

He shook his head. "My wife dropped me off this morning."

"Then whose ute is that?"

Clive's eyelids fluttered shut. His skin looked like old ham, greenish-grey, the stock that gets binned at the end of the week. Belinda wondered if Samuel P. Garfield was right at this minute turning the exact same colour.

"The ute belongs to Mario," Clive said. "One of our delivery men."

"Bullshit," Red said. "They use refrigerated trucks or else the food goes bad."

"Mario restocks our newspapers."

"Okay, good, now we're making progress," Belinda said. "So, where's Mario?"

"Ask *him*," Clive said, glaring at Red.

"Me?" Red said, and scoffed. "How would I know?"

"Lady, he's got blood on his shirt."

Red's eyebrows raised in surprise. He looked down at his shirt at the same time Belinda did. There was a spatter of stains amongst the blue checks. She stepped back.

"You mean *this* blood?" Red said. "Nah, mate. When I got car-jacked, I punched the bastard and busted his lip. There's nothing more to it than that."

"He's an escapee," Clive whispered. "From the jail."

"Me?" Red said. "Come off it."

"Clive, are you telling me you actually *saw* him attack Mario?"

When Clive didn't answer, Red said, "You know what I think? *He's* the escapee. Now the excitement's given him a heart attack. Now he's too crook to leave under his own steam."

Belinda looked from one man to the other. "Well, maybe you're both escapees."

"Or maybe neither of us are," Red said, "and we're all just getting a little paranoid."

Belinda's mobile rang. It was Todd.

"Where the hell are you?" Todd said. "The old man is on his way out."

"I'm stuck at a service station. There's been a prison break and my car got stolen."

"You're *what*?"

"I know, it's crazy, but I can't get out of here."

"Then ring a cab," Todd said, and hung up.

Good idea. She thumbed buttons.

"Who are you calling?" Red said.

"A taxi."

"Sweet. We can skip out and leave Mr Chain Gang for the cops."

Belinda shook her head. "No, the three of us are going together. If Clive is having a heart attack, I'm not leaving him here to die."

"Well, okay, but it's your funeral."

"Don't be ridiculous. He's hardly dangerous in that condition."

Red shrugged. "You never know. He could have a weapon."

Belinda hesitated. "A weapon…?"

The call picked up to a recorded message. "Thank you for choosing Woodson Taxi Service. We're experiencing high demand. Your call is in a queue. An operator should answer your call in…*fifty*…minutes."

Belinda hung up.

A fresh wave of emergency vehicles, sirens wailing and lights flashing, whizzed past the service station.

Oh Samuel, I'm sorry, Belinda thought.

The last time she had visited him in his apartment at the retirement village, he had been drunk, his knee banged up and bruised a deep, violent purple. *How on earth did you do that to yourself?* she had said. Samuel didn't realise what she was talking about until she pointed out his injury. Shaking his head and laughing, he had said, *How the bloody hell would I know? Shit tends to happen on the odd occasion.*

Might this be her final memory?

She must get to the hospital and tell him goodbye, tell him that she loves him, forgives him. Could she jog all the way there? She was forty-nine years old and overweight. Hadn't exercised since high school. If she tried to jog, she'd probably have a heart attack too. She raked a hand through her hair. Okay, if she went outside, tried to flag down a police car, would that be a dumb thing to do? Would it?

"Give me your phone," Red said. "I'll call some people."

Clive sat up. "Don't do it. He'll summon his cronies."

"Summon my *what*? Shit. Lady, you want to get out of here or not?"

Red had a cartoonish look on his face, a larger-than-life grin, eyes popped wide, a parody of innocence. It reminded her of Todd when he'd been a boy. *Todd, did you eat my Easter chocolates? No, sis', I'd never do something mean like that.* Belinda wasn't skilled at reading people, but her gut told her that Red might be lying.

She held the mobile behind her back. "Who do you want to call?"

"Some people to come get us. A couple of mates."

"Don't trust him," Clive said.

Red snorted. "Listen, if I was a bad guy, I'd have snatched the phone away from you by now, wouldn't I?"

Valid point. She was about to hand him her mobile when it rang.

Todd again. "You'd better hurry. The hospital's going into lock-down."

"Can't you pick me up?" she said. "I'm at the servo on the city side of town."

"You want me to leave Dad?"

She thought of the times that Todd had forgotten Father's Day and Samuel's birthday, how rarely he'd visited the retirement village, and her temper started to rise.

"Please," she said through her teeth. "I'm stuck."

"You want me to go out on the roads, are you crazy? Don't you know what's happened? The convicts that organised the riot and the jailbreak were picked up in cars. The rest are running for it. The town is crawling with fugitives. People are getting pulled out of their vehicles left, right and centre by these bastards."

"Todd, it'll be a half-hour round trip for you."

"No way, forget it."

"Get stuffed then!" she said, and hung up. She should have known better. Todd cared only about himself. She tightened her jaw to stop the tears.

Red held out his hand. "Give me your phone."

"Don't do it, lady."

Red rapped the counter with his knuckles. "Okay, where's *your* mobile phone, Clive? Why aren't *you* ringing anybody? Answer me *that*."

Another valid point. Belinda looked from one man to the other, waiting.

Clive said nothing. He rubbed his breastbone. The gesture reminded her of the day Samuel had stopped the lawnmower to grimace and press at his ribcage.

"Excuse me, I'm going to be sick," she muttered.

The door marked TOILET UNISEX was at the rear of the store. She walked carefully, holding onto shelving units. She opened the door.

With a cry, she brought both hands to her mouth.

The man's body, naked except for underwear, socks and shoes, lay wedged between the toilet and the wall. He had closely shaved hair and a staved-in skull. The concave depression on the side of his head had most likely been made by the fire extinguisher sitting discarded in the basin.

Mario.

Over her initial shock, Belinda held her breath and leaned closer.

The skin of his cratered scalp was bruised but unbroken. There was no blood. She went to press fingers to his throat to check for a pulse but in the next moment understood that it wasn't necessary. Bile and stomach acids rose. She had to step over Mario's legs to get to the toilet. By accident, one of her shoes dragged lightly across his shin, and she jumped at the contact. Dry heaving, she bent over the toilet bowl.

At the bottom of the clear water lay a set of car keys.

The urge to vomit left her.

Mario had been attacked in here. His keys had dropped into the bowl. The assailant hadn't thought to check the toilet.

But was the assailant Clive or Red?

One of them had discarded their prison greens and stolen Mario's clothes. Clive had pointed out the blood on Red's shirt, but the blood had not come from Mario after all. Therefore, Clive's use of a false clue would suggest that he was the escapee... wouldn't it? Or perhaps both of them were innocent and someone else, long gone, had killed this man. Belinda trembled and her head pounded.

There was no way to retrieve the keys other than by hand. Repulsed, she dipped her fingers quickly into the cold water and grabbed them. She wanted to wash with soap, but doing so would mean lifting the fire extinguisher from the basin, which would foul the crime scene for police. Instead, she dried her hand on the back of her trousers. The silver ring of keys sat cold in her palm. Now, she had the means to get to the hospital. It was awful, but still...*thank God*. She left the toilet.

Standing next to Red was a stranger.

Like Mario, the stranger—a man—wore only briefs, socks and sneakers. He was heavily muscled with a tattoo sleeve along one arm.

"Hi there," he said, and smiled. "Sorry I'm not decent. I got mugged."

"They took his clothes," Red said. "They can't make a getaway in prison greens."

The tattooed man said, "What's that in your hand?"

Belinda put the keys behind her back. "There's a dead man in the bathroom."

Tattoo's face registered shock. Red compressed his lips into an angry grimace.

"It's got to be Mario," Red said. "Clive, you murdering *prick*."

"Mario's dead?" Clive called, his voice a rasping wheeze.

"Yes," Belinda said. "Well, I'm not sure if it's Mario. There's *somebody* dead."

The Cyndi Lauper song had finished, replaced by something peppy and synthesised; a ridiculous contrast. Belinda giggled and sobbed at the same time. She took a few steps. Her knees knocked. She could feel herself starting to break. When she had all three men in sight, she stopped and held out the keys.

"I think these belong to the ute. My father's in hospital and he's very ill. Dying. I'm taking the ute and I'm leaving now. It's not stealing, okay? It's an emergency."

"Beaut," Tattoo said. "We'll catch a lift with you."

Tattoo looked big and scary, like a bruiser. To be honest, like a *jailbird*. At least, Belinda's idea of a jailbird. Was she being prejudiced? Sleeve tattoos were popular amongst young men these days. Young women, too. He was probably a personal trainer. She read the papers, the critiques on Millennials; she knew that almost everyone on Instagram was either a tattooed personal trainer or a diet guru. Bottle-blonde women with washboard abs tugging at their bikini bottoms, men with beards and man buns flexing their biceps—

Turning the keys over in her hand, she noticed the ID tag: NICHOLAS FLYNN.

Good God.

Shaking, holding up the keys, she yelled, "Clive, his name isn't Mario."

Clive rolled his eyes. "It's a nickname."

"Dirty bastard," Red said. "I told you he was suss from the get-go."

Belinda marched along the aisle towards the counter, keys held aloft, heart booming. "Go on, Clive, tell me Mario's real name." She slammed down the keys and leaned on the counter. "Well? I'm waiting. Tell me."

Clive shook his head and worked his lips silently for a few seconds. Then he whispered, "I called him Mario. He called me Luigi."

"What?"

"It's a game. Mario and Luigi."

"A game? I don't understand."

"Forget it," said a voice, and Belinda jumped.

Red had snuck up on her again. He closed one hand gently around her elbow, the other over the keys on the counter.

"We should get out of here," he said. "Your dad needs you."

She nodded, exhausted, and allowed Red to turn her around. He put his arm about her shoulders and steered her down the aisle towards the glass doors. The music had changed again to a sad Crowded House song. If Red had a jacket, she was sure he would be placing it around her shoulders right about now. The corny thought made her laugh. Then the image of Clive wielding the fire extinguisher and bringing it down on Nicholas Flynn's head made her feel ill and faint.

"Is she okay?" Tattoo said.

"Just a little shook up," Red said. "Like all of us."

"Fair enough, let's go," Tattoo said.

The automatic doors opened. The fresh air revived her.

Red helped Belinda into the back seat of the ute. She permitted herself the luxury of crying for a moment, shedding only a few tears. *Samuel, I'm almost there,* she thought. *Hold on. Please hold on.* Fumbling, she clipped the seatbelt.

The engine started up. The radio was playing the same Crowded House song. The ute began to move. Belinda opened her eyes. Red was behind the wheel, Tattoo in the front passenger seat. Red turned right towards town. They drove in silence for a time. On the other side of the road, a conga line of emergency vehicles whipped by, fast enough for air turbulence to rock the ute.

Of all the days for a prison break...

Upon reflection, however, it seemed apt. Almost funny. Samuel P. Garfield had long been chaos personified. Belinda smiled and felt better.

"If you continue along this road," she said, "the hospital is first left after the roundabout."

"Got it," Red said.

Tattoo twisted around and smiled, his hand out. He had kind eyes. "Can I borrow your mobile?"

"Of course," she said, and put it in his palm. "Your family must be worried sick."

Tattoo threw the phone out the window.

"Hey!" Belinda sat up and clutched the front seats. "What the hell?"

Red took the roundabout at a slow, measured speed. The grey

brick of the hospital loomed large.

"There!" Belinda cried, pointing, voice cracking. "Take the next turn-off."

The men didn't seem to hear her.

"You got any friends nearby?" Tattoo said.

"Only back in Melbourne," Red said.

"Nah, there'll be coppers on every road. I know a place in Warrnambool."

The hospital flew past. Belinda clawed at the window and tried to open it, tried to open the door. Everything was locked.

"Let me out," she begged.

Tattoo propped his elbow on the centre console and showed her a pocketknife. The blade looked small in his giant hand. Stunned, Belinda sat back, interlaced her fingers, put her clasped hands in her lap. She could almost hear Samuel's familiar rebuke: *Hell's bells, girl, you're even stupider than you look.*

Red glanced back. "You know, I thought you'd be shitting yourself by now," he said, and nodded at Tattoo's knife as if it had slipped Belinda's mind.

"Please let me out," she said. "Please. I won't tell anybody."

"Nah, sorry," Red said. "If push comes to shove, you're our bargaining chip."

Her eyes filled with hot tears.

Tattoo, gazing back at her, looked sheepish, almost apologetic. He folded the knife and tucked it inside his sneaker. "We're not hard cases, all right?" he said after a while. "Take it easy. We're not going to hurt you. Are we, Lyndon?"

Red didn't answer.

"Lyndon?" Tattoo continued. "We're not going to hurt her, are we?"

Belinda slumped back in the seat and considered the facts as she now knew them.

That morning, someone had stolen a bulldozer from a roadside construction site and driven it through one of the prison's high brick walls. A number of inmates—those who had instigated a riot in anticipation of the bulldozer's appearance—escaped. They had associates waiting in cars to pick them up. Other inmates saw the sudden hole in the wall and took their chances, running out on foot.

Would she die today, on the very same day as her father, Samuel P. Garfield?

Yes, Belinda decided.

Yes, it seemed more than likely that she would.

November 9th 1989

With most of the staff doing rounds, the tearoom on the Psych Ward lay empty. Dr Ian Webb took a seat near the window, sipped his takeaway coffee, and opened the manila folder. The first page, a referral letter from the ER department downstairs, began:

> Dear On-Call Neurologist,
> Please assess Mrs Leah Moore, aged 46yrs 2mths,
> for sudden-onset recurring hallucinations.

Ian scanned down the page. Mrs Leah Moore had self-presented via taxi to the ER yesterday afternoon, conscious and lucid. The initial examination had found no regular medications, pre-existing conditions, acute illnesses or infections that could account for hallucinations described as "full sensory".

Interesting. So, *every* sense was involved. Sight, sound, touch, taste, smell. Perhaps even proprioception, the spatial awareness of one's own body? Ian rubbed a forefinger back and forth over his moustache and read on.

Patient reported no recreational drug use. Blood tests normal. A CT scan taken last night had shown what appeared to be a calcified area in the left temporal lobe. *Aha*, Ian thought, *now we're getting somewhere*. This morning's MRI images suggested the small, high-signal-intensity area may well be an angioma. He sighed and nodded. Well, yes, a bundle of abnormally dilated blood vessels could wreak all kinds of havoc on the brain.

He flipped the manila folder closed.

Once, in his salad days, something rare like this would have filled him with adrenaline, curiosity, joy. He used to be such a pain in the arse at dinner parties. Yabbering about interesting cases to anyone who would listen. Back then, his wife Felicity had thought his enthusiasm quite charming. For many years, he had kept detailed notes, intending to write a book on the more fascinating neurological disorders he had encountered. About a decade ago, he couldn't remember exactly when, he had stopped keeping notes. The archive box of handwritten pages was kicking around somewhere. In the garage, probably.

Ian faced the windows to finish his coffee. The leaves of the red Japanese maples flamed bright and cheery. He wished he were outdoors in his garden this week instead of consulting. His chrysanthemums may have aphids by now, and the rose beds needed preparation. *God knows, Felicity wouldn't perform these duties.* Besides, he hadn't slept very well last night. In fact, he hadn't slept well for a long time. A challenging case required heart and gusto, and today, Ian didn't feel much of either.

The patient, Mrs Leah Moore, was in a two-bed suite a few metres down the hall. The other bed was empty. Good. Ian despised talking to patients in front of bystanders. Mrs Moore, sitting up against a few pillows, happened to be staring at the maples outside her window with the kind of longing that suggested she, too, wished she were outside instead of cooped up within a hospital. She looked around at his footsteps. An attractive, middle-aged woman, clear-eyed, thin, with greying hair loose about her shoulders, no make-up.

"Hello there," she said. "I'm Leah. You must be the neurologist."

"That's right. Dr Ian Webb. Please call me Ian."

He shook Leah's hand and pulled up the visitor's chair to sit down. She gazed at him, serene, the corners of her mouth lifted. Unusual. Patients with sudden neurological problems were, as a rule, disoriented, agitated, distressed. But she might not be as lucid as she seemed.

"How are you feeling today?" he said.

"Fine, thank you."

"Good," he said. "Do family members know you're here?"

"My brother does, yes."

Ian consulted the referral letter. "But not your husband?"

"I'm divorced. And my ex wouldn't be in the least bit interested."

The patient seemed coherent, at least enough to answer simple, direct questions. Ian closed the manila folder. "They tell me you've been experiencing hallucinations. For how long?"

"A few days. Maybe weeks."

"Weeks? And you've waited all this time before seeking medical attention?"

Leah shrugged. "I thought I was *remembering*. Sometimes an episode from your past simply pops into your head, don't you find? And it's such a lovely memory. I didn't mind revisiting it." She smiled, just enough to show dimples in her cheeks. "Turns out the memory was revisiting me, instead. I didn't understand the distinction. Not at first."

"Ah. Precisely when did you understand the distinction?"

"When the memory became real."

Ian crossed his legs. Hallucinosis, perhaps; a common disorder of perception in alcoholics. Yet Leah's blood and liver function tests had been normal.

Ian said, "The memory became real to you?"

"Yes."

"Real in what way, exactly?"

"Why, in every way you can think of." Leah gestured about the room with open palms. "As real as everything around us. As real as you and me sitting here together."

Ian nodded. Leaning over, he grabbed her chart from the end of the bed and checked the medication schedule for tranquillisers, opioids, beta-blockers. Nothing of the kind. Interesting. Leah was stone-cold sober. Poised, calm within herself. He replaced the chart.

"That's fine," he said. "Please tell me about your hallucination. If you wouldn't mind."

She settled back against the pillows and clasped her fingers together to rest her hands against the bed linen, the very picture of tranquillity. This gave him the creeps. Such incongruence… Perhaps she was having a transient ischaemic attack? He pulled the chair closer to the bedside. Her face had symmetry and appeared to be perfectly functional; no drooping of one side characteristic of a stroke. If Ian were twenty years younger, he'd be jumping in his chair right about now, thrilled at the novelty of the case. As it was, he felt a strange, pervasive kind of unease. He almost wished the empty bed on the other side of the room was occupied.

"It's about a boy," Leah said. "A young man I fell in love with a long time ago."

Ian took the pen from his coat pocket and began taking notes. "Go on, please."

"We're at the train station. On the platform. And we're saying goodbye. We only have a few minutes before my train arrives. A few minutes together that have to last a lifetime."

"Because you might not see him again?"

"Never ever again."

Ian looked up from his notes. Tears glistened in Leah's eyes. Her face looked drawn and haunted, so terribly grief-stricken. The uneasiness left him in a rush, replaced by shame. How on earth could he harbour such an unprofessional feeling as *unease* towards a patient?

"It's all right," he said, patting her arm. "So, this hallucination is based on a real event."

She nodded.

"That's fine," he said, "Please tell me what actually happened."

She managed to laugh. "Goodness gracious. Where do I start?"

He offered an encouraging smile. "At the beginning?"

"I'll try." She wiped her wet eyelashes and took a deep, steadying breath. "When I was eighteen years old and just out of high school, my grandfather died. He left us some money. Paul, my older brother, convinced me to go backpacking with him around Europe."

"Ah yes, of course," Ian said, and guffawed despite himself. "Backpacking around Europe. That used to be the rite of passage for most young Australians way back when."

264

Ian had crossed the pond, too. Not after high school, no—he'd had some twelve years of med school to slog through first—but immediately after finishing his internship, at the age of thirty, he'd thrown in his apartment lease, sold his Honda Civic, and spent most of his money on a plane ticket. While travelling, he'd had barely two cents to rub together. Could only afford to visit Southern Europe, used to free-camp on roadsides, some days eat just one cheap meal in order to save for a bus trip, a rail ticket, the occasional stay in a *pensione* to enjoy a mattress, a bath, the security of a locked door. Every day an adventure. He'd had a full head of hair, dark curly hair worn to his collar, and the kind of big brown eyes that used to attract pretty girls with a single, lingering stare. And now? Well, now he was bald, eyes buried under wrinkled folds. An old man for many years; invisible to pretty girls, naturally. Their indifference had hurt at first. Invisible to women his own age, too. Invisible to Felicity.

"Ian?"

He blinked. Leah was staring at him.

"Apologies," he said, feeling his cheeks redden. "You reminded me of my own European trip. Please continue."

"My brother and I had enough money to travel for two months. Then we went to London and took jobs."

"Is that right? What a coincidence. I lived in London too, for a time."

"Oh, such a wonderful city!" Leah's grin was infectious. "So grey and cold with thousands of awful pigeons, but such a vibrant place. Humming with energy. Don't you think?"

"Oh, absolutely," he said. "That's how I remember it. The perfect description. It looks dead but feels alive. I don't know what the place is like these days, of course…"

"Me neither. Probably just as grey and cold. And still full of pigeons."

They both chuckled. Ian moved his chair closer. "Go on, please."

"Paul and I took a bedsit. It was all we could manage. Goodness, rent was astronomical."

"It certainly was! I rented a bedsit too. A mansion carved up by landlords. On each floor, several rooms had to share a communal kitchen and bathroom."

Leah touched the back of his hand. "Exactly. Oh, how funny. It's like we're twins."

Ian, heart thrumming, strained to remember his old London address. *Bennett Park Mansions*...or was it *Bailey*? Something like that. And the suburb? He couldn't recall. The mansion had been a five-minute walk from the Tube station. Which station? He couldn't remember that, either. On the Tube map he'd kept in his wallet at the time, the line had been coloured silver, hadn't it? Wasn't that the Jubilee line?

Leah was saying, "Paul got a job in a sandwich shop. I signed with a temp agency and ended up in the advertising department of a magazine, cold-calling to sell ad space. We earned next to nothing. The rent alone took most of our pay."

Slumming it. Oh yes, Ian remembered that part very well.

When he had run out of money while travelling—spending his last *Thomas Cook* cheque in Barcelona on a train ticket—he'd fled to London and taken the first job offered to him. A builder's labourer. Hauling bricks, pushing wheelbarrows. He'd been in his physical prime without even trying, without even realising. In bed, pretty girls—nameless girls, a different one every few days—used to run their hands over his lean abdomen, cooing and caressing. He would flex and relax his forearm so that his *pronator teres* and *palmaris longus* muscles would appear to "breathe" in and out, in and out. And yes, that ridiculous and juvenile display certainly got his bed-partners going. But he was a different man now. He had morphed into another person altogether, somehow. Dear God, if thirty-year old medical graduate Ian Webb, he of the tousled locks and the big brown eyes, could see himself now... What would he do? Recoil in horror, that's what. Assuming the younger Ian even recognised himself at all. This morning, while trimming his white moustache, he had glanced into the mirror and, for a moment, saw an old and ugly stranger looking back at him.

"That's where I met Alexander."

Ian said, "I'm sorry, what?"

"I met Alexander in the magazine's advertising department,"

Leah said. "There were six of us in an open-plan office." She wiped a tear from her cheek. "He used to watch me."

"Watch you? In a way that you liked?"

"In a way that I didn't understand. He was English, you see, and I was very naive. More so than other girls my age. I thought he hated my Aussie accent." She smiled. "One of the other women enlightened me; a New Zealander, another temp. When the two of us were having lunch, she told me, 'Alexander wants to jump your bones', and I replied, 'No way'. But I started to pay attention after that."

"And your New Zealand friend turned out to be correct?" Ian said.

"Yes. Soon after, Alexander became my first love. Oh, I'd had a couple of silly boyfriends in high school, but this was something else. This was real."

"I see. First love. A physical relationship?"

Leah picked at the bed sheet. "Not really. Just hugging, kissing. I mean it was the first time I'd ever fallen in love. Alexander was twenty-two. He said he didn't want to rush me. He said it was my decision. That's rare, isn't it? Kind of chivalrous, don't you think?"

Ian recalled *en masse* the dozens of women he'd bedded while in Europe, the blur of their forgotten faces and forgotten names, his lies, his wheedling and cajoling, his curly hair and big brown eyes. He swallowed. "Yes," he said. "It's rare."

"Then the wall came down."

"The wall? You're talking figuratively, I assume. Your own defences came down."

"No. I mean the Berlin Wall."

An electric jolt shot along Ian's spine, forcing him upright in the chair. "What?"

"The Berlin Wall came down."

"And you were in London?" he said. "When it happened?"

Leah nodded.

Goddamn. Ian had seen it live on TV. November 9th 1989. At home in London's Bennett or Bailey Park Mansions, while frying a cheap *poussin* on the stovetop, the tiny television set announcing the news. Shocked, Ian had turned towards the screen and witnessed what he had never expected to see in his lifetime: the reunification of East and West Germany. Another bedsitter at the kitchen table, a melancholic Swede named Filio, had begun crying. For what reason, Ian could no longer recall.

And now, the hairs raised on Ian's arms, up the back of his neck.

"You saw it too," Leah whispered. "While you were in London. Didn't you?"

He nodded, unable to speak.

She said, "Paul told me that we had a chance to be part of history. That we should quit our jobs, let our bedsit go, travel to Germany." She sniffed, tried to smile. "At home, I have a bag of cement chips from the Berlin Wall. At least, they were chips when I collected them. They crumbled into grey dust years ago. But still, how many people get to experience such an important event first-hand? As it's unfolding? Tell me. How many?"

Ian found his voice. "Not many."

"And Paul, well…let's just say he has a persuasive personality." With the flat of both hands, Leah swept away the last of her tears. "We began to save our money. I didn't want to leave Alexander, but what could I do? So, I told myself the sensible thing: it was a holiday romance, a case of puppy love, nothing more."

Leah stopped, froze.

Her complete immobility was shocking. Involuntarily, Ian held his breath.

The absence seizure rolled through her in stages.

He recognised the signs. Hands fell loosely upon the bed linen, mouth dropped open, eyelids flickered, eyes rolled back so that only the whites showed. Interesting. Probable diagnosis: temporal lobe epilepsy triggered by the angioma.

Ian leaned closer, scrutinising her, keeping track on his wrist-watch as the seconds ticked by. Fifteen seconds, twenty… This was an atypical absence seizure. If Leah didn't come out of it within the next thirty seconds, he would hit the alarm. Nursing staff would converge. For the first time in years on the job, he felt galvanised, short of breath, his heart slamming against his ribcage.

Leah came back, suddenly, all of a piece, wide awake as if she'd never been gone.

And with such joy in her face.

Such light.

Ian said, "You were on the train platform with Alexander, weren't you?"

"Yes." She held her clasped hands up to her chin and, for a moment, looked like a girl. "Oh, yes I was there. I was *there*."

"What do you remember?"

"His eyes. His arms around me. The smell of his cologne, the sooty electrical smell of the train station. His lips on mine." She laughed. "And his scratchy vest against my cheek. He likes to wear woollen vests under his jacket. His mother knits them, you know. She lives in Patras. I told you he's half Greek, didn't I? As a joke, I call him Alexander the Great."

"Anything else you can remember? Did you see other people at the station?"

"Plenty. It's a double platform, one train on each side."

"What time is it?" Ian said.

"About nine in the morning. I've spent the night with Alexander. Not the way you might think," she added, "but at his flat all the same. Talking, holding hands. He wants me to stay in London. Asked me to stay. Begged me to stay."

The light disappeared from her face.

Ian said, "Tell me, when you got back to Australia, what did you do with your life?"

She looked out the hospital window for a while, gazing at the flaming red leaves. "Nothing much," she finally said. "I married. Had two children."

"Being a mother is something to be proud of."

"My son drowned in a neighbour's pool when he was three. My daughter overdosed while out celebrating her sixteenth birthday with friends."

"Christ almighty." Ian sat back in the chair. "I'm so very sorry."

"Thank you. Do you have children?"

Yes, an estranged son, who had not spoken to him or Felicity for years. In fact, they didn't even know where Marcus lived any more. That's how many years had elapsed.

"No," Ian said at last. "I don't have any children."

"You have your career," Leah said. "I never had one. I worked part-time in supermarkets, bakeries, department stores, drycleaners. My husband drank and liked to cheat on me. We divorced after our daughter passed."

Ian felt a tightening in his throat. It was a sensation he hadn't felt in a long, long time: the urge to cry. Dear Lord. At what point does a promising future segue into a disappointing present? In his own case, he couldn't say for certain. Perhaps after the last argument with Marcus. Perhaps around the time he had stopped taking notes for his book. After Felicity had moved into the spare room. After Ian had begun to ruminate during sleepless nights over the many choices he had made, after he had begun to second-guess himself, to contemplate the roads he had left untravelled. Had they been better roads? Perhaps. Or perhaps not. Who could ever know? No one could ever know. The contemplation of it might drive you mad.

"I'm not coming back next time," Leah said.

Ian broke from his thoughts.

Leah had her teeth clenched. Unshed tears glittered in her eyes.

"Not coming back?" he said, flustered. "What on earth do you mean?"

"I'm staying."

Ian slid the pen back in his coat pocket and rubbed at his moustache. Leah's defiant gaze didn't waver. "You mean," he said, "that you intend to stay on the train platform?"

"Yes."

He put his hand over hers. She didn't pull away.

"Leah," he whispered. "Listen to me. It's an hallucination. Not time travel."

She shook her head, spilling tears. "You're wrong."

"Leah, please, be reasonable. Time travel? That goes against science. Against nature."

"I don't care."

"Against everything we understand about how the universe works." Ian took her hand in both of his and squeezed it. "We all have regrets. God knows I do. But there's no going back. There are no do-overs. What's done is done."

Leah began to smile. The light came back to her face, even as the tears kept falling. "Let me tell you how the memory ends," she said. "The train pulls up. I kiss Alexander one last time. I get on the train. The doors shut. He's watching me through the windows. I'm watching him. The train begins to pull away. I'm staring into his eyes, staring, staring, trying to burn him into my brain, and you know what? I did. He's there. I can feel him."

"He's not real. Please believe me. Alexander is not real."

"I've finally got another chance," she said. "And I'm taking it."

Another chance.

Ian wanted to go back to November 9th 1989 when he was cooking that *poussin* in the kitchen of Bennett Park Mansions, and Filio was crying. If given another chance, Ian would stay in London. Forget about returning to Australia. He would forge his life in a different direction, get a position at an English hospital, meet and marry another woman, father a child that didn't hate his guts.

"You believe me, don't you?" Leah said.

Ian blinked, his body shivering full-length. "I don't know."

She intertwined her fingers with his. "Come back with me."

"What? How?"

"Don't you want to at least try?"

Ian's throat constricted once more, aching.

Leah sat up in bed, eyes shining. "Here it comes. I can feel it coming over me again."

The manila folder slid from Ian's lap. The pages scattered across the floor. His heart boomed and banged. "Are you sure?" he said. "You can actually see the train station?"

This was just an aura she was experiencing, like the precursor to a migraine, he knew that. He *knew* that.

"London is getting nearer," Leah said. "I'm only eighteen. Without my brother, I'll be too scared to stay. Help me, won't you? Please help me."

Muscle tension drained from her hand.

Ian gripped her deadened fingers. His future danced through his thirty-year old mind. Every door lay open, limitless. So many open doors to choose from. So many.

"Goddamn it," he said, gasping. "All right. I'll look after you like a brother."

He concentrated on the smell of gas and frying *poussin*, wanting to believe, hearing again the reporter's excited voice yammering from the TV set, grainy images showing people atop the Berlin Wall with a few attacking it with pickaxes and hammers and chisels, and over everything, the sound of Filio crying in the kitchen, crying and wailing.

Ian squeezed Leah's hand and prayed.

Prayed for the old man in the mirror, for his lost youth, lost life, another chance.

Leah's eyes rolled back.

Story Publishing History

All stories are copyright Deborah Sheldon. All stories are original to this collection, unless listed below (first publishing instance).

"Baggage" first published in *Sketch* 2010.
"Basket Trap" first published in *Page Seventeen* 2011.
"Beach House" first published in *Australian Reader* 2010.
"Blue Light Taxi" first published in *Tamba* 2010.
"Broken Things" first published in *All the Little Things That We Lose* collection by Deborah Sheldon, Skive Magazine Press 2010.
"Burnover" first published in *Positive Words* 2009.
"Cash Cow" first published in *All the Little Things That We Lose* collection by Deborah Sheldon, Skive Magazine Press 2010.
"Crazy Town is a Happy Place" first published in *Tincture Journal* 2014.
"Family Album" first published in *All the Little Things That We Lose* collection by Deborah Sheldon, Skive Magazine Press 2010.
"Family Business" first published in *Mayhem: Selected Stories* collection by Deborah Sheldon, Satalyte Publishing 2015
"Farm Hands" first published in *Island* 2009.
"Flashpoint" first published in *Crime Factory* 2014.
"Fortune Teller" first published in *Shotgun Honey* 2014.
"Free Lunch" first published in *Short and Twisted* anthology, Celapene Press 2010.
"Getting and Giving" first published in *Prima Storia* 2009.
"Hot Dog Van" first published in *Mayhem: Selected Stories* collection by Deborah Sheldon, Satalyte Publishing 2015

"Lopping and Removal in Three Parts" first published in *All the Little Things That We Lose* collection by Deborah Sheldon, Skive Magazine Press 2010.

"Lunch at the Trout Farm" first published in *All the Little Things That We Lose* collection by Deborah Sheldon, Skive Magazine Press 2010.

"Man with the Suitcase" first published in *All the Little Things That We Lose* collection by Deborah Sheldon, Skive Magazine Press 2010.

"Muscle Fatigue" first published in *One Page Literary Magazine* 2015.

"One Grand Plan" first published in *Crime Factory* 2012.

"Paramour" first published in *All the Little Things That We Lose* collection by Deborah Sheldon, Skive Magazine Press 2010.

"Parrots and Pelicans" first published in *Polestar Writers' Journal* 2006.

"Party Animals" first published in *All the Little Things That We Lose* collection by Deborah Sheldon, Skive Magazine Press 2010.

"Risk of Recurrence" first published in *Southern Ocean Review* 2008.

"Road Rage" first published in *FreeXPresSion* 2008.

"Rooftop" first published in *Queen Vic Knives* 2010.

"Shootout at Cardenbridge" first published in *All the Little Things That We Lose* collection by Deborah Sheldon, Skive Magazine Press 2010.

"The Caldwell Case" first published in *Australian Reader* 2007.

"The Sequined Shirt" first published in *Australian Reader* 2009.

"Waiting for the Huntsman" first published in *Eclecticism E-zine* 2009.

"We Have What You Want" first published in *Polestar Writers' Journal* 2010.

"White Powder" first published in *dotdotdash* 2011.